RUN OUT

Dream Horse Mystery #2

CANDACE CARRABUS

Witting
Woman Works

Publisher: Witting Woman Works

Cover design by Molly Phipps

ISBN-13: 978-0-9896057-8-6

❀ Created with Vellum

This one goes out to my extended family with love.

CHAPTER ONE

Certain men should be required to wear a sports bra when riding.

That's what I was thinking as I boosted an overweight guy onto Fawn, a stout quarter horse mare who could carry him without straining anything. Although she did let out a little grunt of protest when he plopped onto the saddle. His parts bounced recklessly. And by parts, I mean man boobs. Moobs.

I'd read a recent study that said riders could throw their horse's balance out of whack if they didn't wear the right under-garments.

I couldn't unsee the moobs, but I could ignore them as I mounted my horse—correct undergarments in place—and set off for the relative cool of the woods. Here it was, late August in Missouri and there was no sign of the heat letting up or rain coming down.

Unfortunately, there was no sign Winterlight Farm would discontinue public riding anytime soon, either.

The girl behind me waved. Lisa was about my age and the most confident of the group. She rode a petite gray mare with black mane and tail named Oreo. I smiled and returned my attention to the trail. Guiding five inexperienced customers is not my favorite way to start the day, but it's not like I have a choice.

Nope. According to the mysterious trust fund set up by my absentee parents, Viola Parker—me—must keep a job for one full year before I turn thirty. *And*, get a glowing letter of recommendation at the end of it. Not only that, I wasn't to know the contents of the trust until the year was up. So, I could be wasting my time out here in God's country. Otherwise, I'd still be back East competing the top jumpers for blue-ribbon crazed owners with more money than sense.

Well, maybe. Truth is, it's unlikely anyone back there would hire me again.

Straightening my spine, I let out a breath and released my frustration, the gentle movement of my horse's stride soothing me. Even though it was still early, sticky heat dampened my skin like a steam bath.

Our path meandered along a ridge for twenty minutes before crossing a valley with a creek running through it. The horse's hooves made only the barest muffled thuds, lifting the scent of warm dirt to my nose. My dog, Noire, riffled underbrush hoping to flush a squirrel.

"Where's Mr. Malcolm today?" Lisa asked.

"Out of town," I answered without turning. I didn't want to discuss Winterlight's owner, who also happened to be my lover.

Lisa didn't take the hint.

"What's it like working for a hottie in a kilt?"

I rolled my shoulders and cracked a couple of kinks out of my neck. Malcolm is a hottie who wears a kilt, and we'd become involved shortly after I'd arrived, despite my rule to not get in bed with the boss.

"He's good to work for," I said. "Fair."

The man was actually a rare and irresistible package of passion, kindness, intelligence, and looks. Too often I wondered what he saw in me, but not enough to break it off.

"Oh, come on, Vi, spill."

Birds swept by, twittering a happy tune, and a rabbit hopped out from under a bush. I half expected Snow White and her seven dwarves to march into view and break into song. If only to make Lisa shut up.

"We've never gone this way before," said the girl riding behind Lisa on Smitty. I think her name was Sue.

"It's cooler," I said, thankful for the change in subject.

"Yeah," piped up Lisa's boyfriend. "Almost makes it bearable to wear this stupid hat."

Deep breath, bite tongue, don't say what I'm thinking. *If you fall off, that stupid hat might save you spending the rest of your life eating through a tube.*

Before I left the east coast, my cousin Penny made me promise I wouldn't smart off. My inability to keep my mouth shut has cost me a couple of jobs in the past. I twisted backwards, giving the complainer a look that was probably lost under the brim of my helmet—the stupid hat he referred to. Yes, I made everyone wear them, whether they rode English or Western, and whether it was their first or thousandth time getting on.

"Liability insurance," I said.

"Yeah," Lisa said. "And if you fall off and crack open your head, I won't be the one spoon-feeding you and weeping."

Nice couple.

I tweaked the reins and Cali halted. "There's a ravine ahead. We're going down, first."

"Going down," the chubster snorted.

Freaking moron. A moron with man boobs. I sucked in another deep breath.

"Your horses know what to do. Sit up straight and keep your heels down. It will feel like you're leaning back. Any questions?"

"When are we going to run?"

Same voice from the back. I tilted to the side so I could see him. "This is what—your second or third time on a horse?"

He shrugged and gave me a *so what?* look from where he strad-
dled Fawn. She ripped a mouthful of dust-encrusted leaves from
the side of the trail.

"When you can keep your horse from eating while she has a
bit in her mouth, you might be able to handle running." *But please
put on a sports bra first.*

Titters from the peanut gallery. I'm glad I can be so freaking
entertaining.

He jerked the reins to pull up Fawn's head. I regretted saying
anything and made a mental note to put him on a less forgiving
horse next time. One who would turn around and bite his leg. We
didn't have a horse like that, but I could dream, right?

Just a couple more boarders or horses in training and we'd be
able to stop renting to the public. In case I haven't mentioned it,
I hate giving trail rides.

I clucked, and Cali moved off, placing her feet carefully on the
loose stones and gravel. After a hairpin turn, the trail dropped at a
forty-five degree angle before leveling out to cross the creek. The
horses would take care of themselves so long as none of the riders
did anything stupid, like suddenly yanking one rein and pulling
their mount off balance.

Everyone remained calm as we descended. Noire splashed in
the creek, which had been reduced to not much more than a
trickle by the lack of rain. Her black coat blended in with the
dusky shadows of the ravine. We were nearly at the bottom when
something large suddenly moved through the woods, and my dog
shot off barking and snarling, making a racket snapping branches
as she crashed through the underbrush. All the horses jumped.
Lisa shrieked. The guys cursed.

Cali spun in the direction Noire had gone. She was still barking, probably chasing some deer. My eyes stayed on the horses,
making sure none of them bolted and the riders' butts were still
connected to their saddles.

Lisa dropped the reins wrapped both hands around the saddle horn. She'd gone pale.

"Everyone okay?"

"My foot came out of the stirrup," Sue said.

"Just hang on till we get to the bottom and I'll help with that."

Cali's black-tipped ears pricked tight, and she didn't move when I put my leg on her. Her nostrils flared. We heard coyotes howling often enough at night, and neighbors reported seeing bobcats in the area. Those weren't usually predators horses needed to fear.

The woods went quiet, and I waited, listening, but the horses became restless, rustling the crisp leaves underfoot and nipping at desiccated weeds. We walked on, made the level area creekside, I fixed Sue's stirrup, put the reins back in Lisa's hands, and we crossed the shallow stream.

To my relief, Noire came panting back, took a long drink, then laid down in the water to cool off before trotting alongside me and Cali.

"Who was that?" Lisa asked.

"What do you mean, *who*? It was some deer."

"I know what a deer looks like," Lisa said. "Four legs. That was a person."

A person? This deep in the woods? My focus had been the safety of the group. Thick trees and dense brambles made seeing anything almost impossible. Whatever—whoever—it was had been gone in a flash.

What would anyone be doing this deep into the property? It wasn't hunting season. A neighbor wouldn't have run off. I'd tell Malcolm when he got back from his current business trip. He'd know what to do.

Pushing down the churn of anxiety in my gut, I said, "We're going to trot up this hill. Lean forward a little and hold the horn so you don't slip back."

Cali didn't hesitate this time when I urged her forward. But even in trot, her glance and ears kept straying to the right.

People could be predators, I reminded myself. I'd seen it up close and personal. Predators of the worst kind. The kind that horses—and humans—very much needed to fear.

CHAPTER TWO

As we returned from the successful ride—meaning everyone stayed on and there was minimal screaming—Zoe slouched in to work. Her pace and posture conveyed the put-upon sixteen-year-old doing something she resented, but I knew better. Mucking stalls wasn't high on her favorites list, and when she picked up the pitchfork, she was slower than a slug in summer, but she loved being around horses as much as I did. The gleam in her eyes reminded me of me at that age.

She grabbed a halter and lead line and ducked into the pasture, going straight for Honey, the only horse I'd allowed her to ride.

"Hold up there, kiddo," I said from Cali's back.

She froze and gave me a wide-eyed stare. She often got that bunny-being-stalked-by-a-cat look about her, and it made me wonder. Not something I had time or energy for right then, though.

Riders dismounted. I hooked my leg over my saddle's knee roll and loosened Cali's girth. She tossed her head like she always did. "You're late," I said to Zoe. "Again."

"So?"

Insolent little... "So, let Honey go and help with these horses."

Her gaze slid away, and she huffed, then yanked the halter over Honey's ears.

The mare didn't care—she was getting out of work—but I did. I nudged Cali closer, leaned down. "If I catch you taking your frustration out on a horse again, you're done. Got it?"

Man Boobs sniggered, but at a glare from me, he shut it. Maybe Zoe'd be on time tomorrow. Maybe I expect too much? Over the years, a few people have mentioned that I'm very demanding. There's nothing wrong with having high standards, though, or expecting someone to be on time.

Zoe had shown up two months before looking for work, and Malcolm'd insisted help would allow me to spend more time riding. I couldn't argue with that, but we couldn't afford to pay her much, either. All she wanted, she said, was to be around the horses.

She stroked Honey's ears by way of apology, and we all felt better. I did, anyway.

With the riders gone, she and I hosed off the horses and sprayed them with fly repellent before returning them to the pasture. It was the season of horseflies, bot eggs, and cockleburs. Bug spray wouldn't keep the burrs from twisting tails into dread-locks, but it would prevent itchy stings and those sticky little yellow eggs the bot flies lay.

We set to cleaning stalls before it got any hotter.

After about half an hour, Zoe broke the silence with "Sorry I was late," from the next stall over.

"What happened?"

"Oh, you know. I stayed up to watch some old movie with Mrs. Erdman."

At least she was honest. But Mrs. Erdman was ninety if she was a day. Zoe lived with her for free in exchange for helping out. "Mrs. Erdman stays up late watching movies?"

Zoe snorted in a very teenaged girl kind of way. "No. She falls asleep in her chair and snores with her mouth open while her cat snoozes on her chest."

"At which point, you could go to bed so you can get up in time for work."

She didn't say anything for a while.

Finally she offered, "I guess." She dropped the pitchfork into the wheelbarrow with a clang. "But then, she'd be in that chair all night, and she should go to bed, too, shouldn't she?" Zoe came to lean in the doorway of my stall. "Eventually, I put out the cat and help Mrs. Erdman to her room."

I stopped for a moment, wiped sweat on my shoulder, and stretched my back. "Why doesn't she go to bed in the first place?"

Zoe shrugged. "She says it makes her feel old to go to bed early."

We both laughed.

The girl had been quiet in the beginning but had begun to come out of her shell. She was far from a chatterbox, which suited me fine. I hoped I'd been wrong about the fear, but there was still that occasional startled bunny look.

"Tell Mrs. Erdman it's for her own good."

Zoe considered this for a moment then shook her head. "You ever tried telling someone that old to do something?"

I smiled and went back to work. "I see your point."

After forking the last of the wet straw into our wheelbarrows, we took our loads to the manure spreader.

With the immediate chores completed, I could now exercise the privately owned horses. But it was at least ninety-five degrees already with humidity to match and we didn't have an indoor arena. I went into the tack room to cool off and fortify myself with coffee before dragging a horse and my sweaty self into the sun. Hot coffee. Sounds weird on a hot day, I know. Everyone else I'd met out here preferred iced tea, but I was almost as addicted to coffee as I was to whipped cream straight from the can. Of which I had none.

It's too much to expect a person to give up whipped cream *and* swearing at the same time. But I'd done it on a dare for Malcolm. Proved I could. For a few weeks, anyway.

I sipped my almost-as-strong-as-espresso brew and sank into the tack room's ratty love seat. Some combination of the heat, unrestrained man boobs, and the possible poacher in the woods had my head pounding. What I needed was a couple of painkillers and a quick nap to make me fit for company. That and a run to the store to stock up on whipped cream. Enough was enough.

Keeping a cold can of creamy goodness close to hand was the only way to deal with relentless heat, sniggering customers, potential poachers, and recalcitrant help all while not swearing. Not out loud, anyway.

For a moment, I considered sending Zoe to the store. That would be irresponsible, right? Instead, I sent her to scrub water troughs—easy duty on a sweltering day—and slunk upstairs to the cozy apartment that came with the job.

Falling asleep was easy. It always is. Resting, though...

The dream begins with fog. Out of it trots Wastrel, smelling of heaven like always. Much as I loved that horse, I'm not happy to have his ghost vividly appear behind my eyes again. I've slept dreamlessly since JJ died, as I had all my life before coming to Winterlight.

Then, Wastrel started galloping through my nights, digging into things I didn't want to know about, forcing me to piece together obscure clues and solve a crime that had nothing to do with me.

I'd thought we were done.

Hoped we were done.

I was wrong.

I am determined to ignore him. My dream self turns my back, but I can't keep it up. He's so sweet, and we play for a few minutes. First, he won't let me near him, our usual game, but soon he's at my side crunching a carrot I produce from the pocket of my pants.

Then, he's tacked up, I'm aboard, and I can feel the constriction of a show coat around my shoulders, the tall collar of the ratcatcher at my throat. My heels are deep in my sleek black boots, and we've picked up canter. We circle and gain speed, clearly preparing to jump a course. Just like the old days. It feels so good to be on his back again, I smile.

The fog clears and the competition arena comes into focus, the striped rails and panels, the flowers and grass. I can hear the crowd and smell Wastrel's sweat. It's the jump off. His head is up, ears forward. I've memorized the course. The first fence is a blue vertical, then we have a sharp right to the combination...

No. This is the last time I rode Wastrel, the last time I rode a grand prix.

We are *not* going through this again. I don't care if it's just a dream. I yank one rein, but he's galloping, ignoring me. I lean back, shove my legs forward, and pull with all my might just as it all explodes.

"No!"

I thrashed awake and landed on the floor with a thump, breath whistling in my throat, heart hammering my ribs, Noire licking my face. Blearily, I sat up and leaned against the bed, forcing the dream fear down. But shaking it, shutting out the memories, was impossible. I pressed the heels of my hands against my eyes, hearing the splintering wooden jump, the shattering of my heart, and tearing flesh—Wastrel's and mine.

The day of that accident, I awoke in intensive care, hooked to every machine the hospital had. They told me Wastrel had been put down. Later, when my body had healed, I'd abused alcohol beyond all limits, but nothing had dulled the pain.

The first time Wastrel appeared to me in a dream was a few days after I arrived at Winterlight. Somehow, he told me the accident wasn't my fault. He'd wanted to end it. I'd always known he didn't like competition, but his owner forced it, and we'd gotten through it together.

That's why I had to pay attention. I hadn't heeded Wastrel the first time he visited, but he'd truly been bringing me helpful messages, even if they were hard to decipher.

Why that horse show? Why the course where we crashed, he died, and I got carried off on a stretcher? What mystery might be brewing now? I didn't want to find another dead body or rescue anyone.

For the time being, I put it out of my mind. If last time was any indication, Wastrel would return when next I closed my eyes, and I'd try to make sense of what he showed me. A trip to the store for whipped cream was essential now. I grabbed a peach and went downstairs.

Zoe came in, soaked but smiling. "Do we have any more customers today?"

"No." I took down a bridle and decided that staying inside to clean tack made the most sense. "But Ciquala, Miss Bong, Barbie, and Gaston all need exercising. We'll ride later after it cools off."

"We?" she squeaked. She went pale.

"Yes. You'll ride Ciq while I ride Miss Bong, and then you'll ride Barbie while I ride Gaston. They're good horses. You'll be fine."

"Don't you usually gallop them?"

By her wide eyes and thin lips, I'd say she had a fear of galloping. But I felt the need for speed. Malcolm and two of our boarders liked to fox hunt in the winter. Part of my job was keeping their horses fit for that.

With a frustrated sigh, I said, "I galloped them all a couple of days ago. Today, we'll mostly trot."

She nodded, unhooked a bridle and sat. I got out the saddle soap.

It should have been soothing. I like cleaning tack. But the

dream...dread had my gut churning on anxious anticipation of whatever was coming down the pike.

Noire scratched on the door to go out, then raced to the front of the barn, barking at a bright yellow car that pulled in and stopped.

Zoe and I followed my dog. "Is that a taxi?" I asked.

"Looks like it." She zipped out the back door saying, "I'm going to check on Fawn."

Had the taxi spooked her? Fawn didn't need checking. We had to talk. I wanted no surprises for the rest of my time at Winterlight.

All four of the taxi doors opened, and the trunk lid popped up, but only the driver got out. He went to the back and produced several large suitcases. What the hell? My stomach did a scared flip. I almost cut through the back door just like Zoe had. Changing the subject and running away were my two favorite modes of defense.

Curiosity and the weight of responsibility kept me rooted in place. With Malcolm away, I was in charge. But why hadn't the passengers gotten out?

I walked toward the front of the barn. Some sort of discussion or argument was going on inside the vehicle.

A hand grasped the taxi's door frame and an elderly man emerged from the front seat, pulling himself tall. He had thick gray hair sweeping back from his temples and forehead, and a full beard and mustache. He cradled several potted plants against his chest as if they were his only and most prized possessions. I'd never seen him before.

A younger man got out of the back seat. Also tall, thinner than the first, his hair sporting glints of silver.

The air, already still and shimmery with heat, grew stifling, backing my breath up into my chest. I recognized the unmistakable profile first, the nose with the slight slope, well-defined lips, strong chin.

Images from the dream kicked my gut and made me sway with the same disorientation I'd felt as Wastrel and I began the course.

From the other side of the cab came a woman in large sunglasses and a simple sleeveless black sheath, her dark hair slicked back into a signature chignon.

I put one hand against the wall. The other covered my chest, willing my heart to continue beating. Where had they come from?

The elder man's eyes drank in the scenery like a prisoner released from solitary. He put down the plants, slammed the taxi door, picked a handkerchief from his pants pocket, mopped his face.

Zoe came up behind me. "Is that weed?"

Leave it to the sixteen-year-old to jump to the most optimistic conclusion.

"Tomatoes."

"How can you tell from here?"

"My Aunt Trudy has tomato plants she defends militantly—as that guy likely does," I said with a short nod in his direction. "I can tell by the way he holds them."

"Like a bomb?"

"Like a baby."

CHAPTER THREE

The woman spoke first. "Is that you, Viola?"

"One-hundred-thirty-seven dollars and fifty cents," the driver said.

Without glancing away from me, she said, "Make yourself useful, Adrian. Pay the man."

The words came out clipped, cultured, the accent well practiced.

Zoe moved her hand back and forth in front of my face. "You there?"

I shook my head.

The scene had gone all razor-edged black-and-white contrasts except for two colors that stood out: the shiny red of the woman's dangling earrings and the yellow cab.

Adrian handed over a stack of bills and the cab left, raising a cloud of dust to blow through the barn.

The woman coughed delicately. The two men, both tall and fit looking, made no comment. I remained where I stood, clammy and queasy.

Keeping my voice low, I told Zoe, "Stay here."

"Who are they?" she whispered back.

I gazed at them a moment longer, trying to make the two in front a different pair of people. But their lean figures and elegant features refused to become anyone other than who they were.

"My parents."

CHAPTER FOUR

Zoe, like the good teenager she was, or maybe more like the friend she was becoming, ignored my directive and followed when I took a couple of jerky steps toward the front of the barn. Forward, when every cell screamed *back*. Compelled in the direction of pain instead of away from it, my feet betraying my heart.

My insides were frozen, my brain locked up, and the rest of my body rigid. I stopped. Zoe stood beside me.

"Aren't you going to say something?" my mother asked.

She and Adrian had taken a tentative step closer, too, and stood silhouetted in the square opening of the building. The older man wiped his face again and watched. My mother turned to my father.

"Why won't she say anything?"

He'd finally pulled his gaze away from me to take in his surroundings, a view which must have been so alien, them having spent nearly their entire lives in urban European locales.

"This...must be...a surprise," he said, as if the thought had just occurred. Whether this comment was meant for me, his wife, the as yet unidentified man, or himself, it was hard to tell.

Shock was more like it, but my brain had begun to function

enough for me to clear my throat and ask, "What are you doing here?"

"A fine welcome," my mother said.

"You weren't expecting them?" Prickly awareness laced Zoe's tone...but I couldn't gnaw that bone just then.

"Not. At. All." I paused to drag in a shallow breath.

"Are you going to leave us standing out here in this heat?" Again, she turned to my father. "I told you we should get a hotel."

"What are you doing here?" I repeated, more loudly. "How did you find me?"

Zoe's body jerked as if she'd been slapped. "You hiding out here?"

My eyes cut sideways. What the *hell* made this kid so finely tuned?

"Not exactly. I'll explain later."

Clearly, my parents and their traveling companion intended to stay.

Needed to stay? The thought came as a surprise.

Why, on a day when I had no whipped cream and Malcolm wasn't home? His steady strength beside me would bolster my ability to cope, to maintain my sanity. Without him near, I felt even less hospitable than usual, so much so I could begin to dislike myself.

What did they want? I gestured at he of the many plants.

"Who is this?"

Adrian and the elder looked at each other while my mother lifted her chin and longingly studied the cab's dust cloud. Color leached back into the scene, their faces pale against the pasture and trees behind them. For a sec, they were all etched in stark profile, like a pre-Raphaelite painting.

Again, my breath hitched. Even with age, the older man's face was my father's.

My father, who'd always claimed to be an orphan, shrugged,

shoved his long fingers in his pockets, and turned his gaze to the ground. Guilty, guilty, guilty.

My *grandfather*—Jesus, who else could he be?—who until that moment had never existed, lifted his shoulders in a resigned version of the same shrug and added a heavenward roll of his eyes for good measure. Then, he flicked a glance over his shoulder so quick, I almost missed it. He smiled and shifted the pots he held from one side to the other. They were all—plants and people alike —beginning to wilt.

My mother crossed her arms and looked like she wanted to tap her foot. "That's Giacomo."

Giacomo straightened his spine and nodded at me. "Giacomo Russo," he said in a voice raspy with stories waiting to be told. Something in my chest—my heart I suppose—did a big thump.

With a fatalistic sigh, I walked through the barn, past my parents, and up to Giacomo, taking one of the plants. He hesitated, just for a blink, then handed it over with a grateful smile. His eyes skittered to my parents, subtly rolled again, then met mine with a gleeful gleam.

He and I were going to get along just fine. I picked up another of the plastic pots.

"Come inside."

I led the way to the house, a distance of about three hundred feet up a dirt and gravel driveway that would ruin my mother's high heels.

I could have grabbed one of their suitcases. I didn't want to. I could have hugged them. That was out of the question. I could have dredged up an iota of welcome. If they were...welcome.

As I trudged toward the house, I came to grips with my main feeling.

Fury.

I was absolutely, completely, totally enraged they had invaded Winterlight. Despite all the craziness since I'd arrived, I realized right then I'd come to think of the farm as *my* place, too. Not just

Malcolm's. I'd been embraced here, respected. Looked up to, even. I belonged in a way I never had before.

I could not share this place with them. *Would* not.

At the same time, curiosity sprinted to catch up. Although they'd abandoned me as an infant, they'd also created the trust fund that had driven me here. The mysterious trust fund—amount undisclosed—that could be my ticket to freedom, or might be next to nothing.

How did Giacomo fit? What had Wastrel been trying to tell me? Is this what the churning and the dream were about? I really needed a fresh batch of whipped cream.

By the time I reached the porch, my need to understand what the hell they were doing here had almost shouldered aside my anger. Almost.

From behind me came the sound of wheeled luggage bumping and scraping up the drive, but no conversation, no questions, no demands.

Noire trotted to my right, and Zoe stuck to my left.

"What do you want me to do?"

Her concern, and her unexpected loyalty, touched me.

"Keep an eye on things in the barn. Clean more tack."

"Clean tack. Got it."

I set the tomato plants on the porch. My parents caught up. I thanked Zoe and held the door. They dragged their bags over the threshold into the front room. Giacomo came up the steps slowly, his restless eyes taking in the sturdy lines of the old farmhouse, and as near as I could tell, counting the windows. He set the plants he carried next to the others.

My father had hauled up two large way-beyond-their-prime Louis Vuitton soft-sided suitcases. My mother managed to bring in one small carry-on which she dropped the moment they entered. Three or four more frayed pieces leaned against each other in front of the barn.

They could stay there all night for all I cared.

My parents could, too.

Zoe caught my eye before turning toward her chores. *Yell if you need me* she telegraphed. The kid knew something about difficult parent-child relationships. I just wasn't sure what it was.

I let the screen door slam and stifled a satisfied smirk when my mother jumped.

"I suppose you'd like something to drink." I headed down the hallway to the kitchen.

There, I leaned against the counter and hyperventilated. *Why* hadn't I gone out for whipped cream when I had the chance? I got an ice cube and held it to my forehead, then slid it down my neck. The sense that the top of my head might blow off passed, and I fixed four glasses of iced tea, adding sugar to one for my dad and lemon to mine. My spidey sense told me Giacomo would be content with whatever I gave him. But I couldn't remember how my mother took hers or if she even deigned to drink ordinary tea. After all, she was no ordinary woman. At least, not in her estimation.

When I returned, she perched on the edge of a flat, backless bench, her strong dancer's legs neatly crossed at the ankle and her hands in her lap, pulled tightly into herself as if too much contact with the real world might dull her shine. My father struck a forced pose of nonchalance by the fireplace, his arm resting along the white mantle.

God help me.

Giacomo settled back into the sofa like a stone sinking into mud. His white button-down shirt had dark stains beneath the arms. The ancient striped tie hanging loosely down his front had a couple of spots on it.

I passed out the drinks. Dad thanked me and tipped it back. Mom looked doubtful—or was that disdain in those downturned lips?—and didn't take the glass. I plonked it on the table next to her atop the latest issue of *Horse Illustrated* and dropped myself onto the end of the couch opposite Giacomo.

My grandfather—did I really have an extended family?—and I sipped tea.

I'd asked what they were doing here—twice—and had yet to receive an answer. As we stared at each other, I did a little calculating and came up with the number five.

Five months.

The sum total of time these two had ever spent with me since I was born. Small wonder I felt no connection but plenty of resentment. The chance they'd developed a sudden flash of parental love didn't exist. Which meant only one thing...

They needed me.

God help them.

I glanced at the clock above the fireplace. My mother's sharp gaze followed.

"Are we keeping you from something?"

"There's always work to do," I said as evenly as I could.

"Honestly, Viola, you never change," she said. "You look well, by the way. The country agrees with you. Aren't you glad to see us? It's been a long time."

Sixteen years. *Not nearly long enough.*

"Since we're being honest, no. I'm not glad to see you. Why should I be?"

"Vi—" my father started, but not unkindly.

"*Viola,*" my mother cut him off. "What an awful thing to say."

Dad put his hand on her shoulder and murmured a soothing, "Not now, *Gem Gem.*"

His pet name for my darling mother, Gemma Marie.

She tossed his hand away and rose, smoothing her dress. Dad pushed her back to the seat. She sat with a huff, thinking better of whatever scolding she'd been about to hurl.

Exactly how I'd issued from these two defied logic, but there it was. How Adrian might have issued from Giacomo was clearly another story altogether.

My mother produced a wadded-up tissue from some hidden

pocket and dabbed her forehead. "Viola, can you please turn up the air-conditioning? It's positively sweltering in here. I don't know how you stand it."

"I'm usually outside," I answered, leaning forward, drinking more tea, and refusing to blot the sweat on my upper lip. "We don't keep the AC on when no one's in the house, except in the bedrooms upstairs. Perhaps you should go to a hotel. The nearest one is thirty minutes down the highway. I'd be happy to give you a lift. You won't be able to hail a cab out here."

Oh, the satisfaction I'd get from flinging their luggage into the back of my pickup and making them cram into the cab with me, my mother straddling the shifter. I almost smiled.

Giacomo grunted, but exactly what aspect of the conversation he was punctuating, I don't know. My parents glanced at each other, communicating silently like they must have done on the dance floor for years. A hunted look flickered over my mother's face. There and gone in a flash, quickly replaced by her renowned haughtiness. This time, it was her profile that caught me off-guard, as if I'd suddenly seen my reflection off a storefront window out of the corner of my eye.

Spooky.

My father's face gave less away. You wouldn't think I could read them so well, but he reassured her with his eyes. *Follow my lead.*

"Vi," my father said. "We'd like to stay here with you."

His usually smooth tenor caught briefly on the words *with you.* He sipped the last of his tea and added, "for a little while."

"A little while?"

The phone rang. Grateful for an excuse to get away and desperate to hear Malcolm's voice, I dashed to the kitchen and grabbed the receiver.

"Malcolm?" I nearly shouted. "You won't believe—"

"It's Clara. Why are you yelling?" she asked. "Did I see a taxi over there?"

God bless our neighbor, Clara.

"Yes. Yes, you did."

"Ever'thing all right?"

After a deep inhalation, I exhaled noisily through my nose.

"Guess not," she said. "You need pie? Just pulled a rhubarb custard out the fridge. I might could bring it over on the Gator." She sniffed, then sneezed. "Woo. Think I got cinnamon up my nose."

Relief made my knees turn to water. Clara was as far as you could get from my mother, and tough, too, didn't take crap from anybody. She had a sixth sense about when I needed a piece of straight-from-the-oven—or fridge—pie, a commodity that flowed endlessly and magically from her kitchen. The Gator was her favorite new thing—a six-wheeled utility vehicle with a dump bed she used any excuse to take out for a drive.

"My parents are here."

"Why, I didn't know they was comin' to visit. Why didn't you tell me? I woulda baked a cake."

Company was always cause for celebration in Clara's book.

"They just showed up. Pie works fine."

"Oh, I forgot. Your parents done you wrong and you don't exactly like them."

I hate them, I almost blurted. Truth? I didn't know them well enough to expend the energy it took to hate.

Which was easier to say than do. Or not do.

What I felt was confused. Beneath the anger, and entwined with years of frustration and unanswered questions that had produced an ill-adjusted and equally ill-tempered adult, lay a child.

A child still longing to be loved.

Aunt Trudy and uncle Victor—the people who raised me—loved me, of that I was sure, even if they tended to keep their emotions close. But sometimes, they tried too hard. They knew I had a giant, gasping wound. Their attention didn't make up for knowing my real parents had abandoned me. By choice. Not by necessity. The little girl inside still howled with the pain. But I'd always thought this hurt was one my father understood, a thread that connected us despite almost never being together. After all, he'd been left on the steps of an orphanage still slick with afterbirth.

Or so I'd always been told.

Now, it appeared, the story—our connection—had unraveled.

Clara's voice brought me back to the present. "Vi?"

Much as I wanted someone else in the house, anything to buffer the fire that had leapt to life in my chest, dragging Clara into it wasn't kind.

"Now probably isn't the best time. I'll call you later if we need the pie."

"I got Cool Whip."

My insides went all squiggly. It wasn't as good as the canned stuff but worked a treat in a pinch.

"Bring it over."

CHAPTER FIVE

Zoe would surely want pie, too, I thought as I slowly returned to the front room. I'd call her in, and we'd make inane small talk. The inevitable confrontation—the one I felt pressing against my insides—would be avoided, or at least, postponed.

When I got there, Adrian and Gemma turned their heads to look at me. Dad wore a hopeful half smile. Mom tried to hide behind her cultivated disdain, but fear lurked in unexpected shadows around her eyes and tightness at the corners of her mouth.

Giacomo's head lolled on the couch cushion. He snored, his open mouth revealing a decent set of teeth.

Prickly heat rushed my neck and scalp. The air in the room, already heavy with damp, congealed at my temples and tripped down my spine.

I needed to get out. Now.

My parents sharing the air I breathed didn't help. Adrenaline propelled me forward.

"Have to do something outside."

The screen door slammed against the wall then squeaked back

into its frame behind me.

"Stay here," I ordered over my shoulder.

As if they'd set so much as one of their highly esteemed and insured toes inside the barn. As if they'd lower themselves to learn anything about me or what I cared about.

My heart clogged my throat. Despite the unrelenting sun burning my head—or maybe because of it—I ran.

Noire bounded up as if this were a game, shaking water off her pelt, smelling of the pond.

A gazzilion thoughts and questions collided in my brain.

Needed to call my cousin, Penny. Did she know my parents were stateside?

What would Malcolm say? If he was smart, he'd fire my ass.

No, we had a contract.

I jogged past the luggage, into the barn, and stopped, breathing hard. I stood there a moment with my eyes closed. The scents of fresh straw and hay and sweat and horses and leather all mingled together like distinctive perfume in my nose.

It grounded me.

Malcolm needed me. My job was safe.

I was a selfish bitch.

That was nothing new. I'd had only me to look out for me for so long, it was hard to shake the habit.

I went to the tack room and called Penny. She answered on the first ring.

"Hey," I said, "that was fast. You sitting on the phone?"

A slight hesitation. "No." A note of distress, quickly covered. "I'm waiting for the doctor to call."

I gave myself a mental head slap. Penny was due to have a baby in a couple of weeks.

"Is everything all right?"

"Probably nothing serious."

Too fast an answer. Crap. All my worries flew out the window. Well, most of them, anyway. "What aren't you telling me?"

"Nothing, really. It's fine."

"You've never been a good liar."

She sighed. "Remember how I was a little short of breath?"

"That was weeks ago. You're just getting it checked out now? *Penny*." I said her name like I say Noire's when she rolls in something dead.

"*Not* helping," she scolded.

"Sorry."

Penny and I were like sisters, seeing as how we'd been raised together. Almost twins. Her parents took me in while her mother —Aunt Trudy—was pregnant. I was just six months older than my sweet cousin. But she often took the role of the more mature older sister.

"It could be a couple of things," she said. "I might have to spend the rest of the pregnancy in bed."

She could use the rest. But this wasn't the way she'd want to get it. And her husband wasn't exactly the nursemaid type.

"But then everything will be all right?"

"Yeah, yeah. Everything's going to be fine."

I'm not sure who she was trying to convince, me or herself.

"How's everything there?"

Something in her voice, a forced lightness, a reluctance to hear the answer to a question she felt compelled to ask.

I tried to keep it down, but couldn't stop new anger from bubbling up.

"You knew!"

"I'm sorry. It's not my fault, I swear. It was Mom. She said she wanted to send you a birthday card. She must have given your address to them. It wasn't me, I swear!"

I closed my eyes and shook my head. My birthday had been back in May, right after I'd gotten here. I'd never gotten the bogus card.

"I believe you."

Did it really matter how my parents found me? So long as it

wasn't Penny—the one person in the world I could depend on.

Noire barked, and I heard Clara's Gator coming down the road, reminding me she had pie.

And Cool Whip.

"I'm going to call you later," I told Penny sternly, taking my turn as bossy older sister. "And you're going to tell me what the doctor said, okay?"

"Okay." I heard her shift. The big belly must be hard to situate comfortably.

I should be there to help her, not halfway across the country in the middle of nowhere.

"Thanks, Vi," she said.

"What are you thanking me for?"

"For believing me. For not being mad."

I never could stay mad at her. "You should have warned me," I said, but not with malice.

"I tried. Your phone isn't accepting messages. Forget to charge it again?"

"I guess." The wonder was I hadn't broken or lost the thing. The temptation to throw the electronic gadget against the wall was overwhelming at times. I sighed.

After a pause, this time to sip her coffee—I know her better then myself—Penny asked, "Is it awful, them being there?"

"How awful it is remains to be seen. It was a shock, that's for sure. But they just arrived a little while ago along with someone named Giacomo. Do you know *why* they're here or who he is?"

"No. And I'm pretty sure Mom and Dad don't know, either. Mom said, 'you know how they like to be mysterious.'"

She imitated Aunt Trudy's smoky voice so perfectly, I laughed, but quickly sobered.

I sighed again, rolling my shoulders to release a mote of tension. "They're a mystery, that's for sure."

"What does Malcolm think of all this?"

All the muscles in my back seized up.

"He's away on business right now so he doesn't know yet."

"You can fill me in when you call later. I'll be here. Frank's bringing home Chinese."

That, at least, was something.

As I stepped out of the tack room, I saw the Gator slow. Clara peered down the darkness of the barn aisle, trying to determine if I was inside or up at the house. Noire sniffed her, checking for doggie treats, and Clara probably figured if my dog was here, I was, too.

I waved. "We're coming," I yelled.

Zoe looked up from the noseband in her lap. "We are?".

"Yes. Clara brought pie."

"Sounds great."

We joined Clara on the Gator, me taking the passenger seat. Zoe climbed onto the back.

We started up the drive, but Noire turned around, barking.

"What now?" I asked no one in particular.

Sandy's crappy little car sputtered up to the barn. She got out with a wave.

"Hey, ya'll, what's up?"

She was stuffed into a hot pink leopard print sports bra. No T-shirt, as usual. A lavish roll of fat bulged between the bra and the top of her three-sizes-too-small-super-stretch jeggings. Her bleached hair hung stiffly around her shoulders, and the skinny—we use that term loosely—jeans were stuck into unlaced black Army boots.

A smile lifted one side of my mouth.

"My parents are here. We're going up to the house to see them." Couldn't wait to see their faces when they got a load of Sandy. "Clara brought pie."

"And Cool Whip," Zoe added, holding up the plastic tub.

"Sounds like my kinda party," Sandy said. She opened her car door again. "But before we do, I brought you somethin', Vi."

She produced a grocery bag, but I couldn't make out what was in it. Sandy wasn't exactly the gift-giving type, but it fit that if she was going to buy me something, it would come from Walmart.

"Catch," she yelled as she tossed it my way.

I grabbed the bag before its contents conked Clara on the shoulder. Whatever was inside was long, hard, and cold.

Salvation.

I pulled out the can, tore off the lid, and squirted a giant dollop of cream into my mouth.

Chocolate, no less. I usually use plain and reserve chocolate for extreme stress.

"Feel better?" Clara asked.

I nodded, my eyes closed, and passed the can to her.

"How'd you know?" I asked Sandy.

She'd gone back to her car and pulled out two more bags. These, I could see, were full. Perhaps a dozen cans of delicious serenity. She pointed her chin at Clara.

"A little birdie told me."

Clara declined to share. "You need it worse than me."

A happy warmth welled up inside, pushing aside the crazy welter of resentment and old anger as I realized that Penny wasn't the only one I could depend on.

The strain to Sandy's pants as she joined Zoe spoke of imminent outbreak, but she made it without busting loose and dropped the other two bags with a clunk.

Clara shoved the Gator into gear and started forward, neatly steering around the lonely luggage.

I passed my can to Zoe and asked Sandy, "How much did you buy?"

"All of it. But they only had the one chocolate."

Instead of waiting for Zoe to pass it back, I cracked open a can of plain, took a hit, and savored the sweet, creamy goodness. "That's what I call an on-demand anti-depressant."

"Well," Sandy said, opening one for herself, "If'n your parents are here, we're gonna need it."

CHAPTER SIX

W e managed to enter the house spaced out so the screen door skreeked open and slammed shut four times in quick succession.

My family stood and sat right where I'd left them, as if my admonishment to stay put had frozen them in place.

When the door banged closed behind Sandy, Giacomo brought his head up with a snort, and my mother grimaced like her last nerve snapped. Her face glistened with a sheen of sweat, and mascara smudged her lower lids.

Or had she been crying?

This thought threw me for a loop until I reminded myself I had no way of knowing what my mother would look like if she'd been crying.

Or laughing.

Or if she were bored or excited or...

This line of thinking did me no good.

"Back in a sec," I told them and took my hoard of whipped cream to the fridge. Wouldn't Malcolm be pleased to see us so well stocked?

Before returning to the front room, I took one more squirt of chocolate for insurance.

Clara met me at the kitchen door.

"Let's cut this pie before it melts."

Pie might not fix everything, but it was a good start. She jerked open the cutlery drawer to find a sharp knife—her favorite tool.

Sandy came in right behind her. "I'll get plates and forks," she announced. "And napkins."

Zoe followed with, "We all want iced tea right? I'll make more."

Had the stoney glares of Adrian and Gem Gem caused my troop to retreat?

"They scare you?" I asked.

No eye contact. Not a peep.

"Oh, brother," I muttered.

Armed with two cans of plain, I marched back to the front room. I set them down on the coffee table and switched on the giant old air conditioner that had been installed through the wall near the ceiling in one corner. It lumbered to noisy life but quickly began circulating cooler air.

"Our neighbor, Clara, brought over a pie."

Clara carried the jiggly custard dotted with bits of pink from the rhubarb, still clutching the knife between her fat fingers.

This should be good. And I wasn't thinking about the sweet-tart combo now resting on the coffee table. Although that would be wonderful, I was sure.

The first time Clara offered me pie, I refused it. She went still and looked at me as if I'd sprouted a second head, that knife poised to slice off the offending appendage if I didn't come to my senses. I did and never again thought to say *no thank you*.

"And," I added, brandishing my weapons, "we have whipped cream."

My father's eyes lit, but my mother's went glassy as if the sight of so much sugar and fat in one place would put her in a coma.

I should be so lucky.

Sandy brought in a stack of paper plates topped with sheets of paper towels and a handful of mismatched forks. No doubt, my parents were used to gold-trimmed china, expertly folded linen, polished silver, and liveried footmen.

Maybe not the footmen.

Zoe brought in the sweating pitcher of tea and set it on a paper plate next to the pie.

"There," I said. "Mom, Dad, Giacomo, I'd like you to meet our neighbor Clara Davis, my friend, Sandy Houseman, and Zoe Frost. She works for us."

Zoe shot me a mildly annoyed look at not being included in the roll of neighbor or friend, I suppose. I rolled my eyes and swept my arm toward my parents.

"Adrian and Gemma Marie York. And Giacomo Russo."

"My father-in-law," Mom supplied.

I beamed at my friends like a loopy monkey. "My grandfather!"

My last name, Parker, I'd taken from my aunt and uncle. York was the name given to Adrian at the orphanage.

Or so I'd been told.

Was anything what it seemed?

My father pushed away from the mantle and extended his hand to Clara, every move fluid and exact. She took his and he kissed the back of hers, staring intently into her eyes all the while. She shivered and made a little dip like a half-baked curtsey.

Oh, for cripe's sake.

"Thank you for bringing the pie," he said, his voice deeper than when he'd spoken to me. "*Very* thoughtful."

She giggled.

Shoot me now.

"Very nice to make your acquaintances," my mother said. I

noticed her tea still sat at her elbow, untouched, the ice melted. She'd faint from dehydration at this rate.

Sandy lifted her arm in my father's direction as if in a trance. He took her hand and kissed the back of it as sincerely as he had Clara's. Sandy sighed so deeply I thought she might swoon. Romance novel addict that she was, she'd probably never wash that hand again.

I shot a speaking glance at Zoe. Clearly, I'd hurt her feelings by introducing her as our employee rather than as my friend. Would she succumb to his charm, too?

Zoe arched her back and tucked her chin. She stuck out her hand, grabbed my father's, gave it a hard shake and me a decisive nod.

Someone was loyal. Someone had as good a bullshit meter as I did. I'd find a way to repay her for that.

I knelt next to the coffee table, picked up a fork, aimed it toward the center of the pie, and said, "Dig in!"

My mother twitched.

"Just kidding, *Mom*," I said, nearly choking on the word. "You haven't landed in the Wild West."

She sniffed. "I never—"

"Ever had rhubarb custard pie?" Clara interrupted. She inched the knife beneath the first piece, slid it on a plate, and offered it to my mother.

The air in the room froze, and not from the chugging air conditioner. My mother kept her hands tightly clasped in her lap, whether because she was unsure about the delectation or the paper plate, I didn't know.

Then, she flattened them on her thighs.

"Wait, wait," I said. "It's not ready."

My mother's hands spasmed, and she and Clara turned to me. Everyone turned to me. I picked up the nearest can of whipped cream, buried the slice of pie in it, and laid a fork alongside.

I decided to try for that same sexy, sophisticated smile of my dad's. Hey, I have his genes, right? I should be able to pull it off. I'm afraid what was probably on my face was a sly and satisfied grin.

"*Now*, it's ready."

Maybe the beginnings of a smile cracked the careful veneer of my mother's face.

Maybe not.

She passed the whipped cream smothered piece to my father. "About half that size, if you please." She directed this to Clara.

Clara obliged, and I put a little squirt of cream on top.

There, definitely an uptick at one corner of Gemma's mouth, quickly squelched. Was it possible that beneath the haughty exterior lay a real person?

Unlikely.

Giacomo took his without comment and eyed it uncertainly. He took a bite, chewed, smiled, held up his fork, and said, "delizioso," before cleaning his plate.

By the time I'd gotten my piece, my father was hawking for seconds. Clara snagged his gaze and pointed the knife tip at the half of a half left by my mother, then at a full slice. He winked, and she loaded his plate with the larger piece.

My mother ate slowly and dabbed her lips with a paper towel corner.

"That *was* delicious," she said.

It occurred to me I'd have to make dinner for them.

Find a place for them to sleep.

Move myself back to the apartment above the barn.

Tell Malcolm.

Find out what the hell they were doing here. More importantly, how long they intended to stay. This, I decided, could wait until morning.

At which point, I'd need to make them yet another meal.

To hell with that. Surely they could make their own breakfasts?

And even though we'd just had pie, it was about lunchtime. If they'd flown in this morning, they probably needed a decent meal right about now. Not that there was anything wrong with pie and whipped cream.

I might be pissed they'd shown up without warning, furious they were here at all, and freaked to be dealing with them without Malcolm, but I could be hospitable. Just because they'd abandoned me as an infant didn't mean I had to turn my back on them now, no matter how much I wanted to do just that.

Anyway, Giacomo came with tomatoes. And that was a good thing.

"Well," I said, standing and brushing my hands on my jeans. "I'll show you where you'll be sleeping."

My father took my mother's hand and helped her up.

At that moment, the room darkened and all our gazes flew to the window. Heavy clouds had swallowed the sun. A roll of thunder shook the windows, making us all jump. A few drops of moisture patted the porch steps.

"Finally," Sandy said. "Guess you won't need to be watering this afternoon, Clara."

Clara grinned, showing the gap where a couple of molars were missing. She usually wore a bridge. "And a good thing, too," she said. "Pump's about wore out."

Zoe crossed to the door. The rain started to get more serious about its intentions. "So much for working the horses."

"Maybe it'll cool things off a little, and we can ride later," I said.

Zoe nodded, staring through the screen. "Did you want all that luggage to get washed?"

For a moment, I couldn't figure out what she meant.

"Oh, crap." I bolted through the door and down the steps.

"Take the Gator," Clara yelled.

I jumped into the seat and cranked the engine. Sandy slid in beside me, and Zoe ran ahead. She was already swinging the largest piece through the air by the time we reached her. It thumped into the bed. Sandy and I each nabbed a suitcase and flung them on top of the other. Zoe picked up an old-fashioned square cosmetics bag and started running back to the house.

I made a circle as fast as the Gator was able—which was kinda slow. Clara's husband, Hank, grumbled you needed a forty-acre field to turn the thing around. With six wheels, quick maneuvering wasn't what it was made for.

"Hell of a kid," Sandy observed as we rumbled up the drive.

"Lot's of energy," I said.

The kid in question had already deposited the bag inside and was coming back for more.

My parents and Clara stood on the porch watching. Through the curtain of rain, my father had a funny look on his face—a kind of self-deprecating or apologetic frown. My mother looked as if she'd like to worry her lip but couldn't allow her lipstick to get smudged.

We pulled up, and I killed the engine. Clara grabbed a smallish bag and hauled it in. Sandy and I took the rest.

"This one here's on the light side," Clara said when we were standing in the front room again.

Me and Sandy and Zoe dribbled water into little pools around our feet.

"Now that you mention it," I said. "They were all lighter than I expected."

My mother's eyes had a strange glint to them. My father heaved a deep breath.

"That," he said, "is because they're all empty."

CHAPTER SEVEN

I stayed in the apartment above the barn after getting my parents settled in Malcolm's room and Giacomo ensconced in the guest room. If he had any thoughts about the pink comforter and stuffed animals on the bed, he kept them to himself. The room was reserved for Malcolm's eight-year-old daughter, Nicky. But she'd visited in July and wouldn't be back until Thanksgiving.

Surely, they'd be gone by then.

Even though I changed the sheets in the master, dumped my stuff into a pillowcase, and grabbed my toothpaste and shampoo from the bathroom, I knew my mother knew that the master bedroom had, of late, also been mine.

This made me feel darkly guilty. That made me angry. Angrier than I already was.

What the *hell* were they doing here?

With empty suitcases, no less?

On top of that, there was a polite but frosty tension between them that I'd never seen before. Plenty between them and me, but not between the two of them. It wasn't just Giacomo, although I was curious why he had suddenly joined the family after nearly fifty years of nonexistence. I had a feeling the strain was at least partly because of him, but something else was going on, too.

Needless to say, I didn't ask them more questions that night. I simply couldn't be in the same building with them any longer.

So, I sat alone on the couch in the apartment, vegging out in front of the television, avoiding both thought and sleep. With half the whipped cream in the apartment's fridge, and half my new cache at the house, all contingencies were covered. Neither of my parents would use it, of that I was sure, despite my father's enjoyment of it on his pie. They would never risk their figures that way. Giacomo was an unknown. On all levels.

Of course, I wasn't really alone. Noire sat next to me, her glossy black head on my thigh, breathing quietly. Occasionally, she licked her lips, made a soft sound, or moved her legs, and I wondered if she dreamed of her own version of canned whipped cream. She favored hot dogs, and I could depend on them for sneaking pills into her when necessary.

Henrietta, the barn cat, curled against my other leg, then stretched and rolled to her back, showing me her shaved belly. Her stitches were due to come out tomorrow. Sandy, who worked at the vet's office, had promised to come over and do it. I'd removed both stitches and staples from horses, but cats didn't tend to sit still for that sort of thing.

Four kittens had been born in the apartment closet right after I moved in—right in my basket of dirty clothes. Night, all black like his mom, sprawled next to Henrietta. Snowball fell asleep on my shoulder after sucking on my earlobe and kneading my neck, and Tiger and Tigress opted to snuggle into Noire's warmth. Outside, it was hot, but the apartment's AC worked extremely well. It was almost cold.

And peaceful.

I could depend on my critters for comfort and companionship. Except for my old friend Wastrel. He had other matters on his equine mind.

Before long, I'd polished off the last of the can of chocolate whipped cream by way of dinner and fell into a sugar-induced coma.

In the first dream, we'd returned to the horse show. *That* horse show. Jesus. Wasn't it bad enough he'd nearly killed me once? And himself in the process?

Apparently not.

Again, we cantered our circle to start the course, with something feeling off—something I couldn't put my finger on—then right out of the ring and away.

From there, he was standing on cross ties at Winterlight. Right downstairs with all the other horses. His silky coat felt dense beneath my fingers, as if the first cool nights of fall had hit and his pelt had begun to thicken in preparation for winter.

I put him in the pasture with the others and all hell broke loose. My real horse, Cali, immediately paired up with him, which made Captain, her best friend since coming to Winterlight, jealous, and he attacked Wastrel.

Fortunately, you can't hurt a dream horse, and he couldn't damage anyone, either.

Honey got into the fight because she was best friends with Captain before Cali got there, and that made Smitty mad because he had a crush on Honey. But Smitty, being a timid horse, didn't try to defend his turf. Instead, he ran behind a stand of blackberry bushes and hid.

Next, I'm on Wastrel's back again, and we dive off a platform like the circus riders of old. Only we're plunging straight toward a large swath of solid concrete.

I jolted awake with my heart clobbering my ribs, my neck kinked from sleeping sitting up, and stinking from my own sweat.

The cats and dog hadn't moved. Someone blared at me from the TV about the latest, greatest appliance that would make me live forever.

At the moment, that was the last thing I wanted to do.

It was early morning, earlier than I usually started, but sleep was pointless, so I eased the critters away, got up, and stretched.

First thing, I'd check on Smitty. I knew he wouldn't have a scratch on him, but I had to make sure. When I say these Wastrel-hosted dreams are vivid, I'm not kidding. I smell his heavenly scent and feel heat coming off him. Sometimes, I could swear my body ached from the beating it takes during these nocturnal visits.

This time, however, I could thank sleeping on the couch.

I got in the shower wishing it was Saturday. Saturday we had rides scheduled from morning until evening. Exhausting myself with work was exactly the distraction I needed. Plus, Malcolm would be back by then. Sometimes, he checked in when working at a client site, but I wouldn't call him unless it was urgent. If my parents showing up wasn't a level-one emergency, I don't know what was.

Yet, something kept me from making the call. Something like fear. Fear that he'd kick us all out. Fear that I'd use the situation as an excuse to run away—my typical modus operandi when the going gets tough.

Downstairs, I got started as day chased away night. Smitty was fine. The short thunderstorm had tamped down the dust, but not much more, and it wasn't cooler. Gaston worked well. He'd been stiff and resistant to the left when I first started riding him and didn't always pick up that lead, but now he carried himself with balance in both directions. I couldn't wait for Malcolm to ride him so he could feel the difference.

Zoe arrived on time. My day was looking up.

"How're your parents?" she asked.

Miss Bong—also known as Bongo—stood on the cross ties. I didn't pause my grooming rhythm.

"No idea."

I hadn't checked on them. Nor had they condescended to come to the barn.

Fine.

What the *hell* was I supposed to do with them?

Zoe stared at me for a moment, but whatever she saw in my face forestalled further questions. "We have a ride?"

"Yes. In half an hour. Honey, Fawn, and Captain need to be groomed and tacked up. You can ride Smitty."

"Really?"

Smitty was a much nicer ride than Fawn. "Yeah, you're more than ready."

"Thanks!"

She ran to get the horses.

This group of four riders were rank beginners, but the horses were relaxed and ready to take it easy because it was already hot and the rain had made it even more humid than the day before. I let Zoe take the lead, and I brought up the rear, letting Miss Bong's long stride flow into my back to ease some of the tension from my shoulders.

We skirted the fields and Noire happily flushed rabbits. My mind gladly wandered. But I couldn't keep it off the present for long. If the previous series of Wastrel dreams were any indication, these latest ones contained clues. Did these clues point to my parents, or Giacomo, or a different set of people or events entirely?

And what about the unlikely poacher down in the ravine? As soon as I had a chance, I would return with Noire and look for tracks or anything that might indicate someone doing something they shouldn't. Not that there'd be much left to see after the rain.

After a meager lunch of cheese and crackers scrounged from upstairs, Zoe and I sat in the tack room cleaning bridles.

Adrian and Gemma still hadn't made an appearance, and guilt began to erode my indifference. I pulled a rein through a towel soaked in leather conditioner, put it down, and stood.

"I'm going to the house."

Zoe glanced up from polishing a snaffle bit. "Want me to come with you?"

I did.

Wiping my hands on my jeans and sighing, I said, "No. It's time I put on my big-girl panties and face them."

"Hey, they invaded your space. They should be worried about facing you, not the other way around."

I smiled. "You're pretty smart, you know?"

"I know."

"Don't let it go to your head."

She smirked and bent to her task—moving on to the sweaty cheek pieces of Gaston's bridle. I ran upstairs for some creamy reinforcement, then called Noire. I wasn't going to enter the lion's den completely alone.

It was when I stepped down into the aisle that a loud boom ricocheted through the barn. Horses in the field jumped, lifted their heads and looked toward the house. Zoe came through the tack room door.

"Was that—"

"I think—"

The sound had been both familiar and foreign. But my brain was catching up fast.

Again, a crack bent the air, sending a tremor through me. A couple of the horses bucked and took off.

"Shit," I said, starting to run. "Those are gun shots."

CHAPTER EIGHT

I ran. Ran like the devil himself had a bead on me.

Which someone had, once, not long ago, someone evil. But that time, I'd been on a horse. A very fast horse.

Oh god oh god oh god.

Again, I found myself running straight at my fear instead of disappearing in my preferred direction—away.

Wishing I had four legs, I forced more power into the two, sprinted up the driveway, pounded across the porch, and tore the screen door off one hinge getting inside.

Needed to breathe. *Not* picture the images rushing my brain.

No one in the front room.

Sliding down the slick old hardwood of the hallway on the soles of my riding boots, I careened into the kitchen.

There, my parents sat at the table, each reading a section of the days-old local weekly paper. My father wore glasses.

No blood.

Had they killed Giacomo and stashed the body? If so, they were mighty quick.

They brought a gun? Knives? My eyes went to the wooden

knife block near the stove, my thoughts more scattered than the shots that got me here.

"Where's Giacomo?"

My parents glanced up and stared at me. Too calm, too studied.

My mother shrugged and went back to reading.

They were cold-blooded freaking murderers.

"In the garden, I think," my father said. He peered over his reading glasses, then angled his head toward the mudroom and side yard.

We don't have a garden.

With a hand to my diaphragm, I tried quieting my breathing. It whistled like hell's own banshee. "I heard shooting."

The corner of my mother's mouth twitched. She had no makeup on. I'd never seen her without. "So did we," she said without taking her eyes off whatever interesting tidbit of county news had caught her attention.

At this rate, I'd be a cold-blooded killer myself by sunset. Resisting the urge to wrap my hands around the slim column of her elegant neck, I strode past them to the mudroom and peeked through the side door.

Giacomo was out there all right. He'd planted his tomatoes in a neat row, the freshly turned earth looking like a new grave. Planting a garden made a statement about intent. Like, they intended to be here for more than a little while. I pushed the door open and calmly stepped out, that calm being only on the surface. Beneath, my mind caromed like pool balls after the break. I'd been awful quick to jump to the worst possible conclusion about my parents.

The tomato plants' sturdy stems emerged from the freshly turned dirt in a neat row, and the old man hammered a crooked metal post into the ground on one side of it.

I began to breathe.

The shotgun, one of Malcolm's, lay at Giacomo's feet.

"What are you doing?" I yelled to make sure he heard over the clanging. My tone came out more harsh than intended. Hey, I'd just nearly had a heart attack imagining every horrible possibility with regard to people and guns, and I have a vivid imagination. I could be forgiven.

He stopped hammering, looked at me, and took the moment to wipe his high forehead across his shoulder, a hank of his thick gray hair falling into his eyes, then gestured at the plants as if that explained. What was he, a mime?

"I mean, what are you doing with that gun?"

"Crows," he said with a generic sweep of one arm.

I scanned the surrounding trees. "There aren't any."

"Because I let them know. They not welcome."

"By shooting at them?" Whatever happened to good old fashioned scarecrows?

"How else?"

Jesus. I was going to have a *lot* of 'splaining to do when Malcolm got back. I should just call him.

What would I say? *Hey, babe, the parents I haven't seen nor heard from in years dropped by for an extended visit, brought my demented grandfather with them, and he borrowed your gun to plant his tomatoes.*

Yeah. No.

Oh, and by the way, they're sleeping in your room.

This was a conversation better had in person. But I should at least give him a heads-up. I'd leave him a message, that's what I'd do, not with any specifics, but strongly encouraging him to call me before coming home. I could only hope he didn't turn us all out when he got back. He was a very understanding guy, but this invasion might just push him over the edge. I'd seen him mad, seen him handle that shotgun. We didn't want to go there.

He'd also tried to get me to handle that weapon. For my protection when he was away, he said. But I don't like guns. I prefer Willy, the baseball bat I keep next to the bed.

Speaking of, I'd left Willy upstairs when I'd made room for my parents. I needed to get that bat and take it to the apartment.

I didn't know what to say to Giacomo. I didn't think Malcolm would appreciate someone borrowing one of his guns, not to mention the ammunition needed. That probably cost money. Money, I had a bad feeling, neither my parents, nor my grandfather, had.

Gah. *What* was I supposed to do with them?

"You should probably put that gun away."

I should pick it up and put it where it belonged myself. I would, if I could stand to touch it. Which I couldn't.

Giacomo grunted as he tied a string to the metal post and stretched it to a matching one on the other side of the tomatoes. Then, he gently, carefully, draped the vines over the string. Nearby, he had a watering can. Where had he found this stuff?

I really didn't know these people, and I'd entrusted Malcolm's house to them. This is how they repaid me? And his hospitality? By rifling through his belongings?

Noire bounded around the corner of the house, then, gayly carrying a six-foot long branch in her mouth.

I yelled, "No!" but she plowed right through the tomatoes.

The look of horror on Giacomo's face would have been comical if he hadn't simultaneously reached for the gun.

I dove between him and my dog, pushed her away from the plants with one arm, and knocked him to the ground with my shoulder. The gun bounced out of his hand. I snatched it up and stood, panting.

One tomato plant was bent over, but the rest were upright. Giacomo sat, wiping his hands together. He looked at his plants then glared at me.

"What's-a wrong with you?" he asked. Growled, more like, his accent thickening.

A tired old question that would probably never be answered in my lifetime. In this case, though, even I had to admit he had a legit reason for asking. I'd shoved my own grandfather face first into the dirt.

Well. There was me in a nutshell. When it came to choosing between people and animals, people didn't stand a chance. I'd even picked up the shotgun because it threatened my dog. I held it loosely, butt on the ground, the barrel encircled by my finger and thumb. Instinct had made me grab it, but I wouldn't touch it more than necessary.

"Sorry," I said, even though I wasn't.

I extended a hand to help him, but he shook his head and crawled on hands and knees to the injured tomato, tenderly straightening it.

Seeing as how I wasn't getting anywhere with him, I left him to his plants, and went back to the kitchen. There, I grabbed a can of whipped cream from the fridge and went upstairs without saying word one to my parents. They'd made themselves breakfast, it looked like, or lunch. There were plates on the table with crumbs on them. At least they could do that much for themselves.

In the bedroom, I grabbed Willy, the hefty familiarity of the smooth wood calming me. So different from the cold weight of the metal barrel in my other hand. I remember Malcolm telling me it was a Browning. I would call it Browny. Naming it lessened its menace. I could hold something with a name. I didn't have to like it, but I could do it.

The bed had been made. No clothes draped the chair or hung on the back of the door. My parents had traveled much of their lives, so I'm sure they knew how to keep themselves contained.

What about those empty suitcases? They were traveling light. I would have to ask questions at some point. Confront them about what they were doing here and why they had a tomato-crazed old man in tow. But not until I talked to Malcolm. He would know how to approach this. A non-hysterical way to approach this.

Back downstairs, I went to his study. There, in the corner, stood the gun safe, a heavy iron box about five feet tall.

Malcolm was strict about keeping his guns locked up when he wasn't using them. This locker required two keys to open the main door and then another to access a smaller cupboard inside that held a couple of handguns and all the ammo. One of the main keys was locked in Malcolm's desk. He kept the other with him when he was home. When away, he locked that in a filing cabinet. The keys to the desk and filing cabinet were hidden behind books on the other side of the room. The key to the small cupboard he left in the lock.

I leaned Willy and Browny against the desk, relieved to release the cold metal of the gun, and went to the bookcase. The books hadn't been moved, but I pulled them out anyway. The keys were there. I checked the desk. Drawer, locked. Same for the filing cabinet.

Malcolm's precautions notwithstanding, a half-empty box of shells sat on the corner of the desk, and the safe's door gaped, a space like a broken tooth revealing where Browny should be.

Careful not to jar the lethal weapon—for all I knew it was still loaded—I put it where it belonged.

Somebody had a lot of 'splaining to do, and it wasn't only me.

CHAPTER NINE

"You've always told everyone you were left at an orphanage as an infant," I said to my father, trying, and failing, to sound reasonable.

I'd locked the gun safe—for all the good it would do—and gone back to the kitchen.

Adrian tucked one temple of his reading glasses into the neck of his T-shirt and pressed his hands against his thighs.

"I *was* left at an orphanage as an infant."

Gemma rolled the newspaper and held it on her lap with both hands. The movements of her slim fingers mesmerized me. But I quickly brought my attention back to Adrian.

"How is it you suddenly have a father?"

Of the million other questions battling for my attention, the mystery of Giacomo won.

"I've always had a father."

"Not interested in word games, Dad." I lifted my ponytail—frizzy with the humidity—off my neck and leaned against the counter. "I've always had a father, too, but I used to pretend you were dead because that hurt less than the truth."

He had the grace to wince. He exchanged a look with my

mother, or tried to. Her gaze fixed on nothing in particular, unfocused. A stab of alarm tightened my chest.

"To be honest," Adrian said, "we don't yet know the entire story ourselves. Suffice it to say that Giacomo had his reasons—good reasons—for leaving me like he did."

My heart sped up. If he was building some elaborate new justification for why they ditched me, I would scream. I took a squirt of fortitude from the can I still held.

"Somehow," he continued, "he always kept track of me."

This was beginning to sound like a familial pattern. Thank God I'd had the sense to remain childless. Unless you counted horses. And dogs. If that were the case, I had offspring. Offspring I *didn't* abandon.

My mother's knuckles turned white from gripping the paper like a lifeline. "He was living in Florida," she added, as if that helped.

Dad rubbed his hands down his lean thighs. He wore the same gray slacks as yesterday. They were a little frayed at the hems.

"He needed our help," he said.

"So you dropped your dancing shoes, left Europe, went and got him in Florida, and came here?" I slammed the can of whipped cream on the counter and gestured with both hands to either side of my head. "Now it all makes sense."

Still staring into nothingness, my mother opened her mouth to speak, but the sound of a car creeping up the drive drew my attention to the hall where I could see the front of the house.

The first thing I noticed was the screen door angled across the doorway where it hung by the bottom hinge. I made a mental note to fix that before Malcolm got home. The second was the familiar but unwelcome markings of a sheriff's vehicle pulling up to the walkway.

Deputy Joe stepped out but stayed behind the car door, his hand hovering near his weapon, eyes darting from side to side.

"It's okay," I yelled and hurried out so he would see who it was and that I was unarmed. "Hey, Joe, what brings you here?"

Yes, I was on a first-name basis with local law enforcement, and, as far as I knew, good terms.

"911 call reported shots fired."

"Who called 911?"

He consulted a small pad of paper. "Doesn't say. Caller ID indicated Mr. Robert Malcolm."

That would be because this was his place so of course the landlines were in his name. My parents joined me. Without looking at them, I asked out of the side of my mouth, "Did you call the police?"

"No," they said in unison, their voices strained. They went back inside.

Must have been Zoe. I needed to wring someone's neck, and it might as well be hers. Joe's eyes continued to scamper around the yard, pasture, and finally, the porch. Sweat beaded on his forehead. Two giant sweet gum trees made it cooler in the yard than inside, but Joe stood in direct sun.

"My parents and grandfather are visiting, and my grandfather borrowed a gun to scare the crows away from his tomatoes."

Sometimes, truth is best, even if it sounds crazy. Evidently, it didn't sound crazy to Joe. He nodded and relaxed, leaning his forearms on the window frame of the cruiser door.

"They helping you with your new business?"

I closed my eyes, wondering what new level of hell I might be entering now. "What new business?"

"Something to do with being a detective using a dream horse?"

He managed to say this without smirking or laughing, but the corner of his mouth quivered.

All breath left my body. *Sandy*. Damn her. The Dream Horse Detective Agency was her idea, not mine, and not one I was on board with. The dream horse in question, however, Wastrel, well, he was mine, despite all efforts to oust him from my previously uninterrupted sleepy time. I hadn't shared him and his cryptic clues with anyone other than Malcolm, Dex, and Sandy. The guys wouldn't have said anything to Joe.

I added Sandy to my those-who-must-be-strangled list. This was not the sort of thing I wanted people to know about me.

"Uh...yeah." I forced a chuckle that sounded fake even to my ears. "That was just a silly idea we came up with one night. Too much to drink, probably."

I bit my lip. Way to throw Sandy under the stampede. But she had no business blabbing that I was starting a detective agency. Especially when I wasn't.

He leveled a *yeah, I've got your number* look at me before putting on his sunglasses. "Too bad," he said. "Things got interesting here for a while after you moved to town."

"Interesting. Right."

He slapped the car roof. "Well...cows to catch and high-speed tractors to ticket."

I laughed for real. "Good one, Joe."

"Keep it clean, Parker." He smoothed his short dark hair with one hand. "Don't waste our time and resources with nuisance calls."

I backed up a couple of steps. "You got it. Have fun protecting and serving."

He eased into the car seat, gave me two thumbs up, and grinned before backing around to head out.

When I turned, my father had a screwdriver and was fixing the broken screen door hinge.

"I would have done that," I said when I got back to the porch.

"Happy to help."

I stood there for a minute, feeling confused and useless and unsure how to proceed.

"Thanks," I said when he looked at me.

He nodded, and I went inside knowing I should continue the conversation with my parents, wanting to see why Zoe felt the need to call 911, but suddenly, achingly, so tired I could barely move.

I heard the squeaky fourth tread of the stairway and knew my mother had gone up. I'd like to go lie down in an air-conditioned room, too, but that luxury had to wait. Giacomo helped himself to a glass of iced tea from the fridge.

"Cops?" He held the cool glass to his cheek, letting the condensation drip through his beard and onto the front of his collared shirt. No tie today.

"I think my barn worker must have called them when we heard the shooting." I put the whipped cream away. "Let's try to keep that to a minimum from now on."

"I make a scarecrow tomorrow." He shrugged. "It don't work so good as the scattergun."

"I understand."

It's not like it was rare for people to shoot off guns around here, even if it wasn't hunting season. People shot them for fun, for target practice, and what have you. Made no sense to me. Malcolm had competed in the pentathlon when he was younger, which included pistol shooting in addition to riding, fencing, swimming, and cross country running. Which explained his amazing body *and* why he had hand guns. But I didn't know if he hunted. In any case, he had a safe full of both long and short firearms that I didn't like.

"I'm sorry about before," I said to Giacomo. "Are you all right?"

He pulled himself taller. "Eh," he said with a dismissive hand gesture. "Takes more than a shove from a little girl to hurt Giacomo Russo."

At five foot six and a hundred and thirty pounds of muscle, I wasn't exactly a little girl, but I was glad he was all right.

"I'll try to keep my dog out of the garden, and you stay away from the guns. Okay? They belong to Mr. Malcolm."

He poured himself more tea, his back turned for a moment. I didn't like his lack of response.

Going for casual, I asked, "How did you get the gun out, anyway? How did you open the safe?"

Giacomo shut the refrigerator door too hard and everything inside jiggled and clanked.

"How you think?"

"I don't know," I bit out, then took a calming breath before continuing. "That's why I'm asking."

He drank his tea, smiled, his eyes twinkling as they had when we first met, and I had the first hint that when younger, Giacomo Russo had been a charming rogue.

"Easy," he said with a wink. "I pick the lock."

CHAPTER TEN

I *pick the lock. I pick the lock.*

Giacomo's statement, baldly matter-of-fact and unapologetic, whispered through my brain as I put my truck in gear. I didn't need Wastrel to confirm what I felt in my gut. Something wasn't right about this situation.

Dex One could do a background check on the old man. What if he was a clever con artist taking advantage of my parents? He might be, but he was my grandfather, all right. He and dad shared the same profile and endearing lopsided smile.

I put it all out of my mind and headed to the farm implement store to buy a new bale spear. Two days ago, I'd managed to snap the old one after getting stuck in the ditch while harrowing the pasture. Apparently, levering two tons of tractor with a two-inch thick length of steel isn't recommended. Replacing it before Malcolm got back seemed like a good idea. No reason to give him something else to be annoyed about. My parents would be enough.

I'd left Zoe in charge after dressing her down about calling the police.

"Someone was shooting," she'd said. "Guns are dangerous."

"People shoot all the time out here."

Not that it still didn't make my heart leap from my chest every time.

"But I thought—"

"I know what you thought. Just don't be so quick next time."

"Next time?"

"There won't be a next time. You know what I mean."

She frowned, clearly not clear on what I meant. But there wouldn't be a next time, so I let it go.

I also left a message for Malcolm. Nothing hysterical, just a calm note urging him to call me as soon as he could.

Sandy pulled in, hopped out of her car, yanked open the passenger door of my truck, and slid onto the seat before I could say *no*. She slung her arm around my dog. Noire licked her sweaty face. The air conditioning didn't work in Sandy's car. It was feeble at best in my truck but enough that we could keep the windows closed.

"Where're we going?"

Her grin kept me from kicking her out, but I really wanted some alone time.

"Town," I said. "I broke Malcolm's spear."

"His..." Her eyebrows shot up. "Wow. That didn't take long." Her grin widened as I focused on pulling out onto the blacktop. "They don't sell them at the tractor store, you know."

I looked at her.

She snapped her fingers at me. "Earth to Vi. Not enough whipped cream this morning?"

"That thing on the front of the tractor for picking up big round bales? Where else would I get one?"

"Ooohhh...." She rolled her eyes. "You mean the *bale* spear. I got it."

"What else—oh." I snorted. "Very funny. No, I didn't break Malcolm's *spear*. You read too many romance novels."

She shrugged, the movement lifting her generous chest nearly to her chin. A purple tie-dyed sports bra already had the girls hoisted high.

"I didn't think you could read too much," she said in a small voice.

Her hurt tone sliced through my self-absorbed haze. I knew she had confidence issues and looked up to me. Why, I have no idea. I guess it's enough I'm from New York and different. In a Monty Python *and now for something completely different* kind of way. I also knew she had a crush on Malcolm, or used to. Maybe still did. It would be hard *not* to crush on a super-hero handsome guy with a fabulous body who worked around the farm in a kilt. Sometimes without a shirt. God, I hoped he didn't freak when he found out about my parents.

"No," I said. "You can't read too much."

We continued in silence for a half mile of winding road, the fields to either side striped with rows of drying corn and soy beans. Another pickup came from the other direction. Sandy waved.

"Who was that?" I asked.

"I don't know."

"Then why'd you wave?"

"You're supposed to wave to ever'body."

"*Supposed* to? Why?" Waving to the wrong person where I came from could get a girl in trouble.

"It's friendly-like. Anyway, even if I don't know 'em, they prob'ly know somebody I know. Get it?"

I didn't. "So, you wave just in case?"

"No, I wave 'cause it's friendly."

"Nobody around here would recognize me."

"Look, Vi, you got to understand. They. Know." She emphasized her point by poking me in the shoulder. "They know when somebody's new, they know your truck, they know Malcolm, and they know you work for him." Poke. "They also know Clara and Hank. Hell, you're on a first-name basis with the sheriff's deputy." Poke. "Half the county prob'ly already knows your family's here."

"Not a happy thought."

I rubbed my shoulder, and she jabbed her finger into my forearm. "And, you know me. So, if you thinks you're invisible or somethin', you got another think comin'."

I sighed. Invisible was good. "I don't stick my nose in anyone's business, and I don't want them sniffing around mine."

"It ain't so bad." She rubbed her hand over her mouth. "I might of died if you hadn't come lookin' for me that time."

"I—" She'd been drugged, raped, beaten, and left to die, but she could still joke about a man's *spear*. Her spirit inspired me to be better.

"So don't act like you don't care, neither." She crossed her arms under her breasts, nodded, and stared through the windshield. Point made.

Point taken.

A car approached from the other direction. I felt Sandy watching me out of the corner of her eye. I lifted one hand from the steering wheel and wagged it at the other vehicle at the last moment.

Sandy did an extravagant eye roll, the kind that made me wonder if she could see her brain.

"What? I waved. Did I do it wrong?"

"It was too late. And you don't have to use your whole hand. Save that for when it's someone you do know. Just use a couple of fingers."

Waving at strangers. An art form.

"She didn't wave at me."

"Don't matter. You still gotta do it."

I breathed a sigh of relief after we reached the highway without meeting any other traffic.

"Do I wave to people out here?"

"'Course not."

No, of course not.

"Let's go to the drive-thru at McDonald's when we get there," she said. "I ain't had no lunch."

Mine had been craptastic, so while I usually avoided junk food, this sounded appealing for a change. Anyway, they had salads, right?

Sandy squeezed my dog and turned on the baby talk she used when speaking to animals. "Would you like that Noiry-Poiry?"

I ground my teeth, but Noire's tail thumped and her ears perked up.

"Huh, pwitty girly-whirly? Who'd like a nice juicy burger-wurger from Mickey-Ds?"

My dog had more patience than I did. I turned on the radio and tuned her out, mentally making a shopping list for the grocery store. At the top? More whipped cream.

Twenty minutes later we idled in the drive-up line of the fast food restaurant. Noire put her front feet on my thigh so she could pant out the window in anticipation of her burger-wurger.

My truck sounded like it might die at any moment. Malcolm had cleaned and recharged the battery shortly after I arrived in Missouri, but the '99 Chevy had nearly two-hundred thousand miles on it, and I wasn't sure how much longer it would last. With being able to use Malcolm's vehicles occasionally, I hoped to nurse it through the winter until next spring when I found out how much the trust fund was worth. If it wasn't even enough to buy a new truck...

"Think happy thoughts," Sandy said.

"What?"

"You're face is gettin' all tight like it does when you've got somethin' worryin' you."

"It is not." Though it didn't really surprise me. I've never been good at hiding how I feel.

"Hell yeah, it is."

I forced a smile, and we ordered. I joined the junk food frenzy.

Nothing like a little salt and grease to turn your mind to happy thoughts.

As we waited for our turn to pay, Sandy said, "Manroot."

"Huh?"

"It's one of them words from romance novels that they use in place of...you know."

"Penis?"

"Yeah, that."

The car in front of us moved up, and we followed.

"Throbbing manroot," I said after a moment.

Sandy hooted. "I knew you read them."

"Some." I didn't have much time to read.

"Molten rod," she said.

I almost choked. The car in front of us edged forward again, and we got a little closer to the window. Noire's hot breath hit my face. I elbowed her back, rolled up the window, and turned the fan to high.

"Turgid member," I said, revealing that I'd read more than I let on.

Sandy buried her face in Noire's neck to stifle herself.

We reached the first window, and I rolled down mine enough to hand over the money to a cute teenaged boy.

"Swollen shaft!" Sandy yelled just as he gave me my change. I dropped the coins on the ground.

"Holy shit."

She howled with laughter.

"Shut up!" The car in front of us sat there, and I couldn't get my window to work.

The boy leaned down so he could see Sandy, then looked at me and winked. I smiled at him, and we inched forward just enough to get away.

"Are you insane?" Tears leaked from the corners of my eyes as I tried to keep from laughing.

"Oh. My. Gawd. You shoulda seen your face."

I wiped my cheeks, glared at her, and bided my time until we had our food and were once again on the road. When I saw her shove a quarter of her Big Mac in her mouth, I shouted, "Pulsing shaft!"

Meat, cheese, lettuce, tomato, pickle, onion, and special sauce shot forward to hit my windshield. I snorted soda all over my steering wheel. Noire lunged for the hurled bite and swallowed it before we even knew what she was doing.

Half an hour later, the guy at the implement store shook his head as we left. We couldn't stop giggling the entire time we were there. Because, well, *implement* and *spear*.

I'd needed the laugh and felt much lighter while attaching the shiny new bale spear to the tractor. I took groceries to the house, thinking I should have asked my parents and Giacomo if they wanted anything before I went. They had no way of going on their own. And perhaps no money, either. I really should ask whether they did, but had decided I'd wait until Malcolm came home. He'd get the needed intel in a calm and reasonable way. I'd go all demanding and accusatory on them before they said two words, and that wouldn't help. Plus, they'd have to answer him. After all, it was his kindness they were relying on.

My mother watched me put everything away. She wore a short yellow linen dress. With her hair pulled into a pony tail, she looked cool and elegant even with crappy air conditioning.

"I'll make a salad for supper," she said. "Perhaps you'll join us tonight."

We were not ready to sit down and pretend we were a happy family. Something else to delay until Malcolm returned.

"I still have a lot to do down at the barn." I rubbed sweat off the back of my neck and tried to look apologetic. "By the time I take a shower—"

"I know you work hard, Viola."

My jaw locked up. "You know nothing about me." There. It was out of my mouth, out of my mind, my heart. And it came out nice and steady, without heat rushing my throat.

She paused, one hand on the fridge door handle, her back to me. The tendons in her slim forearm pressed against her skin. It didn't make me feel better that she was tense too. I used the moment to stretch my neck and breathe deep before saying, "And I go by *Vi*."

Opening the fridge, she said, "Yes, but I named you Viola."

"Why?" So many questions, but this one had always bugged me.

"I was very young when I had you."

"Barely seventeen, I know," I said to her back, wondering if all important conversations must take place in the kitchen.

"The last thing I studied in English class was Shakespeare's *Twelfth Night*."

Had she even finished high school? The few times we'd been together, I'd been too angry to wonder.

"*Twelfth Night?*"

She put an armload of salad fixings on the counter. "Do you know the play?"

I like Shakespeare but haven't exactly had time to read his entire body of work. "Not that one."

"You should. It's very romantic and funny."

"I'll put it on my to-do list." A long list with little chance of ever being completed.

The effervescent mood brought on by my time with Sandy began to flatten.

My mother slipped an apron over her head—where the hell had that come from?—and began washing a head of romaine. "Viola was an orphan, too, you know. Shipwrecked. A very resourceful and intelligent character." She took out the cutting board and a knife and got a bowl down from the cabinet, thoroughly at home in someone else's kitchen. "Shakespeare's Viola disguised herself as a man for protection but was always forthright and honest in her dealings with others."

I leaned on the counter and watched her fingers work. "Even while deceiving them as to her true nature?" I asked. Was there a hidden message in what she was telling me? I wasn't good with deciphering code. Let alone discussing literature with my mother.

"Yes. She had secrets." She sent a tentative smile over her shoulder. "Don't we all?"

"Some more than others. Me? I'm an open book." I glanced at the clock. It was already five, and I did have chores waiting.

My mother hid whatever non-verbal response she might have to my comment by keeping her back to me and chopping carrots.

She used the knife blade to slide them into the bowl on top of the lettuce and said, "I won't spoil the end of the story." She turned toward me and pushed a stray hair off her forehead.

I sidled to the kitchen doorway and set my shoulder against the frame with my arms crossed. It was a little closer to the exit, and I was desperate to escape this awkward veiled conversation. "Feel free to share spoilers," I said. "I doubt I'll read it anytime soon."

"All right. Well, along with talk of madness, there is a great deal of deception and mistaken identity."

"Sounds like real life."

"Yes, well. Viola doesn't only impersonate a man, she also takes the role of someone of a lower class than herself."

"You gotta do what you gotta do." I pushed away from the doorframe. "You're sleeping in Malcolm's room, and he'll be home tomorrow, so I'm not sure what we'll be able to arrange after that."

She nodded and followed me down the hall. An itchy feeling between my shoulder blades told me she still carried the knife.

"The story seems to be about love," my mother said to my back. "All kinds of love."

She was definitely trying to drive home a message, here, but it was a little late for her to go maternal on me. I hoped she didn't intend to make her point with the knife. Given how dense I can be, I understand why someone might feel like that was the only way to get my attention. On the other hand, Sandy's poking had been enough for one day.

At the porch, I turned to my mother and took the bait. "So, what is the play really about?"

"I think it's the secondary title that has more meaning. It's also called *What you will*."

I've taken my share of literature classes where the teachers make you deconstruct stories to death. In lieu of knowing what an author intended, they make it up. My mother appeared to have rambled into water over her head with this one.

"I'm a little tired for a Lit 101 quiz, Mom."

"I know, Viola—Vi. I guess what matters is that even after all the confusion, in the end, Viola finds love and happiness."

Sounded like the sappily-happily ever after of all romance books.

Too bad it was all fiction.

CHAPTER ELEVEN

S leep is my favorite. Well, second favorite. Riding is my number one most loved activity.

But sleep...I know a little Shakespeare, too. Sleep used to be like death to me, the temporary end to *the heartache and thousand natural shocks that flesh is heir to,* as Hamlet said. Like floating on clouds of whipped cream, sleep was sanctuary, or used to be, before I came to Winterlight, before Wastrel started visiting. Now, I felt more like Henry IV when he wondered *O gentle sleep, nature's soft nurse, how have I frightened thee?*

Not that I couldn't go to asleep. That was easy. And staying there worked as well. But it wasn't a sanctuary. It wasn't gentle.

And falling asleep with the words *what dreams may come...* drifting through...not my best idea.

Wastrel takes me down a tight city street. For a change, I ride him bareback. No show clothes, no competition ring. No jumps. The clip-clop of his hooves on cobblestones comforts me. Diesel fumes, garbage stench, and the reek of day-old frying oil assault us. But it is quiet. Early, by the slant of light glancing off the brownstones making a canyon of the narrow lane. The cars parked to either side are older, putting the era at around the sixties, maybe. We've never time traveled before.

Up ahead, a man wearing a hat and suit walks away from us down the middle of the road as if he owns it, his step jaunty. He carries a bouquet of white flowers with dark greenery. Not roses. The blooms are too flat and have too few petals. I want to get a sniff, if only to rid my nose of the stink, but Wastrel refuses to go closer.

We follow the man when he cuts between two cars and onto the sidewalk, then goes through a door into a narrow entry to slap his gray fedora onto a hook. A horse wouldn't have fit in the entry, but I'd resigned myself to the unnatural physics of dreams.

The man goes up an equally skinny flight of stairs taking the steps two at a time. I'm not even sure I'm still on horseback at this point, but I can't change my direction or control anything that happens. I must wait and watch what Wastrel shows me.

A shaft of sun coming through a tall window brightens a tiny square landing and lights up the man's wavy dark hair as he goes through a door without knocking. A flash of profile before he ducks in, too fast for me to tell if he's someone I know.

The scene shifts to nighttime. The change jolts me, and I grab for Wastrel's mane. We're floating above a car creeping along a narrow country lane, headlights off.

We're back on the brownstone landing, and I feel menace, something dangerous coming behind us, but I can't turn away from the man in the suit and the woman who greets him with open arms and a bright smile.

We veer back to the country scene and another man, out of the car now, also carrying white flowers. These I can smell because the air in this place isn't clogged with car exhaust and cooking food. Gardenia. Love them.

He goes up a couple of steps, his gait tired but eager, unlocks a door and closes it quietly. Like the other scene, I'm behind him, can't see his face, and in this locale, nothing of the surroundings is clear, as if the edges of a painting got smudged before it dried.

I'm jerked back to daylight, to the man and woman hugging. Dizziness rocks me for a moment. She exclaims at the flowers. I feel the love they have for each other but also the stealthy darkness coming up the stairs. It's going to swallow us. I try to yell. I'm not sure who I'm warning or what the risk is, but no sound comes out of my mouth.

The woman looks right at me—through me—and her eyes go wide with horror. She puts her hand out. *No* she screams.

There's a loud boom.

The noise pulled me right out of bed to my feet where I swayed and caught myself on the bedside lamp. It tipped over and broke. I groped for the wall switch and flicked on the overhead light.

Noire stood on the bed, startled awake by the sound of glass breaking, then pricked her ears toward the window and let out a low woof.

The clock said it was two in the morning. I scrubbed my face, still half in the dream, wondering if the shotgun blast had been real.

A shotgun. A man driving on a country lane. Shit.

I bolted through the small living space, down the stairs, and out into the barn sprinting through it on the balls of my bare feet. Vaguely, I knew the chunky gravel of the drive dug into my soles but ignored it.

The house was dark, but with many of the windows open, shouting came through. A shriek cut the air, and a light went on upstairs.

As I slammed up onto the porch, I noticed Malcolm's SUV parked over on the side.

What the hell was he doing here?

The front door didn't give when I rattled the knob.

"Malcolm!"

As I ran around to the mud room, I couldn't be sure I'd made any sound, just like in the dream. The side door was locked, too. I punched through the glass pane, flipped the deadbolt from the inside, and jumped across the threshold, hoping to clear the shards.

I skidded down the hallway like I had earlier and made for the stairs, grabbing the round newel post and using it to fling myself halfway up.

Light and anger spilled from the main bedroom.

My breath came in short gasps as I took in the bizarre scene. Malcolm stood in the doorway holding his shotgun in one hand, the barrel pointed straight up. His other hand gripped a hunk of my father's nightshirt and held him at a stiff arm's length. Dust and plaster floated in the air along with the smell of gunpowder. I didn't bother looking for the hole that must be gaping in the ceiling seeing as how everyone appeared to be alive.

The sound of the toilet flushing told me where Giacomo was. My mother sat on the edge of the bed, leaning forward. Her sleek, dark hair hid her face, and she held her head. The strap of her peach nightgown had slipped off one shoulder.

Malcolm's features were set and hard. I'd seen that look when someone had kidnapped his daughter and tried to kill me. I didn't like having it directed at anyone I knew.

Dad's eyes flashed hot and angry. The set of mom's shoulders made me think she was in pain. When Giacomo joined us, still zipping his fly, ill-contained amusement danced at the corners of his mouth. He had the gall to wink at me. Whether that was meant to be conspiratorial or reassuring, I have no idea.

This was my family.

And I was in a shit-ton of trouble.

CHAPTER TWELVE

For a long moment, no one spoke. We stood frozen in a whacked-out tableau that made me imagine I'd fallen into a Shakespearean scene. No telling whether the play was tragedy or comedy.

"Somebody start talking," Malcolm said, his voice equal parts taut, tired, and tough.

Robert Harvey Malcolm, laird of Winterlight, had returned to his keep and was not happy about its condition.

He had that sweet rumpled look he always had when he came home from a business trip. A bit of beard, his wavy surfer hair mussed from running his hands through it, tie loose, and sleeves rolled up to expose his freckled forearms.

They all stared at me, and if ever I wanted a hole to open beneath my feet, it was then. Was I the one who had to start?

"Mom," I said, "are you all right?"

"Mom?" Malcolm said loudly enough that Hank and Clara, a mile away, likely heard.

"Yes." I kept my tone even. "And you can let go of my dad."

He looked at me like I'd grown a second head. "They're. In. My. Bedroom."

"He hit me with the gun," my mother said, her voice faint. She moved her hand to expose a red welt blooming on her forehead.

Shock rooted me in place. My father said something in another language, a bad word, by his inflection. Malcolm released him at the same time dad slapped his hand away and joined my mother on the bed, putting his arm around her shoulder. She flinched, and he started to pull away, then drew her against him and rubbed her arm.

"Are you dizzy?" I asked. She shook her head. I turned to Giacomo. "Get some ice."

He nodded and went down the stairs. My fingernails dug into my palms. My right hand throbbed. I'd forgotten I'd punched out a window. I held it behind my back. Unlike my mother, I've had a lot of practice ignoring pain.

"Queasy?" I asked her. I've never been hit with a gun, and I always wear my helmet when riding, but I've still managed to concuss myself, and I know the fuzzy headache it brings.

"No," she said, and I hoped it wasn't that bad. Without looking away from her, I said to Malcolm, "I called you earlier."

"I've been traveling all afternoon, Vi. Forgive me for having the courtesy to not return your call after midnight."

My father stood and drew my mother up with him. "Come, Gem Gem." He scowled at me as if this was all my fault. Malcolm and I moved aside to let them by.

When they reached the squeaky stair tread, Malcolm slammed the bedroom door so hard the windows rattled. A chunk of plaster hit me in the head.

"I didn't know what to do," I said. "They showed up yesterday, along with Giacomo—my father's father—"

Malcolm held up his hand to stop me. He set the gun against the wall and took my mother's place on the edge of the bed.

"Did it occur to you to call me *yesterday*?"

It had. I'd dithered, too afraid to risk it, sure I could handle everything on my own. That would be true if all the actors in this drama were horses instead of people. Or dogs. Them, I could deal with. People, not so much.

"Yes and no."

Looking at the weariness on his face, knowing that it was more than jet lag, I realized that once again, I'd blithely rushed into a relationship, and yet again, I'd royally screwed it up. With Malcolm, I'd actually paused to consider the ramifications of getting involved with him. For about a minute.

This would have happened sooner or later. I'm a freaking mess magnet. My parents' arrival just moved up the inevitable.

He scooped both hands through his hair, and when he spoke, his voice had softened. "I finished up early. Wanted to surprise you." He rested his elbows on his knees, his thick thigh muscles straining the fabric of his khaki slacks.

"Instead," he continued, and I realized his tone had gone too soft, "I walk into my house and get attacked by a stranger wielding one of my own guns. Can you imagine?" He squinted at me. "Mind telling me why the hell the old man had my shotgun?"

Still soft, but with an inflexible edge. Damn Giacomo. Hadn't he agreed to stay out of the safe? The shock had worn off. Murky exasperation took its place.

"Mind telling me why the hell you clocked my mother with that gun?"

He stood and came toward me, close enough for me to feel the heat of his anger. I flattened myself against the door.

"The old man snuck up behind me when I came in the bedroom." His voice rose, but still, his tone remained reasonable. "It was dark—because I wanted to surprise you. It all happened so fast..."

I'd seen this deadly calm side of Malcolm once before. I'd hoped to never see it again. He paced to the other side of the bed, and I held my breath.

"Didn't take much to get the gun away from him, but by then your father was yelling in French and your mother was up and moving. Did I mention it was dark?"

I nodded.

"And that I was expecting you?"

He hadn't, but that was a given.

"She shoved me."

"My mother?" That seemed so out of character as to be made up. She was pushy, yes, but not physically.

"Maybe she thought I was the old man?"

I shrugged. "Maybe." More likely she stumbled into him.

"Reflex," he said.

"Reflex?"

"I thought I was being attacked, Vi. That something horrible had happened to you. You can't imagine what went through my mind in those moments. I defended myself."

Against my mother, who, for all her haughty superiority, was incapable of attacking anyone. I pictured the terrifying moments in the dark when no one knew what was happening.

He paced back toward me, jerking on the knot of his tie, yanking it off, and slinging it toward the back of a chair. It slithered to the floor. Kind of like my heart.

I'd done this to him, brought this scare under his roof. I supposed that made us even. After all, it'd been his ex-wife and her lover who'd kidnapped Nicky and tried to kill me. They'd wanted to kill Malcolm, too. Anything to get their hands on the farm. The lover impaled himself on a bale spear during a brawl with Malcolm, and the ex was cooling her pedicure in jail, awaiting trial. Their scheme had failed, in large part because of me and Wastrel.

He came over to the tall dresser by the door and put his wallet and phone on top, just like he always did. I'd caught my breath from the mad dash to reach them, and now it left my body in a whoosh. I knew him. Knew his habits, his likes and dislikes. We'd immersed ourselves in each other for weeks working side by side during the day when he could manage it, riding, putting up hay, fixing fence. At night, our bodies learned each other's contours. Our fingers knew the touch that made our pulses race, our lips and teeth, where and how much pressure to make our breathing hitch.

And our hearts, well, I could speak only for mine. I'd been ignoring it, but in noticing that simple, everyday gesture, I knew it was gone. I would miss him. Miss this place.

When I first came to Winterlight, Malcolm had mentioned creating a partnership of some kind. I wanted to wait until I learned the trust fund's value. Then, all the craziness happened, and the partnership idea hadn't come up again. Even though he said he was worried something awful had befallen me, I knew what had to happen next. What always happened next. Enough was enough. Expecting him to take this latest incursion on his sanity with equanimity was too much.

I put my good hand on the doorknob. "I'll go pack. We'll be out of here by tomorrow."

He stopped in the act of kicking off his shoes and fixed me with a stunned glare. Then his gaze dropped to my right hand. Dang it. I moved it behind me again. It really hurt. I needed an icepack.

"I'll work until you find someone else."

We had a one-year contract but only had to both agree to break it. I'd never get the trust fund, but my parents needed it worse than me.

Once again, the look on his face indicated I'd grown a second head, or maybe antennae. He started unbuttoning his shirt and put his back to me, his shoulders stiff.

"Run away when things get tough. Is that all you know how to do?"

In that moment, I hated him. Because it was true.

"That's not fair," I blurted. "I'm doing this for you."

He whipped his button-down shirt across the room and spun on me. "Bullshit. You're doing it for you because it's easier than staying put and working through things."

In that moment, I also hated Dex One. He'd done a very thorough background check before Malcolm hired me, and there was no denying my history.

"I *have* tried. It's not working." Lame. So lame.

Malcolm crossed his arms and leaned down so his face was right next to mine. I tried not to inhale his enticing scent—soap and starch and sweat.

A long breath wreathed my shoulder. Some of the tension left him. All of it settled on me.

"No," he said.

I turned my head away. He was still the boss of me, though he never asserted that authority. If he didn't agree...I'd leave anyway. It wouldn't be the first time I'd quit an untenable situation, consequences be damned. But for once, I wanted to stay, and not only because of the trust fund. This was my parents' fault.

I hated them, too.

He grabbed my wrist. "You're bleeding."

"Don't change the subject. That's my tactic. It's better this way."

His head snapped up, but I wouldn't look at him.

"Better than what?" he asked sharply, then continued to breathe over my ear and neck.

I shivered. "I'm having dreams again," I whispered. "I think it has to do with my parents. I don't know what's coming, but after last time..."

My voice stumbled over the images I tried to keep locked in a closet. A dead body in the manure spreader, galloping from a madman with Nicky struggling in front of me, being held at gunpoint, Malcolm and the bad guy grappling at the edge of a hay loft.

Squeezing my eyes tight, I shoved the thoughts back into the dark where they belonged.

Malcolm's hand lifted toward my face, and I recoiled, but he would never hit me, so I tried to cover it. Too late. I could feel his incredulous stare willing me to look at him. I gritted my teeth against the urge to turn into the warmth of his palm poised an inch from my cheek.

"Better than what?" he asked again, gently this time. He cradled my damaged hand, brought it up where he could see it, kissed my bruised and bleeding knuckles, then lowered it again.

"Better than putting you through this craziness that follows me wherever I go. You don't deserve any of this."

"Vi. Life isn't fair, and it isn't about who deserves what. What do you truly want?"

I wanted to sink into him so far that I'd never have to come up again. It hurt to breathe, and my neck felt like a noose had tightened around it. I wanted to stay.

"I don't want you to leave," he said.

I squeezed my eyes tight and forced air past the constriction in my throat.

He touched his forehead to mine. "I heard you," he said. "When you screamed my name outside." The pads of his fingers stroked my jaw. His thumb caught the tear I didn't even know had spilled. "Admit it. Some of the same thoughts that went through my mind went through yours."

I nodded and risked a glance at him, his beautiful face fractured by the moisture in my eyes. The quiet fury had fled. His finger hooked the deep armhole of my ratty tank top and traced the edge of it until his knuckle grazed the side of my breast. My heart and body arched, reaching for him.

"This is a good look for you," he said.

A silent, relieved, and happy laugh huffed out of me. "Are you sure?"

He had one hand on my ribcage now and the other slid behind my head. He pulled me into him, to the place that felt like home. The rapid beat of his heart matched mine.

"Sure I like this look on you? Oh, yeah." He emphasized his point by sliding his hand down to fondle my butt.

"No, about..." I angled my head toward the hallway, the stairs, and all the rest. "Them." After a pause, I added, "me."

"You're not getting away that easily but, oh, let us never, never doubt what nobody is sure about."

I slumped in his arms. "Please, no more Shakespeare."

"What? That was Joseph Belloc, poet." He took my shoulders and moved back so he could look at me. "You need ice on that hand."

He tugged a fresh T-shirt over his head and gave me one as well. His was soft from wear and hung down to the middle of my thighs. I hadn't exactly been thinking about my lack of clothes when I tore down here. Being wrapped in his shirt was like being cocooned with his kindness. I'm a sucker for kindness.

We went into the hallway, me leaning on him because my knees were weak from relief. The stifling heat outside his air-conditioned bedroom hit me like a wet broom.

"What do you have against Shakespeare?" he asked.

"Nothing." I sniffled. Weak, that's what I was. And more grateful to him than I could express. "My mother was trying to tell me something earlier using the characters and plot of *Twelfth Night*."

He paused at the top of the stairs. Muffled voices drifted up from the kitchen, the sound of ice clinking, a soft laugh from my mother.

"Ah," Malcolm said. "Viola disguised as Cesario. Interesting."

The breadth of the man's knowledge. A trip to the library to brush up on all this was in my future. "I...I think she was trying to say she named me for her."

His gaze dipped into mine and skimmed right down to my soul. I honestly didn't know what he saw in me. But the fact that he saw *something*, something that made him say *no* when I tried to run, gave me hope. Hope for me, hope for us.

"Well, Viola-not-disguised-as-anyone-but-herself. No one's sleeping. Why don't we go downstairs and ask?"

CHAPTER THIRTEEN

Downstairs, Giacomo stood under the porch light's glow sipping a tumbler of red wine. Moths circled his head like planes backed up at LaGuardia. My mother sat at the kitchen table, eyes closed, holding a package of frozen corn to her head. Next to her were the fragrant gardenias in a glass vase. My father paced between his wife and father as if unsure whether either could be trusted on their own recognizance.

The moment we hit the hallway, he stopped and came toward us. Thinking to head him off, I moved in front of Malcolm.

"Dad—"

He didn't even look at me. "We're very sorry Mr. Malcolm—"

Malcolm held up his hand. "We'll sort it out in the morning. Is your wife all right?"

"I'm fine," she said from the kitchen. "If you knew how many times Adrian's clocked me in the head with his elbow during practice, you wouldn't be worried."

Not exactly. I'd be *more* worried. If only because my mother used the term *clocked*.

My father winced. He stared at my mother, but she didn't open her eyes. He glanced over his shoulder to where Giacomo still stood just outside the screen door, his back to us, the half-empty tumbler dangling from his fingertips.

Dad's voice hushed. "It's just that Giacomo needed our help. We were ready to come home anyway, and we hadn't seen Vi in so long..."

Malcolm sucked in a deep breath, but before he could say anything to stop this sudden torrent of information, I pinched his butt. We might not find out why I was named Viola tonight, but Dad looked desperate to spill, and I wanted to hear what he had to say. Even if it *was* nearly three in the morning.

Malcolm's free hand grazed his scalp again, and a memory flashed in my brain of Aunt Trudy threatening to snatch me or Penny bald if we didn't do what she wanted. This triggered a brief pang of homesickness at odds with my desire to stay at Winterlight. If I were a sailboat, I'd be rudderless in high seas. Then, Malcolm gave my hip a squeeze to let me know he understood. That anchored me.

He pivoted and walked toward the living room at the back of the house, and, most likely, his stash of single malt Scotch. I grabbed my father's wrist and dragged him after us. We passed the wide office doorway, a room that originally was for dining. The gun safe hung open, again. What compelled Giacomo to lie to me and pick the lock—twice—to keep a weapon close?

Dad started to lower himself into Malcolm's leather recliner but I shook my head and pointed to the matching couch. He sat slowly, as if second guessing his decision to follow me, and I plopped next to him. Meanwhile, Malcolm poured about an inch of amber liquid into his favorite cut crystal glass. After a moment, he added another half inch and got down a second glass to pour an equal amount in it. He handed one to me, and I passed it to my dad. My head needed to remain clear.

"Let's start with Giacomo," Malcolm said after sitting on the edge of his recliner. It tipped forward with a squeak. "Why did he need your help?"

My father studied his hands where they rested on his thighs. "He wasn't completely clear on that. He only said he needed to get out of Florida right away."

"Wait," I said. "How did he even know how to find you if you were given up for adoption as a baby?"

He reached over and took my hand. His was cool and smooth against my callouses "That's a good question, Vi, and I still have a lot of my own." He sighed. "When he first called, I didn't believe him. I wanted to, but I never trust anything that sounds too good to be true. He knew details about the orphanage and the exact date I was left that no one else could know." He lifted his eyes to mine. "I admit I was thrilled by the prospect of being reunited with my father."

"So you just believed him?" I wasn't sure the details Giacomo knew couldn't be had for the right price. "He could be anyone. He knows how to pick locks." Could my parents really be this gullible?

He chuckled. "You have your mother's skepticism. Gemma insisted on a paternity test. It was positive."

"You do look like him," I said.

Malcolm took a fortifying swallow of Scotch, and I longed for a shot of whipped cream. But getting it would require leaving, and I didn't want to miss a word.

"So," Malcolm said, "you dropped what by all accounts was a very successful dancing career and rushed to Giacomo's rescue. Even though you don't really know what kind of trouble he's in? And you brought him here?"

Uh oh. Maybe we should have left this till the morning.

Dad sipped his drink and looked across the room to Malcolm. The two men assessed each other over the fumes of their liquor. I would have pegged my father for a wine drinker, but the strong peaty flavor didn't appear to faze him.

"We're broke," he said with a shrug. "The career hasn't been all that successful for a while. It was time for a change. In case

Viola didn't mention it, most of the luggage we arrived with was empty."

"I hadn't gotten that far," I said.

"We needed a place to regroup," he continued. "Frankly, we had nowhere else to go. Giacomo was adamant about not returning to New York, so here we are."

"You could have called first," I said.

"We could have—"

I fixed him with a glare to deflect my guilt at not calling Malcolm when they arrived. Having this trait in common wasn't exactly something to celebrate.

"We should have, you're right. It was your mother's idea. She thought it best to not give you warning."

He put the crystal glass to his lips, tipped back an unhealthy swig, coughed, and wiped his mouth.

"I find it best not to argue with her," he said.

I exhaled forcefully and gave Malcolm a helpless look.

Dad brought my attention back to him. "What would you have said if we had called?"

I answered that without hesitation. "No."

"Exactly. She was right."

"Can you parse the particulars later?" Malcolm asked. "I'm more concerned with whatever kind of trouble Giacomo's in."

On cue, Giacomo appeared in the living room doorway.

"Someone's after me," he said with no trace of accent. "And he wants me dead."

CHAPTER FOURTEEN

Giacomo claimed there had been an accident long ago, someone had been hurt, but it was all an old misunderstanding, and the man who was after him wouldn't track him here. He clammed up after that. Deep creases of fatigue dragged his eyelids down, as if he'd been carrying a burden for a long time. We were all tired, and Mom was making noises about getting back to bed. Malcolm gave in and said we would talk more in the morning. He grabbed a few things from upstairs and we went to the apartment.

If Wastrel came knocking, I didn't hear, and it was good to rest dreamlessly, even if only for a few hours, even if I felt like I could sleep for a week. But only if there were no dreams.

In the morning, Malcolm helped feed the horses, and we decided to go for a ride before it got hot. I wanted to show him where we thought we'd seen the trespasser. I left a note for Zoe, and we got Gaston and Cali ready.

"Whoever it was," he said after mounting, "they're long gone by now."

He settled himself with a happy sigh and patted the big chestnut's neck. Malcolm usually rode in boots and breeches, but he hadn't thought to get a pair the night before. Neither of us wanted to disturb anyone at the house at the crack of dawn, so he wore jeans and used a western saddle. Gaston tossed his head as Cali edged over to him. I tweaked the rein to keep her from getting too close. She was as likely to nip his neck as nuzzle it.

"I'll call our conservation agent and let him know someone might be poaching." He led us up the driveway past the house.

"Okay." I rode up next to him, and Noire caught up with us, too. "But I still want to go down there and look around."

"Lead the way," he said with a smile had nothing to do with riding or poachers.

I knew he wanted me in front of him so he could watch my butt. Men. Sheesh. One track mind. My parents and Giacomo were here under dubious circumstances, we might have a poacher, Wastrel had roared back into my nights, and all Malcolm cared about was the view.

Fine.

I urged Cali to the front. She swished her tail in Gaston's face, and he let out a horsey grunt of annoyance. I arched my back and stood in my stirrups for a moment so I could wriggle my hips, all under the guise of stretching my heels down and finding my balance. An appreciative groan came from behind. I flashed a grin over my shoulder.

Cali jogged a few steps thinking this all meant it was time to go faster. As an off-the-track thoroughbred, she was always up for speed. I let her move out. She picked up a good working trot, tucked her chin, and rocked her back up under my seat. Coiled within her rippling muscles were a couple of playful bucks waiting for the right moment. Said bucks didn't usually unseat me, but I stretched my heels deeper just in case.

At the edge of the alfalfa field, we had a nice straight path with springy footing. A gallop would do us good.

Five minutes and several in-stride bucks later, Malcolm and I were side by side in the cool of the woods, laughing like kids as the horses walked on the buckle, catching their breath.

"We'll move your parents into the apartment," he said.

"What? No." The apartment was mine, part of our contract, my pay. So what if I'd been ready to walk the night before? "Why should I give up my space?"

"You sleep at the house. With me."

"I know, but—"

"Why should I give up *my* space?" he countered in an unusual show of possessiveness.

I chewed my lip. "What about Giacomo?"

"The couch in the apartment pulls out. It's a little tight, but the entire place is air conditioned. They'll be more comfortable."

I grumbled something along the lines of not caring about their comfort.

"Giacomo will be farther from the gun safe, as well."

That would be a good thing. He'd be farther from his plants, too.

"He planted a garden."

"That was fast."

"He brought tomato plants with him."

"From Florida?"

"I guess. I haven't really talked to them."

"You have to."

"I was hoping you would."

I'm such a freaking coward.

He reached across the space between us and took my hand. His was warm and strong, his touch comforting and soothing, the way it must feel to a horse when you stroke their neck.

"They're still your parents. And your grandfather. You've never had one of those before, have you?"

I hadn't. My maternal grandparents died before I was three. Penny's paternal grandmother was still alive, but she lived upstate and we rarely saw her.

He squeezed my hand. "We'll do it together, a little at a time. It'll be all right, you'll see."

"What about my dreams? I can't make any sense out of them, but what if—"

His cell phone chirped. Goddamn thing. I never bring mine riding. Call me a purist, but when I'm on my horse, I want to concentrate on that. No distractions. It was an ongoing disagreement between us.

He reined Gaston to halt, pulled out the device, consulted the screen. "I have to go back."

I huffed. "Okay." I started to turn Cali around.

"You don't have to. Take your time. I'll let your parents and Giacomo know they need to move down to the apartment."

We hadn't exactly agreed to that, but what could I say? At least he wasn't kicking them—or me—out.

Deep down, I knew he was right. Not just about the apartment, but about my having to deal with them. It was going to be a while before I'd admit it, though. God, I wished he was kicking them out.

That wasn't the kind of guy he was, and, of course, that was just one of a long list of reasons why I liked him. More than liked him.

Yeah, it would be a while before I admitted that, too.

I rode close, took his arm, pulled him to me, and kissed him deeply, trying to infuse that with some of the appreciation and gratitude I felt.

He made a yummy sound and ended it. "If we don't quit, I won't make it back to work."

Pointing my chin at the ground, I said, "We have privacy here."

"Tempting," he said. He held up his phone. "But this client has a problem only I can fix."

A lock of his hair had escaped his helmet and stuck to his

skin. I stroked it back from his temple. "Okay, Superman. Go rescue them."

He picked up his reins.

Words wriggled around inside me trying to escape. I couldn't seem to put them in a sensible order. "Just..."

His eyes searched mine. "Just what?"

I blew out my breath. "Just thanks."

"For what?"

Geez. Couldn't the guy accept my freaking gratefulness and let it go?

"For being you," I blurted, which was both more and less than I'd intended to say.

He smiled in a way that might have revealed more than he'd intended as well, gave me a salute, and eased Gaston into a slow canter back toward the house. Noire followed, but when she saw that I was staying, she came back. Cali pawed and tugged at my hands, wanting to catch up and pass the other horse. She couldn't help herself.

I turned toward the ravine. Noire loped ahead, stopping to sniff at the base of a tree, then continuing. A red squirrel scampered away, and she sprinted after it, but it streaked up a trunk to a high branch before she could reach it. It sat there chittering at us until we were farther up the trail.

Early morning sunlight slanted through the trees flecking us in splotches of yellow. Birds sang. I'd learned some of their calls and recognized the staccato *ki-ki-ki-ki-ki* of a pileated woodpecker even though I couldn't see it in the dense green canopy.

We started down the steep hill. The sun wasn't high enough to dispel shadows from the ravine yet, and my eyes took a moment to adjust. The scent of damp earth rose up. Cali tensed, remembering the fright from last time. Noire stayed near. No deer or poachers to chase this morning. Cali sloshed through the creek, a little higher thanks to the too brief rain, and I dismounted on the other side. Off the trail, the underbrush was thick and heavy with dried wildflowers, seed pods, and burrs. I reminded myself I'd need a shower as soon as I got back to check for ticks and wash away the chiggers.

Thorns caught in my T-shirt and scratched my arms. I walked slowly, leading Cali with one hand, holding branches aside with the other. I scuffed my feet in the leaves and twigs on the ground, the swish and crunch reminding me of fall. Despite the heat, it was only a few weeks away.

What was I looking for? No idea. Nothing in my dreams so far led me to suspect there was anything or anyone here. And I still wasn't convinced we'd seen a person at all.

Noire lent her superior sense of smell to the search, and a little farther ahead, she stopped and started digging, snuffling and pushing dirt with her nose.

The area around her had been disturbed. Not disturbed exactly, but cleared. As if... I grabbed Noire's collar.

"Quit." She jerked forward. "Leave it." She looked at me, not understanding why I'd keep her from doing her job. "Sit." She sat.

Something or someone had been here. Had cleared a small area as if for a tent or a sleeping bag. The leaves were pushed aside and the dirt beneath smoothed. No sign of a fire. We would have seen smoke from the house, and with everything as dry as it'd been, a fire wouldn't have been safe. Another clear area led to the creek edge. I kicked around some more, wishing I had brought my phone for a change. It wasn't very smart, but it had a camera.

I continued in the direction our trespasser had run, believing now that a person had been here. A strip of reddish-brown fabric hung on the four-inch thorn of a honey locust. The spikes grew in star-shaped clumps right out of the trunk like sea urchins attached to dock posts. The tree was a menace to human and animal alike. I pocketed the material and gave the tree a wide berth. Ahead, the ground rose steeply and the creek tucked under a rock outcropping to the right.

The sun chose that moment to crest the ridge behind us. It sparked on a shiny object halfway up the hill, and I tugged Cali toward it. Our shadows blocked my sightline, and I lost track of it for a moment, chiding myself for dragging my horse through the woods after what was probably a worthless piece of quartz. We moved to the side.

There.

A pale aquamarine marble glinted at me. It sat atop a handful of dull limestone rocks like a diamond set in lead, looking as absurd and out of place as a pair of shiny international ballroom dancers did on a dusty horse farm in Missouri.

CHAPTER FIFTEEN

We meandered through the woods for another half hour, the marble a heavy lump in my pocket. Having gotten her silliness out on that first gallop, Cali maintained a loose-jointed walk. She'd taken to trail riding well despite the competitive streak inherited from racing. Noire trotted in our wake, occasionally stopping to sniff or dig. All of us were enjoying the relative coolness of early morning. None of us were in a hurry to get back. But I could stall for only so long, would have to deal with my parents and face whatever mystery Wastrel had dreamed up this time.

If only it were all truly a dream.

By the time I rode into the barnyard, heat waves shimmered over the barn's tin roof. I stopped for a moment looking from the house to the apartment, wondering if Malcolm had already talked to Adrian and Gem Gem. The idea of having them upstairs from where I spent my day sounded as appealing as getting in a sauna. Noire made a beeline for the water bowl. Oh, right, we were already in a sauna.

I took Cali into the barn, untacked, hosed her off, and left her in a stall with some hay. Then, I made my own beeline to the air-conditioned tack room. I stood for a moment, listening. No sound came from the apartment. I went up, got some whipped cream and a glass of ice water and plopped down at the kitchen table, staring out the window.

Noire curled at my feet. Having my dog near always made me feel better, even if she panted hot air on my leg. But no matter how many times I told myself everything would be all right, nothing changed the feeling I'd swallowed a cup of eels.

Footsteps climbing the stairs heralded Zoe, and I tried to pull myself together, but it was a man's voice that came from the hall.

"Did someone kill the cat and forget to tell me?"

"Dex?"

"The same." He strode into the kitchen and dragged me up into a hug.

As if all the attention from Malcolm wasn't enough, Dex One was no slouch in the affection department, either. Dex One was Dexter Hamill, retired mounted cop and sometime PI. His horse, Ciqala, lived at Winterlight.

He smiled, and the corners of his coffee-colored eyes crinkled. His usual military buzz cut had grown out since the last time I'd seen him, and he'd grown a mustache. Wisps of graying blond hair brushed the collar of his polo shirt. He must have needed a different look for the last job.

"Got more of that water?"

"Of course." I started to get a glass for him, but he motioned me back to my chair.

"It's hot," he said, as if I hadn't noticed.

"Thanks for letting me know."

He got a glass, filled it, then settled his lean hips against the counter. Moisture clouded his snowy polo shirt, making it cling to his muscled torso.

"Nice 'stache," I said, hoping he wouldn't notice when my nervous knee started up, bouncing erratically beneath the table.

Dex One didn't miss much. I might be diverting my anxiety by admiring his pecs, but he could tell I was worried.

"Something you want to tell me, Miss Parker?"

I stood to get more water and force my jumpy knee to quiet. "What do you mean? Is there something you want to tell me?" I kept my gaze on the ice cube tray but could feel his eyes on the back of my neck.

"Something's bothering you."

I laughed a little as I sat again and swirled the ice in my glass. "You a mind reader, now?" But what was there to say? Wastrel was back and there was nothing I could do about it. Anyone in the vicinity could be in mortal danger. Aside from that, my parents were in mortal danger from me.

"Don't forget, I did your background check. I know how your mind works." He waggled his eyebrows.

I began to feel better. Dex had that way. But even though he flirted, he'd once said he loved Malcolm like a brother. His allegiance was, and always would be, to Robert Harvey Malcolm.

"I'm fine," I said. "Just a little tired."

He reached under the table and steadied my jittery leg. "That's my girl."

I wasn't his girl, I was Malcolm's. But Malcolm was also my boss and would be for another eight months. I had to stay at Winterlight that long if I wanted to receive the trust fund. Even though the amount was a mystery, it represented independence.

At least, I hoped it did.

If I'd been smart, I never would have let my relationship with Malcolm be anything more than that of employer-employee.

I'm not always smart.

Dex One leaned closer. Unlike me, he smelled good, like he'd just stepped out of the shower. Provocative, the scent of freshly scrubbed man when I was all sweaty and stinky. My overheated skin prickled with awareness.

Maybe I should have responded to his advances instead of

falling for Malcolm. Dex One was more my speed—a no-expectations kind of guy. Not that Malcolm had put any pressure on our relationship. But he was definitely a long-term kind of guy. Me, not so much. Even at the ripe old age of twenty-nine, I still wasn't sure if I was ready for commitment.

My friend Harry had called me cold backed not too long ago. When that term was applied to a horse it meant she had a sore back and didn't want a saddle or person on her. I'd resented it at the time, but the truth was, I didn't want anyone on my back, either, then or now.

I forced myself to rally. "You're right about the heat. I don't think I'm going to ride anymore today. Hey," I said to change the subject, "Have you talked to Renee lately?"

Renee was Dex One's sometimes girl friend. When I first arrived at Winterlight, she was there often, but her sister had become ill, and she'd moved in to care for her shortly after. That was in Kansas City, so we hadn't seen her for a while.

Dex pushed himself away from the counter, giving me his sideways suspicious PI look.

"She's fine. She'll be here for Dex Two's gala next week."

"I look forward to seeing her," I said, wishing he and his skeptical look would move along. "Malcolm's up at the house."

"Let's go up together."

"I have work to do."

"You just said you aren't going to ride. What are you not telling me?"

I put my hands out. "Okay. Okay. My parents are here and Wastrel is back."

He jerked like I'd cuffed him on the chin. "Good God, woman."

"Right? It's hard to imagine one person being so lucky."

"I'm not sure which to be more concerned about."

"Me neither."

"Do they know?"

"About Wastrel?"

He nodded.

I shook my head.

"Which came first—the dreams or the parents?"

"Dreams."

"Were they in them?"

"No. I mean, I don't think so. It's hard to tell sometimes. I have no idea if there's any connection."

He went to the window, sighed, and scratched the back of his neck. "Anything else I should know about?"

I hated to get him all worked up about what might be nothing. But he'd been really mad last time when I hadn't told him all there was to tell. Problem was, I didn't know what was significant.

He faced me, eyes narrowed again like he could see under my skin. Dang. I'd hesitated too long.

"Tell me."

It was my turn to pull back. I wouldn't want to be a criminal he wanted something out of.

"Wednesday morning, one of the riders thought she saw a person running through the woods."

"And?"

I crossed my arms. "And what?"

"Don't play games with me, Miss Parker. I know you."

"You're a real pain, you know that?"

Leaning down so he got close to my face, he said, "I can be a bigger pain, if you like."

"No thanks. I went back today. It looked like someone might have been camping there. All I found was this." I showed him the marble.

He took it and held it up to the light. It sparkled and reflected the sun just as I imagined the Mediterranean would on a day like today. He frowned and gave it back.

"Anything like this in your dreams?"

"Nope."

"Maybe you should ask that horse a few questions."

"Yeah, I'll make a list and submit it to his assistant."

"You're his assistant."

"Not funny."

With a glance at his chunky black-ops watch, he said, "Well'p, too many bad guys, not enough time." He dumped his glass in the sink, gave my shoulder a playful punch, and turned to leave.

"Wait, that's it?"

Without turning around, he said, "You'll tell me if there's anything I need to know."

Not a question. Again, I hesitated too long.

He gave me a look. "Right?"

My turn to sigh. "Yes."

"Okay then. I'll stop at the house to see Malcolm and meet your parents."

"There is one thing. My parents brought my grandfather with them. My father's father. Maybe you could check him out?" I hated to put Dex on Giacomo's tail, but something about the old guy didn't add up.

"Why? Wait...grandfather? Isn't your father an orphan?"

"That's what I'd always been told."

"I'm on it." He turned again.

Zoe met him at the top of the stairs.

Her eyes skittered over Dex One then slid away. "Oh, sorry." She turned to go.

That stupefied bunny look had darkened her features again. I didn't like it. Maybe I should have Dex check up on her, too.

Dex flipped on the charm. "How do, miss?" He swept his arm toward me. "No need to run away. Friend of Miss Parker's?"

"It's okay, Zoe. Dex was just leaving."

He winked, gave me a *we'll-talk-later* nod, and strode out.

"Who was that?" she asked after the screen door slammed downstairs.

"Dexter Hamill, private investigator. Ciqala belongs to him."

"I thought Miss Bong belonged to him."

"She belongs to Dex Two." I canted my head toward the stairs. "That was Dex One."

"That's confusing."

"Once you see the Dexes together, you won't confuse them. They're as different from each other as their horses are."

Zoe got a glass of water. She still had her back to me when she said, "He's pretty *hawt*."

"*Haught*?"

"Yeah, you know. Good looking. Great body."

"Oh, you mean *hot*."

Through the back window, I could see the subject of this observation standing by the fence petting his horse, the muscle definition in his arms evident even at a distance. I couldn't fault her taste, but...

"He's too old for you by at least twenty years."

"You've already taken Mr. Malcolm." She guzzled her drink. "You can't hog all the hot guys."

I didn't want to have this conversation with Zoe or any other sixteen-year-old. "They are few and far between, I agree. But they're both too old for you."

She gave me a *whatever* shrug. "I can look, right? Why the limp?"

"Half his leg is missing. A horse fell on it. He wears a prosthesis."

Confusion scrunched her features for a long moment. Or maybe it was deep thought. I imagined Dex One's hotness level plummeting.

In a throaty whisper, she said, "That's über-hawt."

CHAPTER SIXTEEN

It's not like the men of Winterlight can't take care of themselves. Quite the contrary. Both Malcolm and Dex One are smart, fit, and crack shots. Both can spot bullshit a mile away. And it's not like I'm the jealous type. Who has time for that? I had no proprietary ownership of said men. Part of me wanted to claim Malcolm for my very own, a part buried deep. But I wasn't ready. Anyway, I couldn't, not with the craziness of my parents and my friendly neighborhood dream horse.

Just the same, possessiveness surged through me, biting and dark. Who did Zoe think she was, calling Dex and Malcolm *hawt*?

I rose and refilled my water glass. "Up for a little riding lesson this morning?"

Zoe's hazel eyes flashed wide, and she beamed around a big bite of pretzels she'd found in the cabinet. With a vigorous nod, she mumbled, "I'b lub thad."

"You can ride Smitty again. It isn't getting any cooler, so hurry up."

She ran downstairs to get him ready. I chased my water with another hit of whipped cream before following.

By the time we got to the riding arena, I'd cooled. My temper, that is. My intention had been to teach her a lesson, but not about riding. Getting back at her for proclaiming Winterlight's men *hawt* was the truth. I decided she hadn't really meant anything by it, the men could defend themselves, and it was too damned hot to give a shit.

Plus, she's a good kid, if a bit too easily spooked. I still wondered about that, but did I have the brain space to work another mystery? Nope. I sent her into a working trot.

My agreement with Malcolm stipulated I didn't have to teach lessons even though it would bring much needed income to his bottom line. Working with Zoe didn't count. It was a way to pay her for the hard work I forced her to do.

Halfway around the ring, Smitty stuck his nose out and his trot started to fall apart. Zoe leaned forward and her posting gained too much air.

Whoa now, I whispered. "Shorten your reins," I said to Zoe. "Sit up straight. Steady him." Steady yourself.

It was groups of little kids bouncing around on—and falling off of—ponies I couldn't handle. Private lessons for adults, though? Maybe I should consider it. Surely it would be better than the trail rides.

Or not. I can talk myself into or out of anything. But if it would help Malcolm...

I brought myself back to Zoe and Smitty. "At C, ride a twenty-meter circle."

She looked around in a panic.

"You're coming up to it. It's at the middle of the other end of the arena."

I'd added the dressage markers after coming to Winterlight. I didn't expect her to be familiar with them, but she made an effort to bend Smitty and ride a roundish shape. More like an egg. She'd pulled him together but now her reins were too short, her hands were posting along with the rest of her, and Smitty's head was getting higher and higher. At X, an invisible maker dead center of the ring, he began to drift sideways toward the gate, his eye rolling to me in a plea for help.

"Halt," I said as they sidestepped past me.

Zoe yanked the reins, Smitty tossed his head, and they stumbled to a stop. After a moment, they both huffed out a breath.

"I'm sorry—"

I held up my hand. "Don't apologize. You're doing fine."

"I am?"

"Well, yeah, if what you were asking for was an oval with your horse bent to the outside and a discombobulated leg yield at X."

"That's not what I asked for."

I put my hands on the reins and gently tugged them through her fingers to give the horse some slack. He wiped slobber on my side in thanks. "Are you sure?"

"What do you mean?" Confusion scrunched her cheeks.

"Horses almost always give you exactly what you ask for," I said.

"But I—"

"But you have to be very sure, very clear of what you're asking."

She looked toward the woods for a moment. "I was steering him with my right rein to turn on the circle."

"Yes you were."

"So, why was he going the other way?"

"What was your body doing? Your legs? Seat? Weight?"

Her shoulders slumped. "I don't know."

"Your body communicates with your horse as much as your hands. More, actually. What about your mind? Were you thinking about where you going?"

She rolled her eyes. "No. I was wondering how Mrs. Erdman is doing."

This took me by surprise. Nice of the kid to worry, but how much could a ninety-year-old lady be doing in this heat? "Mrs. Erdman? Wait, she has AC, doesn't she?"

Zoe nodded. "Yeah, but she borrowed my car to go see a friend."

"She has a driver's license?"

Her lips curled in, then she frowned. "I didn't ask."

Christ. "I hope you have good insurance."

"I—"

A horrible shriek came from the barn. Smitty whipped around, nearly dumping Zoe. She gasped and grabbed mane. His front hoof came down hard on my foot. I almost made the same sound that had startled us.

We both spoke.

"What the hell?"

"What was that?"

Howls followed. Garbled yelling. Then a man, I think, keening. *Keening.*

I took a fortifying breath and started running, ignoring my throbbing toes.

It took only moments to get inside. Henrietta the cat sprawled on the tack room steps. Otherwise, the barn was empty. Yelling came from the apartment.

For a second I hesitated, my hand on the doorknob thinking I'd have to start keeping whipped cream down in the tack room. Then, up I went, yet again right toward what I'd be better off running away from. All I could think was, *what now?*

And there they were. My father and Giacomo on the couch, my mother in the bathroom running water.

Adrian patted his father's back, clearly unsure what to do. Giacomo leaned forward with his face in his fisted hands, muttering, and I figured the shriek had come from him. Had he stubbed his toe? Barked his shin? Had my dog laid waste to his garden? What? Gemma came out with a wet wash cloth and shoved it at the old man.

"Can't make sense of what he's saying." She retreated to the kitchen.

I looked to Adrian. One brow lifted, and he cut a sideways glance at his father, conveying more with that simple expression than any words could. The familiarity of it forced me back half a step. I could have been viewing myself in the mirror.

Giacomo lifted his head. I barely recognized him. His face before had been weathered but often wore a charming smile, and he always had a spark of mischief in his eyes. Now, he looked years older, haggard, with a dull sheen of dread clouding his gaze.

His fingers uncurled. In his palm rested the marble I'd found earlier.

"Where you get this?" he asked.

What the hell? Clearly, Malcolm had talked to them and they were moving to the apartment as he wanted. A little heads-up would have been nice. I'd left the marble in a tray on my bedside table thinking it would be pretty in the morning light. In Giacomo's big hand, its opalescence was dimmed, its depths hidden.

Images from recent dreams flashed through my brain. None contained a marble. Cold sweat popped out of my pores.

"The woods," I said. "Why?"

He opened his mouth and that bitter moan I'd heard a few minutes before filled the room again. Tears dribbled over his wrinkles to gather in his beard.

The *hell*.

He made to stand but couldn't free himself from the deep couch cushions. Adrian took his arm and helped. Giacomo slowly straightened, looking like his whole body hurt.

My mother stood in the doorway to the kitchen, looking like her whole body defined disdain. But that was normal for her. Whatever was going on with Giacomo was just the latest in a life-long catalog of people and things she scorned.

"This," Giacomo said, making it sound like *these*. He cradled the marble to his chest. "This belong to Josephine." His voice broke on the name.

"Apparently, she's been dead for forty-seven years," my mother said.

My face, if not my entire body, surely showed disbelief. "Not possible. Who's Josephine?"

"*Sí*." He nodded slowly, eyes on the marble. "Josephine," he whispered. "She was my wife."

CHAPTER SEVENTEEN

Insanity. That's what this was. Maybe it ran in the family. Not a comforting thought, but then, it would explain so much.

It was a freaking marble. There must be millions. True, this one was large and very pretty, but—

"Look," Giacomo said.

He beckoned me to follow as he held the glass ball up to the window, turning it between his thumb and forefinger. Light shimmied inside it like dawn through the crest of a wave.

"Hand blown." He glanced at me to make sure I was listening. "One of a kind." He turned it a little more. "I no see for over forty years." He rubbed his free hand over his mouth pushing his mustache up and away, and his eyes lost focus as he drifted inward, no doubt remembering something from long ago, but he snapped back. "See these bubbles here?"

Bubbles. Yup. We'd roared into crazy town. To humor him, I peered into the orb. For a nano-second, Wastrel galloped there, just as I see him in my dreams, his mane and tail flying up and out—

"'E's Pegasus. See? Like the stars."

I pulled back like I'd gotten too close to a cliff edge, lost my balance, hooked my heel on the edge of a chair, and fell into it. Grabbing the armrests, I bounced back to my feet just as quickly and, without a word, left.

My head pounded in time to my steps as I walked fast through the barn. Zoe had Smitty on the cross ties, running a cold hose over him.

"Hey—" She started.

I gave her the talk-to-the-hand hand and continued up to the house. I needed to get away from them. From this place. If I wasn't already insane, I would be soon.

I flung open the screen door. It slammed the wall and came unhinged again. So much for my father's repairman capabilities.

Malcolm sat in his office working at the computer. Some classical symphony played softly from hidden speakers. He glanced up with a smile, but when he saw me, the smile vanished.

"I found a marble in the woods," I blurted, my breathing too fast.

His brows drew together but he waited, knowing more was coming.

"Giacomo says he recognizes it. He hasn't seen it in over forty years, mind you, but still, he knows this marble because it was hand blown and it's one of a kind and it has bubbles—*bubbles*— that look like the constellation of Pegasus, and that's how he knows the marble belonged to his wife, Josephine."

I put my hands on my hips and paced toward the window. "Bubbles," I muttered. "He was wailing, Malcolm. Crying. It was very convincing."

"You don't believe him?"

I whirled on him. "Do you?"

He leaned back in his chair and switched off the music. "A few months ago I would have said it was preposterous." He rose and came over, putting his hands on my shoulders. "But since knowing you and Wastrel, I'm more...let's say open to possibility."

My body relaxed a fraction the moment he touched me. "I haven't dreamed about a marble for Christ's sake."

"Maybe you will."

I shoved his hands away. "I don't want to have these dreams at all. I certainly don't want my parents here. Or Giacomo, whoever he is and whoever's after him." I pictured the deep sadness in the old man's eyes for a moment. Sure, I felt sorry for him. But... "And I sure as hell don't want to dream about them. Any of them."

"You don't believe he's your grandfather?"

"Oh, I know he is. The resemblance to Adrian is too strong to deny. But what do we know about him? He's been missing—by choice as far as we know—for forty-seven years. Where has he been all this time?"

"Dex is working on it."

"That's good. But will it tell us how my grandmother's marble ended up in your woods?"

My grandmother. I tried to imagine her, to fill in another hole in the family tree. My mother's parents had been gone before I was three, but because they were also Aunt Trudy's parents, they'd been around. I'd met them, and there were pictures in the house I'd been raised in. What had Adrian's mother looked like? Did Giacomo have a picture?

Malcolm took a deep breath. "Dex will find out everything he can." He took my hand and tugged me to his leather office chair, sitting and pulling me down onto his lap. "Whether that solves the mystery of the marble..."

I sat stiffly, not wanting to let go of my anger, not wanting to give in to his embrace.

He stroked my back and gently forced my head against his shoulder. "Let Dex do his job, and try to relax until we have something definitive."

I huffed and tried to put it all out of my mind. But I kept seeing Giacomo's sagging face, his tears, and through them, his certainty.

Malcolm put his hand on my leg, his thumb tracing the seam of my jeans up the inside of my thigh. My breathing slowed as my heart sped up.

He kissed the top of my head. "I changed the sheets," he said.

Such a good man. And I was...not in his league. Silently, I let him soothe and arouse me.

"And patched the ceiling. We're not air conditioning the attic anymore."

I smiled into his chest, tilting my head enough to brush my nose against his jaw.

"You're not alone, you know," he said. "You don't have to face the world by yourself all the time. It's okay to lean on someone else."

His hand crept up my thigh, his thumb making circles all the way.

I'd always been alone. Had never relied on anyone else, never asked for help. People had a tendency to let you down.

I snuggled more deeply into his shoulder and rested my hand at his waist, knowing for the time being at least, I could rely on him. Would it last? Doubtful. But then, if the shootout in the bedroom hadn't scared him off, maybe there was hope.

He wasn't wearing his kilt today, but it was still obvious how he was feeling. Images of dreams, thoughts of long lost marbles, even my anger became slippery, harder to hold onto.

"Have someone in mind I could lean on?"

He shifted me to the side, reached into his pants, and arranged himself. "I have something in mind, that's for sure."

I slid my hand to his crotch and stroked his hard length through the fabric of his jeans. "So I noticed."

"Why don't we——" he started.

"Let's go crease those fresh sheets," I said at the same time.

He laughed and stood, carrying me upstairs. So romantic.

Our clothes flew through the air the moment we crossed the threshold and he slammed the door behind us. The air conditioning felt divine on my bare skin. I didn't look at the patched ceiling, pushing him down on the bed and climbing on top. I nabbed a condom from the bedside table, briefly wondering if my mother had poked through the drawers.

I shoved thoughts of my parents aside. Quickly, I had Malcolm deep inside me. He closed his eyes and let out a throaty moan. He needed this. We both did.

And hour or so later, I snorted awake from a light doze. I didn't want to sleep. Wouldn't, if that's what it took to keep Wastrel away.

Malcolm had his arm around me, his front to my back. I could tell by his breathing that he'd fallen asleep, too. I stretched and purred. His arm tightened, causing a wave of gauzy contentment to spiral through me. An unfamiliar feeling, that. One I could too easily get used to.

I opened my eyes and looked at the clock.

"Crap." I pulled away from him. Hours had ticked by, and I'd more than dozed off. But as was often the case, being skin-to-skin with Malcolm had kept Wastrel away.

He scrambled after me. "Where do you think you're going?"

"I left Zoe alone in the barn with my parents." I already had my jeans on. "Look at the time."

It was nearly four. The whole day gone. But for those hours, I'd been without worry, anger, or dreams.

Bliss.

He rolled to his feet without comment, heading down the hallway to the bathroom, giving me a wonderful view of his superbly muscled backside. Glorious, glorious man. Was it any wonder I drooled when he wore that kilt?

A moment later, I had my T-shirt pulled over my head and hopped on one foot as I pulled my boots up so I could peek between the slats of the blinds to see if anyone had come to visit.

As I watched, Zoe's dirty blue sedan came over the hill to the front of the barn, dragging a great cloud of dust behind it, Mrs.

Erdman at the wheel. I don't know where she'd gone to visit her friend but was glad to see both she and the car returned in one piece.

She rolled down the window as Zoe emerged from the barn with a wave, said something, and went back inside. Mrs. Erdman kept the car running if the cloud of smoke around it was any indication.

Wait. Smoke? It billowed from underneath, poring between the wheels. "What the hell?"

Malcolm came back in and leaned down beside me to see what I was what-the-helling about.

"Who's that?"

"It's ninety-year-old Mrs. Erdman in Zoe's car."

His eyebrows shot up. "Well, good for her. But it looks like..." He jerked the string to open the blinds fully even though he was still naked.

He grabbed his jeans and yanked them up his legs.

"Looks like what?"

"Hurry," he yelled as he pounded down the stairs. "That car's on fire."

CHAPTER EIGHTEEN

Smoke nearly engulfed the big sedan. Somehow, Mrs. Erdman had hooked a mattress on the bottom and dragged it for who knows how far. As we reached the scene, flames licked the front tires and shot from under the hood.

Zoe stood frozen in the barn doorway with her hands on top of her head. "Ohmygod-ohmygod-ohmygod," is what I think was coming out of her mouth.

"Get the fire extinguisher," Malcolm yelled. He grabbed the hose by the fence, yanked the hydrant handle up, and started spraying the car.

The extinguisher? "Get Mrs. Erdman," I screamed back.

I could hardly see her through the smoke. She scrabbled at the door handle and her seat belt, eyes wide with terror. Smoke slinked to the interior. She coughed.

Cold fear tangled my brain.

Malcolm lunged for the door handle but snatched his hand back. He sprayed it with water, covering his mouth and nose as he did.

"That door doesn't open," Zoe shouted. "Get her out!"

My parents and Giacomo came running.

I pushed Zoe toward the tack room, wanting her away from this. "Call 911."

She turned frightened eyes to me. "Are you sure?"

Jesus. "Do it!"

The fire spread to the back of the car and clawed both sides, grasping at the windows.

My father brought the fire extinguisher and started squirting white foam over everything.

I ran inside to get the other hose.

When I came out, Giacomo had used his tie to open the passenger door. He tugged Mrs. Erdman over the console and seat by one arm. She screamed and fought him, panicked and crazy.

My mother ran to that side and got hold of the older woman's other arm. Together, they pulled her out. I sprayed more water. Nothing helped. Noxious black smoke choked us.

"Get her away," Malcolm ordered Giacomo and Gemma.

They half carried, half dragged her inside the barn. Zoe joined them, a glass of water in her hand. Whether that was for Mrs. Erdman or to help put out the fire, I didn't know.

"Vi, hurry up and move your truck."

I hadn't even noticed how close Zoe's car was parked to my truck.

Shit.

That truck might be falling apart, but it was all I had. I sprinted upstairs for my keys. Before I could get back, an explosion rocked the building. Windows rattled and dust shook loose.

My throat threatened to close. They'd gotten Mrs. Erdman clear, but had Malcolm and my father gotten far enough away?

I rushed back down the barn aisle. All of them—Malcolm and my father included—stood just inside, out of the sun and away from what was now a huge fire.

The trunk lid had blown open and the hood had detached

entirely. It sat smoking in the cow pasture. The air reeked of burning rubber as tires melted into the dirt.

Malcolm handed me the hose and took the keys. I kept water flowing while he moved my truck. The paint had been scorched right off the passenger side, but it started and moved so I wasn't wheelless yet.

More importantly, Mrs. Erdman sat up, sipping water. Zoe helped her while Giacomo held her hand.

"Wow, you guys," I said to my parents. "Thank you."

The fire extinguisher—now empty, I assumed—hung from my father's hand. My mother smoothed her hair and blotted her neck with a damp cloth. No one spoke.

I cleared some of the smoke out of my lungs with a hearty cough. "How'd you know what to do?"

Adrian's gray eyes calmly skipped over me, looking me up and down as if we'd just met.

"We might know nothing about you"—he paused to set down the extinguisher—"but you know even less about us."

CHAPTER NINETEEN

As if the fire weren't enough, hot shame now threatened to strangle me entirely. Sweat pricked my scalp. My legs shook, but I recognized that as dissipating adrenaline.

Two things I knew.

One, contrary to my suspicion, my parents were speaking to each other. Otherwise, Adrian wouldn't have been able to fling back at me what I'd said to Gemma the day before.

Two, I hated them. They'd ruined my life once, and now, when I'd finally found a place, maybe even a future, they threatened to do it again.

I needed to get away. From them. From everyone. The apartment was no longer mine. We were already in my main refuge—the barn. Anyone could follow me to the house.

I pivoted, ducked through the fence to the horse pasture, and walked.

Behind me, the squeak of the hydrant handle told me someone had turned off the water. A vehicle came up the driveway. Probably the first of the local volunteer fire department.

I didn't turn. I didn't care.

Toward the middle of the field, a thorny snarl of blackberry bushes shot higher than my head. There'd been precious little fruit in July when the berries started to ripen. Lack of rain had seen to that. Horses gathered in the shade of the oaks and hickories growing on the far side of the dense wall of bushes. That's where I went. No one could see me there.

Clara had domestic blackberry plants in her garden that she watered, and they yielded enough fruit to make blackberry cobbler. I'd eaten it hot with melting vanilla ice cream. The sweet-tart clash of flavors made my eyes burn, but I ate it until my stomach hurt. That had been during my whipped cream abstaining days. I should have detoured to the house to get some before coming out here. The comfort of dusty horses would have to do.

They were drowsy, lower lips hanging, eyes half closed, tails swishing idly. Captain stamped a foot as I ran my hand over his back. Ciquala snorted. Fawn and Smitty stood nose to tail. Cali's head bobbed as I approached. I pressed the flat of my palm between her eyes. She leaned into me, nudging my hip.

I rested my cheek on her neck, my fingers clenched in her short mane.

The pressure of unshed tears crowded my chest and crept into the back of my mouth, the pain worse than the choking smoke, and pushed at the backs of my eyes. I squeezed my eyelids tight, leaned harder into my horse's calm solace, but it didn't help.

An angry sob broke free. Cali shook her head, my grip on her mane too tight. But she didn't move, didn't complain, didn't judge.

Miss Bong moved closer to us. Honey squeezed between Gaston and old Fergus, Oreo on her flank. Even Barbie, who wasn't a bad horse despite having belonged to Malcolm's ex wife, edged near. The mares, always the bosses of the herd, made a protective circle around me even while they nibbled at what was left of the grass at our feet and pretended they were doing nothing. Nothing at all.

And everything.

My legs gave out. I sank to the ground, my face in my hands. Stopped trying to choke back the anger and fear and disappointment and hurt. I didn't try to sort out the feelings. For while I hated my parents, self-loathing always crouched in my belly like a cornered wild animal.

I sat there for a long time. The horses stayed near, their bodies warm, but air moved between them. Eddies created by their tails caressed my skin. The horses took my distress and passed it on to the wind. Slowly, I felt lighter, cooler.

With a sigh, I told myself I had to face my parents. Find out what the heck was going on. Take them shopping. There must be things they needed, especially if their luggage truly was empty. I'd been selfish to ignore them. It's not as if we'd ever been on good terms. Worse, now. Truthfully, we weren't on any terms. I'd decided to hate them long ago based on years of anger at being dumped. Who wouldn't be pissed about being rejected by their parents?

Sitting there with my thoughts circling like vultures did me no good.

I got up and started across the field, thankful Malcolm hadn't felt the need to find me, to console or fix me. The remains of Zoe's car smoldered in the driveway. Inside the barn, it was quiet. I turned on the hose, got a drink, turned it off, and stood there, thinking.

Were they upstairs or at the house? Instead of putting one foot in front of the other to find out, I made sure all the stall-cleaning implements were straight. They hung in a neat row—pitchforks, two brooms, and a large plastic shovel—on the wall to my right. All clean. I always put them away clean. Keeping order in my surroundings brought me a measure of peace. I nudged the broom handle a little to bring it parallel with the pitchfork next to it.

"Perfect," said a voice behind me.

"Shit." I jumped and spun.

My father sidestepped the thin stream of water moving toward the drain. Light on his feet. But a lifetime of dance would do that.

"You startled me." I sounded angry, feelings still bunched between my shoulder blades.

"I see that. Sorry."

Sorry for making me jump or for what he said earlier or for being here or for leaving me? So much to be sorry for and I was sick of it. His gray eyes bore into me for a moment and I nearly flinched, but then they softened, the corners crinkling in good humor.

"I see you inherited my love of order."

He had a love of order? God help me. In my peripheral vision, I saw his gaze roam the wall of faultlessly straight tools, but it was as though he saw beyond to something else.

"Your mother says I have OCD."

My cheeks relaxed. Not quite a smile, but an acknowledgement. "Heard that a few times myself."

Is this how it would be? The slow revelation of small details eroding my carefully fortified walls? Were we alike? Had Gem Gem sent him out to test the water?

Did I have to be so suspicious?

For now, yes. Until I knew more about what brought them here, I had to guard the walls. It's not that I didn't believe what he'd told us about being broke and needing a change. There simply had to be more to it than that.

"As if liking order is a bad thing," he added.

Laughter started, but my cell phone buzzed in my pocket. I hadn't realized I'd picked it up when running out of the house. It reminded me I'd never called Penny back. Checking caller ID, it wasn't her or any number I recognized. Hardly anyone called my cell phone.

Frowning, I glanced at my father. He smiled and gave a nod. Not that I needed his permission. I was torn between not wanting to talk to him at all and grabbing tight to the tenuous connection our exchange had started to create.

I took the phone into the tack room. There was a beat of silence after I answered, then a voice I hadn't heard in a while said, "How you be, V?"

For half a breath, a cold finger stroked the back of my neck, though I couldn't say why. "Holy crap. Harry?"

"How're you doing, gorgeous? It's Michael, now, by the way."

"Michael? When did that happen?" Harry'd always said Michael sounded too serious, so he'd used his middle name, Henry, or the nickname, Harry. Plus, his mother always called him Michael, and he hated that.

"Even perpetual partiers grow up."

"If they don't die from the fun, first," I said. Which I'd often worried he would. "It's good to hear your voice."

"I've missed you."

"That's going too far, and you know it."

"I'm wounded, V. How could you say that? We were always so good together."

"If by good you mean drunk."

"Oh, come now. You can't steer twelve-hundred pounds of horseflesh around a jump course if you can't see straight."

"Not that you didn't try."

"And went completely off course and got disqualified. You were always the better rider, anyway. Not sure why I bothered."

We were silent for a moment, both of us probably remembering the not-so-good old days, and me wondering at how easily we'd fallen into our old banter.

Harry—Michael—was good-looking enough to grace a Ralph Lauren ad. I used to have a huge crush on him and the lifestyle his parents' wealth afforded—the horses his parents afforded. But the partying was too much. First, it was the cocaine paraphernalia I found in the tack room. He admitted to using but swore he was getting help. Stupidly, blindly, I believed him. But when I walked in on him with a man, I walked out and never looked back.

Let's just say he and the other guy weren't having a business meeting.

"Allie and Baba say hello," he said.

That's what he called his parents, Alcott and Babette. They were also charming, and their East Hampton *cottage* had been on the cover of Architectural Digest. As had their Fifth Avenue digs.

Allie and Baba had embraced me and made me feel like I belonged with them despite my origins. Being part of their circle made me feel safe, almost content.

"How are they?"

"Always doing their bit for the economy. They're in Barcelona."

Longing swept through me. I sank into the tack room's ratty lounger, its frayed armrests reminding me of just how low I'd come. "What about you? How are you?"

He'd disappeared the year before and no one knew to where. Or, if they knew, they weren't telling.

I sprang up and paced to the door, determined to push away this dissatisfaction. I'd been content at Winterlight before my parents showed. A deeper, more satisfying contentment than what I'd felt with Harry's parents. Mine wouldn't stay forever. This would get sorted out, and I'd be happy again. Out of the corner of my eye, I watched my father wandering down the barn aisle, glancing up the loft ladder, peeking over stall doors. Was he waiting for me?

"I'm better than ever, Vi. Clean and sober."

Something in Harry's voice made me believe him. "Michael, huh? Finally getting serious?"

He chuckled, his old smugness tucked into the sound like a cherry nestled inside a chocolate. "I'll never be as serious as dear old Alcott, but yeah, I'm getting there."

"Glad to hear it." My responsibilities, not to mention my

parents, tugged at me, but I wanted to catch up with him. Talking like this with an old friend, so easy, was a balm to my battered senses.

Though Harry—Michael—wasn't really a friend, not in the best sense. Because of his addiction, he couldn't be trusted. Or maybe it was me that couldn't be trusted around him. We might have been good together in a certain way, but we weren't good for each other.

"I'm sure you're busy," he said. "When are you returning to civilization?"

"Ha ha. Believe it or not, things are civilized here. I do need to go right now—"

"That's my V, always keeping her nose to the grindstone."

He sounded a little sad. I wanted to cheer him up. To cheer myself by talking to him. "Can I call you at this number?"

"That'd be great. Don't work too hard, okay?"

"Okay."

"Oh, wait, one more thing, before I forget. Remember High-Class Acres?"

Was he kidding? Ed Todd's place had been my dream. Elegant old Colonial, miles of four-board fencing surrounding manicured pastures, a twenty-stall barn with a lounge overlooking the indoor arena. I'd worked for Ed off and on over the years and always entertained fantasies of what it would be like to have a spread like that.

"Of course." I lowered myself back to the easy chair and held my breath. Ed had been like a grandfather to me. And not one who picked locks and stole shotguns.

"There was a fire."

My stomach clenched. Fire? Again?

"I heard it started in the loft. The fire department got there pretty quick, but the west end of the barn is gone. And Ed..."

I gripped the phone. "Ed?"

"He got the horses out, and then he collapsed. He's in the hospital, but it doesn't look good."

"No, no, no." My throat closed up again. I pictured Ed, mostly blind, frantic to save the horses, unheedful of his own safety.

"Right. Well. The point is, the place will be for sale in the next few months."

That was Harry. Skip over the sad part about the lonely old guy no one cared for and move on to the part where someone benefitted.

But I cared. I went to the desk and grabbed a phone book to find an airline that could get me to the Island.

Steeling myself against my worry for Ed, forcing the waver out of my voice, I said, "Been saving your pennies?"

"Never. What a thing to say."

Michael Henry Brown really was a trust fund kid. He'd had a big one, but I suspect he blew through it long ago and now sponged off his parents.

"What are you suggesting then?"

"Rumor has it you're going to inherit a big wad of cash within the year. You can buy it yourself."

CHAPTER TWENTY

Hands on hips, I gazed out the tack room window seeing not the riding ring, but Ed Todd's kind face, hearing his blustery, curmudgeonly voice. I knew he was old, but a world without him? Unfathomable. I wanted to see him. *Had* to see him. Before...before. I wouldn't think the thought.

A glance out the door told me Dad still milled around the barn, obviously waiting for me. Mom probably had dinner going.

How did Harry or anyone else hear about the trust fund? There were *rumors*? Penny and Ed Todd were the only ones who knew why I was in Missouri for a year.

I found the number for an airline and reached for the phone. It rang, making me jump.

"Winterlight F—"

"If you're done pouting, come to the house."

Pouting?

Pain forced its way into my throat again. Was he serious? I tried to glean from Malcolm's tone whether he was. He sounded serious. I didn't need this.

"I have to take a couple of days off."

A slight pause. Maybe he was reconsidering his approach. He should.

"Now?"

"I know it sucks with my family here, but there was a fire and Ed Todd was hurt and..." My voice broke.

"Easy now."

I pictured Malcolm standing in his office staring in my direction. I could almost feel his eyes on me, questing, probing. I turned to look toward the house, even though the barn was between us. Maybe he'd feel some of what I was feeling.

"Ed Todd," he said as if to himself. "That the old guy you used to work for?"

I took a deep breath. "I need to go see him. Just the weekend," I said.

"But you will come back."

He'd softened, his voice soothing as a down pillow. In spite of everything, he wanted me back. There was something else in his tone, an unspoken worry, but I couldn't dissect that right now.

"Yes."

"Cancel tomorrow's rides and give Zoe the weekend off."

"Where is Zoe, anyway?"

"I took her and Mrs. Erdman home."

"Thanks."

"Right now, I want you to come to the house and face your parents. Explain what's going on."

I huffed by way of answer.

"In the meantime, I'll see if I can get you on a flight."

We hung up. My father sat on the steps outside the tack room. I dropped beside him.

"I've been summoned to the house."

He slowly shook his head. "Man, I know that feeling."

Were we supposed to bond now over what a bitch my mother was? Was I more like him or her? I wouldn't have thought either, but a lot of what I'd thought had turned out to be wrong.

He put his hand on my knee.

"Nothing for it but to face it."

He started to rise, but I covered his hand with mine. "Wait." I cleared my throat, forced out a question. "I thought you were mad?"

He put his arm around my shoulder. "Vi, my dear, we can spend our lives being mad over what's been, or we can go forward. Try to be better." He took a deep breath. "I guess we've all done and said things we regret, that we'd change if we could."

I nodded. "It is what it is." Cringe-worthy for sure, but the best I could muster at the moment. I hoped we were discussing ourselves and not just dropping platitudes.

"It was what it *was*," he corrected gently. "But it can *be* different. Better. If we want." He patted my knee. "And we do. That's partly why we're here."

"But not the only reason."

His eyebrows shrugged and a resigned puff of breath escaped, much like the huff I'd just given Malcolm.

I *knew* it, knew there was something going on with them that they'd been hiding. Not that I'd asked, I admit. But the knowing gave my spirit a slight lift.

He stood, pulling me up with him. "We'd better go before Malcolm mounts a search party."

"He is the superhero type."

"Seems like a good man."

"Yes."

We started down the barn aisle. I couldn't believe we were holding hands. What was I, a toddler, for Pete's sake? But it felt so damned good, my hand in his, both of them strong, mine calloused, his not. I tugged him to a halt. He turned to me, saw the questions in my eyes, nodded.

"The other reasons we're here will take a little more explaining."

"I have to go to the Island for a couple of days." Tears threatened, and he squeezed my hand. Reassurance? Understanding? "But I'll be back on Sunday."

He pulled me toward him, neatly twirled me under his arm and right against his side. For a moment, I felt nearly as safe as I did when Malcolm folded me into his arms. My breath hitched on a painful squeeze in my chest. If Adrian had carved me open with a hoof knife I couldn't feel more raw and exposed.

"That's a date," he said, and he danced me out of the barn.

Forward. To something different. Maybe to something better.

CHAPTER TWENTY-ONE

Turned out, the soonest I could get on a flight was early Saturday morning. We stood to the side of a long line waiting to go through security, Malcolm's hands on my shoulders, his thumbs pressing firm circles against my collar bones. I'm not sure he realized he was doing it.

Sometimes his calm presence was overbearing. Part of me wanted to shove him away, do something stupid to rile him. Another part of me craved his touch, wanted to melt into him, never come out.

"I'm fine, really," I said, lifting my shoulders. Not enough to shove him off but enough that he stopped circling and stroked his big hands down my arms.

He nodded. We both knew I was far from fine.

Dinner the night before had been subdued. Since my father and I had agreed to talk on Sunday, the dramatics were postponed. Instead, some silent communication between him and my mother assured a bland conversation about the hot, dry weather, the comforting quiet of the farm, the price of pork bellies.

Their silent communication thing irritated me. Even if they currently were at odds with each other, they were connected.

Their link hummed with exclusion, intimacy, a special rapport, and the simple warmth of a long, affectionate relationship that eluded me.

Or, that I avoided. I get it. I don't need an analyst to tell me I was abandoned so I leave relationships and situations before they can leave me.

And here I was leaving a good job, a potential future, and Malcolm. Running out like a green horse overfaced with a four-six vertical. I had no ground line. No way to measure the height to jump, no way to see what was on the other side.

"The horses will miss you," he said.

I focused on his throat, the glimpse of luscious chest hair peeking out above the collar of his shirt.

When I first pulled into the drive at Winterlight, I told myself I didn't have to take the job, didn't have to stay, didn't have to get the trust fund—amount undisclosed.

I still didn't.

But Malcolm had no way of knowing the thoughts swirling around my brain since the phone call.

He'd made me a round-trip reservation, extracted a promise of return.

But...

The temptation to leave and not come back pulled harder than a runaway.

"The horses will be glad to have attention from you for a change," I countered.

He lifted his chin and squeezed my arms. Like a good rider on a green horse, he calmed and steadied me, gave me space to breathe, kept turning me toward the thing I feared.

We'll do it together, he'd said of facing my parents. Together like my parents? Was that really possible? True, there was tension between them now, but that surely had to do with present circumstances. Malcolm trusted we could figure things out together. I had my doubts. He saw me more clearly than I saw myself. And still, he wanted me to return. His patience and strength made me skittish.

"The cats will miss you."

Being skittish—an almost constant state with me—made me edgy and snappy. "Cats don't miss people. People miss cats."

"Noire will miss you."

"She likes you more than me."

"Only because I sneak her treats."

Another retort waited on my tongue. I was so tired of being snappy. All. The. Time. Harry's call reminded me it used to be a full-time occupation. One that kept me from decent jobs, decent friends. It's why Penny made me promise not to smart off before I left for Winterlight. I hadn't been doing a very good job of it. She'd also made me promise to not drink or sleep with the boss.

Fail. Fail. Fail.

I needed a couple of days away, dreaded the reason I had to go. Out of the corner of my eye, the security line grew, even this early. It made me anxious to get going, to get to Ed Todd.

"I'll miss you," he said finally.

His Adam's apple bobbed. He didn't usually fear speaking his mind, his feelings, but he was worried, probably suspected the thoughts circling my head.

When I didn't respond, he said, "The horses need you even if they won't miss you."

This was closer to truth.

"Remember what Nicky said before she went back to Chicago?" he asked.

Nicky, his daughter-not-daughter. He'd had his share of pain and loss. "I think so." The security line was beginning to distract me.

He repeated what Nicky had told him. "The horses are much nicer now that Vi is here."

Now, I understood why he'd wanted to leave so early. He wanted to tell me things. Things he could have said in the car. But there, I could tune him out. Face-to-face, not so much. God, he knew me. It was annoying. Made me want to lash out.

"Be careful," I said, diverting the flow of whatever he was planning to say.

He stiffened. "Vi, I—"

"Something's not right with Giacomo." Malcolm probably thought I'd meant for him to be careful about whatever else he was planning to say. I rushed on. "I don't understand the dreams I've had. He said someone is after him. Someone was in the woods, I'm sure of it. And there's that marble that was his wife's."

"That's impossible, and you know it."

"You said you could believe it after everything else that's happened. He's been awfully quiet since I found it."

His brows drew together in a suspicious frown. "I don't think he's the chatty type to begin with."

"Just watch your back. And him." After another glance at security, I added, "Don't forget to feed everyone. Fergus had some swelling around his front left ankle. Wouldn't hurt to put a cold hose on it."

He gripped my arms, reminding me how big and strong he is. But he would never use force. Not with me. Instead, his gentle strength could be my undoing. I tensed against him.

"I know you're tough, Vi. But it's okay to feel..." He followed my gaze for a moment and somehow pulled my eyes back to his. "You've been hurt. Deeply. I understand that. You have a right to be angry."

There was a 'but' coming. I could feel it. Old pain fought with the new hope. Goddamn his tenderness.

"Please stop." I struggled to pull out of his grasp. "I have to go." My voice sounded choked.

"No. You need to hear this. You can lean on someone. It's okay to ask for help. You don't have to tough it out alone." He pulled me against him, stroked his hand into my hair and pressed my head to his shoulder. "Don't be afraid. Let me help you."

His other arm wrapped around my back, crushing the air out of me. I loved the way our bodies fit together. Loved everything about us. And that scared the crap out of me. I bit down on the gasp of desperation that arose thinking about a future with him.

I squirmed. He held tight.

He spoke quickly into my ear, his voice a strip of leather encased in satin. "You're more than your anger and fear, Vi. You are smart and kind, loyal and warm hearted and..."

I was beginning to like the list even if I didn't believe it. I let out a long breath, and his hold on me relaxed. "And?" I prompted

His chest jumped with a bark of laughter. "Fun and interesting. I'm never bored around you."

He pushed me back enough to look into my eyes. His were blue like a sunny day at the beach.

"You just want me back to take care of the horses."

"And your parents."

"You had to bring them up."

"It's more than the horses, Vi, you know that."

I pulled my arms from where they'd landed around his neck, hanging on like a bucked off cowboy held a rescue clown. I'd almost forgotten where we were. The airport sounds were suddenly too loud.

Rubbing my eyes, I said, "I don't know what I know except that I'll see you on Sunday."

"You keep your word, too," he said. "That's another thing I like about you, and a very admirable quality."

I nodded. "You're not so bad yourself. And... and..." I forced it out. "I'll miss you, too."

A rueful grin climbed one side of his face. He knew it was the best I could do at the moment. He grasped my shoulders again, kissed my forehead—light as a whisper, strong as a promise—turned me toward security, and swatted my butt. My carry-on, a backpack, slipped off my shoulder. By the time I slid it up and turned to wave, he was gone.

CHAPTER TWENTY-TWO

Penny picked me up and we went straight to the hospital. Ed Todd wasn't there. A nurse told us he'd been moved to a hospice on the north shore not far from where Penny lived.

My heart dropped into my stomach on hearing *hospice*. Penny and I exchanged a look. She put her hand on my arm.

"It's not always for...palliative care," she said. "Some people go for rehab."

We looked at the nurse. She blinked. "That's true," she said.

Which didn't exactly answer the question we'd obviously been asking.

With the hospice close to Penny's house, I could take her home before visiting Ed. Seeing him felt even more urgent than it had the night before. After picking me up at the airport, Penny gratefully let me slide into the driver's seat since her huge belly barely fit under the steering wheel.

"Why didn't you send Frank?" Her husband was a busy plumber, but he rarely worked on Saturdays. "Aren't you due any moment?"

"End of the month. And you know Frank doesn't get off the couch on Saturday unless the pope himself springs a leak."

I nodded, focused on merging onto the expressway.

"Everyone's in an awful hurry for a Saturday morning," I said.

"Aren't you in a hurry?"

"Yeah, but..." Once I'd gotten the sluggish sedan settled in the center lane, I shot her a quick glance. "What?"

"Who are you and what have you done with my sis-co?"

I smiled. We'd started referring to each other as *sis-co* when we were about eight years old. "You haven't called me that in a long time."

"You'll always be my sister-cousin." She circled her palm around her ginormous belly. "With this little guy swimming around, I can't help but think of kids...us."

"But everything's okay with the pregnancy? You?"

"Oh, yeah. Just normal preggy stuff. I can't eat anything without getting heartburn, I have to pee every twenty minutes, sleeping is a long-lost dream, can't sit or stand for too long. It's great." She pressed her side and winced. "I think he's going to be a soccer player the way he kicks."

"You know it's a boy? I thought you were waiting?" Traffic lightened as we got farther east, and I was glad for baby talk distraction. I'd had a few squirts of whipped cream before leaving for the airport and nothing but coffee since. I'd like to say I slept on the plane, but my stomach cramped and my heart beat too fast every time I thought of Ed.

She shook her head. "No. I switch between 'he' and 'she.' Can't very well call her *it*."

"No, you can't."

She reached across the seat and squeezed my hand. "Ed's a tough old guy. He'll be all right."

I sighed. "I've missed you."

"Me too."

We drove in silence until reaching the exit to head north. There, someone cut in front of me to make the light.

"Freaking moron," I said.

Penny took a breath. The kind she took before saying or asking something difficult. But I couldn't take any more bad news. I was about to say something but had to slam the brakes again because of another idiot driver.

Penny braced against the dash. The jolt popped the words right out of her. "Do you still hate it?"

The question startled me. "What? Hate what?"

"The job. Right after you got there, you said I'd sent you to hell."

"No—"

"And now your parents—"

I reached for her but couldn't take my eyes off the busy road and stupid drivers. She grabbed my hand midair and held it tight.

"No," I repeated, more softly this time, gripping her fingers in what I hoped was reassurance. "I did hate it, but I don't, not anymore."

"Because of Malcolm."

I thought about this for a moment. "Not only because of him."

"So, you like it?"

"I love it."

This came out faster than expected, surprising us both. I snorted a disbelieving laugh, would have to examine this thought more later.

"Really? I mean, it must be so different. And you, you're different."

"Am I?"

"You have to turn here," she said, sounding astonished.

"What?" Focused on getting to Ed, I'd almost missed the road to our house. *Her* house. Hers and Frank's. It wasn't where I lived anymore.

"Yeah. I don't know how to explain it exactly," she continued, and I'd forgotten what we were talking about. "But you used to yell at people to get out of your way because they were going too slow for you."

I'd done that a lot all right. But I'd been gone only three months. No one changes that much in so short a time. Do they? I pictured Winterlight, the grassy pastures and horses, rows of corn gilded with soft light at sunset, the stillness of the woods at dawn, felt the quiet, a quiet I'd thought unrelentingly tedious at first.

After another deep breath, I said, "I guess driving a tractor will do that to a person." I stopped the car in front of their white split-level ranch. "Thanks for lending me your wheels. Not sure when I'll be back."

"In time for dinner, I hope."

"Unlikely." I glanced at the clock on the dash. "It's almost time for that now."

"What are you talking about? It's barely midday."

I put the car in park and pressed my eyes. "Right. Sorry. You meant supper. Yes. I'll probably be back in time for that, but don't wait. I'll call when I know more."

She gave me a look I'd seen on other people's faces but never hers. The one that made me wonder if I'd sprouted a second head. Her eyebrows lowered. "Is your mobile charged?"

I dug the ancient flip phone out of the side pocket of my carry on. The battery showed one quarter power. "Yup. I'm good."

Penny undid her seat belt, leaned over to kiss my cheek, and climbed out, one hand on her lower back. If I needed a reminder about birth control, seeing her discomfort would do it.

Ten minutes later, I shoved an oily bag redolent with the scrumptious scent of fast-food fries into my carry on, slung that over my shoulder, found the hospice center information desk, and was pointed to Ed's room.

He looked asleep and shrunken. Why did people shrink when they were in the hospital? Was the air pressure different? In my case, I'd recoiled from the hiss and bump of the machines I'd been hooked up to, from the rhythmic reminders of what had happened to me and Wastrel.

I stood in the doorway a long moment. If there were machines here, they were well disguised. The room was not huge, but homey. Lights were off, curtains drawn, but a soft nimbus from the sun leaked around the edges, giving the space a muted glow. It smelled of flowers, not disinfectant.

A few steps in and I found a chair, put my bag on the floor, set the food on the bedside table.

Ed Todd's skin had a gray tint, as if the smoke had permanently changed his complexion. His breathing was shallow, with too long of a break between exhalation and inhalation.

I caught my own breath, swallowed hard against a swift and devastating punch of awareness of my youth and strength and pure aliveness.

Ed wasn't here for rehab.

One weathered arm lay outside the covers, bruises splotched beneath the crepey skin from elbow to finger. I covered his hand with mine, not pressing or squeezing, not wanting to wake him, desperately wishing he'd speak.

"You saved the horses, Ed," I whispered. Harry hadn't mentioned whether Milly, the skinny white barn cat had gotten out. Harry wasn't much for details.

Ed took a stuttering breath and I swear his nose twitched.

"Been waiting for you," he croaked slowly without opening his eyes.

"Me or the angel of death? You look like shit."

"If death brought fries, I'd invite him into bed."

"Well, don't expect me to climb in there with you."

"You never were any fun." His voice crackled like crumpled newspaper. "Never mind. Your gift always was—"

He began coughing. I put my hand on his shoulder. He waved me away. The fit subsided. "—with animals. Your gift. Stay with that. They need you."

My eyes began to sting.

"Jesus, Ed. Why'd you have to do this to yourself?"

"You said it. Had to save the horses."

"When you getting out?"

The corners of his mouth turned down a little, but quickly bounced back. His eyes opened a crack. "Doesn't look like I am this time."

"Bull. They can't keep you. Come on, sit up." I looked for the bed control, couldn't find it. "I'll feed you some fries. You want a glass of water?"

He sighed, closed his eyes again, licked his lips. "Don't want anything. Hurts to swallow."

My nervous knee bounced, and my stomach went all queasy again.

"Smells good. You eat."

I couldn't.

His fingers fluttered against mine. "Closer," he whispered.

I scooted the chair forward and leaned in, rested my head next to his.

"De...lib...erate," he whispered.

I lifted my head and looked at him, stroked his forehead. "What are you saying?"

His breathing became labored, sawing in and out like a horse galloping a cross-country course.

"I'm calling a nurse."

With surprising strength, he held me in place, gave a shake of his head. "The fire," he rasped.

I tried to see out into the hallway and catch the eye of a passing nurse, but no one was there.

"What about the fire?"

"No...accident."

CHAPTER TWENTY-THREE

I'm trying to jump a hurdle riding a toy stick horse instead of Wastrel. It's my second try. The jump is positioned at the top of a wide but very steep ramp, and the approach is a sharp angle. A jump judge stands nearby. He's telling me I can't make it, I will be disqualified, I might as well quit.

Even I don't think I can make it. The course has already been long and tiring and my legs feel like lead. Wastrel is somewhere nearby, out of my line of sight.

Gripping tight to the toy's wooden handles, I miss the second try and nearly fall off the ramp. I can't see over the top, can't see what's coming if I clear this jump, but I'm determined to do it.

Circling back to give myself as much of a running start as possible, I take huge canter-like strides trying to pump strength and energy into my legs, but it just isn't there.

The jump judge shakes my shoulder, says something. I turn sharply to look at him, my momentum broken.

It's a woman, vaguely familiar.

"Vi Parker?"

I blink and shake off the dream. My hand still covered Ed's, but the light in the room had changed, darkened. The air smelled different, stale.

"It's Susan," she said, "Ed's sister. Do you remember?"

We'd met a few times over the years. I'd been to dinner at her house. "Yes." My fingers twitched. Ed's hand was cold.

Gently, with too much care, she took my elbow, pulled me up, and my stomach dropped.

"He's gone, honey. Thank you for being here with him. He'd been asking for you."

"What?" I thought he'd looked near dead before, but the change was obvious in his sunken cheeks and slack mouth. "No."

My face grew hot. I rose and stumbled back. My chest convulsed and an ugly sob escaped. Susan steadied me, then pulled me into a hug.

"I know, honey. It's hard." She patted my back. "He was a good man. You brought a lot of joy to his life. He talked about you all the time."

Susan is a nurturer. She'd always watched out for her brother, even while raising five kids of her own and being plenty busy with grandchildren. Crying into her shoulder felt as natural as riding a horse.

She rubbed my back some more. "We'll all miss him."

———

They took Ed away. I watched his bed roll down the hall until it turned a corner. I'd never see him again, never work horses with him, never joke with him. The shock had worn off but not the disbelief. My chest began to feel tight but I breathed through it, didn't start crying all over. Susan said he'd be cremated and there'd be no service, not right away at least. She might do something at his farm later, she said. I gave her my cell phone number and current address and left.

When I got to the car, I stopped trying to hold back the tears. It was past midnight. I didn't even know what time he'd died.

Back at Penny's, she'd waited up, sleeping in the recliner. She knew what had happened the moment she saw my face, and I got another round of hugs—awkward around her big belly—and back rubbing. She made me eat pasta and drink a glass of wine and drew me a bath with lavender oil.

Before falling into bed, I checked my messages. One was from Malcolm letting me know everything was fine there, to call if I needed anything or just to talk, everyone missed me, my parents were behaving. This sucked a watery laugh out of me. The other was from Harry telling me to let him know when I was on the Island so we could get together. My return flight wasn't until later on Sunday, but I didn't call him back. Instead, I got on Penny's computer and booked an earlier flight.

I needed to get home.

CHAPTER TWENTY-FOUR

I t wasn't lost on me that I'd been startled by everyone on the Island being in too much of a hurry, that I'd chosen to fly back early instead of getting together with Harry, that when thinking of returning to Winterlight, I'd called it *home*.

What I didn't understand was how this shift had occurred in little more than one hundred days without my even realizing. I'd been working under the assumption that once I completed my year and got the trust fund, I'd return to New York. After all, things wouldn't work out with Malcolm. That kind of goodness wasn't available to people like me. Not long-term. As usual, I'd get out before he could reject me. My heart would be safe. It would be for the best.

This is what I'd been telling myself all along.

I sat in a window seat, leaning against the airplane wall, eyes closed, disinviting contact with the outside world. Losing Ed left me feeling like my insides were scratched raw. The scared creature that lived in me seemed to have dug her way out or died trying. Now there was only a wind-torn hole so big a horse could jump through.

How a person could feel such exquisite numbness and scorching pain all at once defied reason. Actually, that's not entirely true. I'd briefly glimpsed this exhausting stew of wrenching sorrow and howling emptiness when Wastrel died, but I'd been in the hospital and gladly pumped full of drugs that kept me from feeling or thinking. When the prescriptions expired, I'd self-medicated with alcohol.

Which led to my inability to keep a job and eventually landed me at Winterlight. My thoughts skipped around this, though, never staying put long enough to really consider all the connections and implications.

And then there was Ed's near-death revelation that the fire at his place hadn't been an accident. I'd forgotten about it in the confusion after I woke up next to him, dead. Him, not me.

How did he know? He must have discovered something. Had he told anyone else? I had a feeling telling the cops back on the Island wouldn't do much good with only the whispered words of a dying man for proof. And it would only upset his sister, Susan. Maybe I could turn this one over to Dex One to investigate.

Malcolm met me at the airport with a kiss and a hug, took my bag, and didn't try to force conversation. That made for a blissfully quiet ride from the airport to the farm. I couldn't wait to do some hard physical labor. Too bad we'd already baled hay. A few hours of bucking bales under an unforgiving sun would ensure I fell into bed too exhausted to do anything but sleep. Hopefully, without dreaming.

I'd dozed on the plane but hadn't drifted deep enough for Wastrel to visit.

At the house, we walked past Giacomo's small but lovingly tended garden to get to the mud room. For a change, the old man wasn't keeping watch from a chair just inside the shade cast by the big oak out back.

"He's taken to going for walks in the morning," Malcolm said. "For his constitution."

"When did this start?" I'd only been gone overnight.

Malcolm smiled. "Yesterday."

I paused, looking over the plants. They'd already had decent sized green tomatoes on them when Giacomo stuck them in the dirt. Some were beginning to ripen, and I looked forward to my first tomato and mayo sandwich on toast.

Something caught my eye. Dropping my purse on the steps, I went to take a closer look.

"What the hell?"

Tied to one of the stakes as a support for the plant Noire had bent over was my favorite bra, one cup perfectly embracing a single large tomato. "Are you kidding me?"

Malcolm came over. He grinned when he saw what I pointed at, then snorted.

"Don't," I said. "Don't say a word." I knew what he was thinking about. Shortly after I'd arrived at Winterlight, a pair of my panties had gone on quite a journey.

He burst out laughing.

I narrowed my eyes at him. "Not funny."

"But it is."

He was right. Part of me wanted to be indignant, and part of me *was* annoyed, but I couldn't help giggling at another piece of my underwear being used in a way it wasn't intended. Thanks to the last twenty-four hours, even I could see that in the big scheme of things, this was insignificant. Plus, laughing felt good. Ed Todd always appreciated a good joke, and I could hear his voice making a crack about the cup size and number of tomatoes it would hold. As Malcolm put his arm around me, the tattered hole inside began to feel less ragged.

"It's a good excuse to talk to your grandfather," he said.

"Oh, I will. You can be sure of that."

The man himself chose that moment to round the corner of the house at a jog, his face ashen and dripping, Noire on his heels. Giacomo ran up to us and held out his hand. Nestled in his thick palm sat another marble. Unlike the sparkling translucence of the blue one I'd found, this one was densely black and dull as if it absorbed light rather than reflecting it.

We looked at Giacomo.

"The *bastardo* found me," he said. "'E's a gonna kill me."

CHAPTER TWENTY-FIVE

Malcolm led Giacomo inside to get something cool to drink, and I went to the barn to find my parents. Noire followed, bouncing against my leg with joy and slobbering my hand. I bent to pet her.

"Who's a good girl?" Her tail wagged her whole body. "Will we ever find out?" She cocked her head. Her tail slowed. "Just kidding. You're the good girl." I ruffled her ears, and she stood on her hind legs and licked my face. I hugged her. "Come on, you goof."

The horses grazed peacefully, feet stamping and tails swishing. They probably all needed a good dose of fly spray.

Inside the barn, the aisle was swept clean although the tools weren't hanging as straight as I'd like, and a piece of straw threaded the tines of the pitchfork. I'd fix that later.

My father sat in the worn chair in the tack room, wearing his reading glasses, reading one of the horse magazines piled on the coffee table.

"Where's mom?" I asked.

"You're back," he said at the same time.

"Yes, and Giacomo found another marble."

He stared at me as if I'd spoken Chinese. "Gemma's upstairs."

My hand still grasped the doorknob. I wanted to go back to Giacomo. "Can you get her and come to the house?"

He began folding the newspaper with admirable but slow precision and made no effort to get up.

Shaking my head, I took the steps two at a time. My mother sat on the couch, reading a book. I'd concluded they were speaking but clearly things were still strained between them. Otherwise, why would she be up here and him down there? It was time to get to the bottom of all their nonsense.

She glanced up and smiled when I bounded in.

"Giacomo found another marble. He's very upset."

"Another...oh." She stood. "Is he at the house?"

"Yes."

"I'll be there in a few minutes."

I started to say something about Adrian.

"I'll make sure you father comes, too," she said.

I nodded, pivoted, and went back down, wondering whether to be annoyed she'd known what I wanted. Inhaling the healing fragrance of the barn, I committed to not being aggravated by anything or anyone today. I would listen to Giacomo's story without interrupting.

Maybe.

And then, *maybe*, I would take a nap and see if Wastrel had anything to say. The sooner we got this situation—or situations—resolved, the better. Then, we could all get on with our lives.

Separately, if I had anything to say about it.

Giacomo sat at the kitchen table with a cool rag on his head. He had a tumbler of wine in his hand despite it being barely lunch time. An untouched glass of iced tea sat on the counter. Evidently, it hadn't done the job of soothing the old man's nerves.

Malcolm leaned against the counter, arms crossed, patient as the devil. He wore shorts that showed off his muscular legs. I still had on the jeans I'd worn on the plane—I always wear long pants when traveling—and they'd begun to stick to me, but I wouldn't run upstairs to change and risk missing anything. Out the front window, I watched my mother come up the drive at a brisk walk. She looked cool as usual in a white skirt and top. Dad came along behind her at a more sedate pace, hands in the pockets of his slim gray trousers. If reluctance to talk to his father slowed his steps, I could relate.

Once they came inside, we shifted to the living room where we could all sit comfortably. I grabbed a can of whipped cream out of the fridge and took a generous shot as I followed the rest of them down the hall.

In a saucer on the coffee table were the two marbles, one large and bright as a cloudless day, the other smaller and menacing as a storm front.

Malcolm and I exchanged a look. Did he expect me to conduct the interrogation? I frowned and shook my head.

"All right," Malcolm said, settling into his chair and leaning toward Giacomo with his elbows on his knees. "Where did you find the black marble?"

Giacomo swept the wet rag off his head and swung his arm through the air in the general direction of nowhere. "In a nest. In the barn."

"The barn?" I asked. There were a few swallow nests in the loft but you'd need a ladder to see inside them. They were way up in the rafters.

Giacomo pointed, this time more specifically. "The old barn. On the threshold." He wiped his face, took a drink, and looked at Malcolm. "'E's watching me," he whispered. "The *bastardo*."

Malcolm studied the backs of his hands for a moment. "Who is this bastard who wants to kill you?"

Adrian jerked as if he'd been kicked and moved from where he'd been standing beside Gemma's chair. He sat next to his father and patted his shoulder. Giacomo's lips moved but no sound came out.

"Take your time," Adrian said. "We're here to help."

Geez. What psychology Cliffs Notes had he been reading?

"Benito," Giacomo sputtered.

A portentous name if I ever heard one.

He lifted moist eyes to his son. "It's why I wrote you. Why I had to leave Florida. He tracked me there." He shook his head and muttered *Dio santo* along with what I took to be a few curses in Italian.

Malcolm took a deep breath. "Why does Benito want to kill you so badly that he would follow you halfway across the country?"

And invade our lives went unspoken.

"Have you been on the run your entire life?" my mother asked.

My father's head came up. He stared at his wife, then turned to his father. "Is it why you left me at the orphanage?"

Malcolm held up his hand. "One question at a time."

"*Sí, Sí,*" Giacomo said.

Honestly, the man had lived in this country for at least seventy years, and I'm pretty sure he'd been born here. For the life of me, I couldn't figure out why he insisted on clinging to this fresh-off-the-boat persona.

But I'd promised not to get annoyed.

"Benito was in love with my Josephine. And her father, he was the boss, you know? You understand what this means, to be the boss?"

"Like the godfather?" I asked.

He nodded. "Just like that. The boss, he groomed Benny to take over his whole life." A sad smile creased his cheeks. "But she loved *me*." He jabbed his thumb at his chest with pride then spread his hands wide. "Ah. My Josephine. She was so beautiful."

Considering Giacomo's reaction to the blue marble, I sensed this story didn't have a happy ending. "What happened to her?"

Giacomo knuckled his eyes, then grabbed Adrian's hand. "She got pregnant. Her father, he would kill me. We went to Las Vegas to be married. The boss, he was very, very angry, but Josephine, she was strong. She stood up to him. Told him it was what she wanted and that was that."

Adrian looked uncomfortable but whether it was because his father was squeezing his hand too tightly or because it was the first he was hearing his history, I couldn't tell. I sat on the edge of my seat. This was my story, too.

"We had a little apartment. I worked three jobs. She was soon to have the baby." He lightly beat his and Adrian's joined hands on his knee, took another swig of wine.

I stood and went to the window. Something stirred inside me, an uncomfortable oily sensation swirling in my gut. I shot more whipped cream at it.

"One morning," Giacomo continued, his voice tight, "I'm coming home from my job at the toll booth. I know she will have breakfast waiting. It's later than usual, light already because I stopped to buy her favorite flowers—white camellias."

I turned to stare at him, the scene from my Wastrel dream coming back full force, stealing my breath. The city, the narrow stair leading to an apartment, the woman waiting within. The dark malevolence stalking up the stairs.

Giacomo took a long sniffling breath. My mother produced tissues from somewhere, gave them to him, walked over to stand beside me.

"They followed you," I said. "Benito and another man."

Giacomo's eyes found mine. "How you know this?"

I shook my head. "Good guess."

His eyes narrowed in suspicion, but he went on. "Yes. They follow me. Benny and his younger brother Eduardo."

I dug my fingers through my hair. My stomach seethed with anticipation. I wanted to shout about the shooting, to end it, but I bit my tongue and let him tell it.

"They came to kill me. To take Josephine to her father, force her to marry Benito. But she sees them when she opens the door. They are right behind me. I can see it in her face."

His eyes were wide, remembering, his lips trembling. The pain was sharp and fresh for him, and I felt it in my chest. My mother pressed her fingertips to her temples, and my father stared at my grandfather, helpless to stop or change the story, needing to hear all of it.

On a choking sob, Giacomo said, "I turn. He fires."

His shoulders shook as he stopped trying to hold back. I barely understood him as he told the rest.

"He missed me. He hit Josephine. My Josephine."

My father's face, usually such a study in cool confidence, crumpled like a heartbroken child's. I took a hit of whipped cream and offered the can to my mother. She declined, covered her mouth with her hand, but didn't go to her husband. I didn't know who to try to comfort, and I'm not very good at it, anyway, so I just stood there trying not to throw up.

Giacomo took a moment to steady himself. "I grabbed the gun. We struggled. I didn't want to kill anyone. I just wanted to get to Josephine. But it went off again. And again. I didn't know who was hit. They ran away."

This hadn't been part of my dream. I'd woken with the first shot.

"Later, I found out Eduardo died. Benny, he lost his eye."

"My God," Adrian whispered. "What about Josephine...what about my mother?"

"She went into labor," Giacomo said. "Right there at the top of the stairs, with her life bleeding out. She had the baby. And then...and then..."

My mother murmured, "Jesus, Mary, and Joseph," under her breath and knelt in front of Giacomo, taking his head to her shoulder.

"She died in my arms," he sobbed. "She died, and I ran away. I took you to the orphanage and I ran away. She told me, with her last breath, she told me to keep the baby safe, keep him away from her father. To love him enough for both of us." He leveled a long look at his son that was so filled with longing and anguish, my stomach twisted.

"What do I know about taking care of a baby?" he asked. "I did what I thought was best. But I never forgot. I stayed in touch with the sisters at the orphanage. They kept our secret. I called when I could. They told me about you as you grew up."

"Where did you go?" Malcolm asked.

"To the cargo ships. Took a job as a seaman and sailed the next day."

"For how long?" I asked.

"Until a couple of years ago."

That was nearly fifty years of running.

"And then you checked yourself into a nursing home in Miami and started growing tomatoes?" Adrian barely disguised the misgivings in his voice.

Giacomo shrugged. "I couldn't do the work on the ships no more. My back. The nurses, they treat you good at those places. I thought I was safe from Benito after all these years. But the tomatoes, no, I had them all along. Josephine gave them to me when we married. The seeds were from her grandmother's garden in Italy."

"Surely not the same tomato plants that are outside," I said.

He nodded. "I save the seeds and plant them every year. I will make you the best sauce you have ever tasted."

That was something to look forward to. If he survived whatever Benito had planned for him.

"What about the marbles?" Malcolm asked.

Giacomo stretched one hand toward the saucer, couldn't quite reach. My mother picked them up and held them out. He took the blue one.

"This was Josephine's. Her father gave it to her. I was in a hurry when I left or I would have taken it. I took the baby and the seeds and the clothes on my back. Benito, he must have found it later."

"He *was* camping in the woods." I looked at Malcolm. "He must have dropped it when Noire went after him."

"Maybe," he said. "Probably."

"And this one?" My mother pointed at the black marble in her palm.

Giacomo pulled back, didn't pick it up. "That," he said, crossing himself, "is the sign of the eye thief."

CHAPTER TWENTY-SIX

Giacomo stared at the black marble in blank terror. Gemma looked at him as if he were a large, infuriating insect. Adrian gaped into the middle distance, probably trying to wrap his mind around this horror story that was his.

And mine. Geez. My grandmother. His mother. My mother was many things I didn't like, but at least she was alive. And that meant the possibility existed to fix things between us.

Malcolm scooped both hands through his hair and looked at me with exasperation. If he was going to pin the blame for this on me...I stopped myself. He is a reasonable man. If he hadn't blamed me when Giacomo blew a hole in the bedroom ceiling, he probably wouldn't blame me for this, either. Maybe he saw the momentary doubt in my eyes, because his softened. He came over and wrapped his arms around me.

By God his strength was reassuring.

"I need to call Dex," he said quietly. "Stay with them. Find out what *the sign of the eye thief* means. Can you do that?"

I nodded.

He squeezed me tighter. "It will be all right."

"How do you know?"

"Because I said so."

"Oh." I smiled. "Okay, Superman."

He patted my butt and turned to the others. "What is Benito's last name?"

Giacomo snapped out of his daze, ran a hand over his face, took a breath. "Columbo. Benito Antonio Colombo."

Malcolm went to the office.

Mom saved my having to inquire about *the sign*.

"What does it mean?" she asked. "The eye thief?"

"Because I shot out his eye," Giacomo said. "When he kills—he killed many times for the boss. Always, I see it in the paper. Always, it is a sign for me. 'E comes in the night and cuts out your left eye and replaces it with a black marble like that." He covered the left side of his face with his meaty hand. "'E's coming."

My mother turned to me. "We should leave." Her eyes stayed on me for a long moment then dropped to the floor. "It isn't right to do this to you and Malcolm."

"Where would we go?" my father asked.

"Yes, where would you go?" I echoed. Honestly, at the moment, I wasn't sure whether I wanted them to stay or leave. But if they had somewhere else to go, maybe they should.

My mother's shoulders drooped. That was all the answer I needed.

"Dex will know what to do," I said. "In the meantime, how about some lunch?" Food always made everything better.

I squirted whipped cream into my mouth and headed to the kitchen. There, a quick inventory told me we needed to go to the store. Especially if we were in for a siege.

I made grilled cheese sandwiches and we ate in silence. After a little while, Malcolm joined us.

"Everyone sleeps in the house," he said. "I have an air mattress. Giacomo will sleep on that in our room. Gemma and Adrian will take Nicky's room. Dex will be here later with a few of his men. Someone will always be keeping watch."

Giacomo looked up. "I get the scattergun?"

A line appeared between Malcolm's brows even though I could tell he was trying not to scowl. I could just imagine what he was thinking.

"Yes," he said, then he directed his attention to my parents. "Do either of you know how to use a gun? I mean really use one, not just hold it."

They shook their heads. He already knew how I felt about them. He'd tried to get me to learn how to handle the shotgun back in May and I'd refused. When push came to shove, I'd let Dex One give me some quick instructions with a pistol, but when the time came to use it, I'd been disarmed in a blink.

"I'll keep Willy close by."

Malcolm gave me a reproachful look. "I don't want Benito getting close enough that you could use a baseball bat."

"You are right, Mr. Malcolm," Giacomo said. "But he is cunning, Benny is. He prides himself in getting close to his target. He don't use a gun if he can help it. He cripples the victim with a knife, first. "

My father had been quiet, but now he spoke up, his voice thinned by revulsion. "Do you mean to say that he sneaks up on a person and takes out their eye before he kills them?"

Giacomo had refilled his wine glass, emptying one bottle and helping himself to another. He thumped his chest and belched. "*Sí.* Exactly that."

"Fucking hell," my mother whispered.

Everyone turned to her, shocked. My feelings about her flip-flopped. Suddenly, she was someone I could like. A couple of swear words shouldn't matter, but to me, they revealed more about her than she probably intended. I smiled.

"Yes. Fucking hell," I said. "And we're going to need more wine."

"We'll give Dex a shopping list," Malcolm said. "For the time being, no one leaves the farm. And no one goes anywhere alone."

"Put whipped cream on the list," my father said, taking a generous hit from one of my cans.

We all turned to him, just as surprised by that as by mother swearing.

He shrugged. "What? It helps."

"It will make you fat," my mother said.

"I should live so long."

Gemma's lips stretched into a thin line, but she dropped it.

Giacomo took another slug of wine. Malcolm rolled his eyes heavenward. I suppressed an exhausted and giddy laugh.

Who would have thought the threat of an eye-stealing murderer could bring out everyone's best?

CHAPTER TWENTY-SEVEN

We worked in pairs to get my family moved from the apartment back to the house and settled. Despite Malcolm's concern, I kept Willy to hand. He strapped a pistol to his belt, handed Giacomo the scattergun, and loaded the rest of his arsenal, hiding weapons strategically around the house and barn, making sure everyone knew where they were, just in case.

As the day progressed, clouds heavy with the potential of much-needed rain gathered in the west, the first promise of a good soaking we'd seen in weeks. I had no reason to feel happy, yet thoughts of cool moist air, less dust, and greening grass made my steps lighter.

Dex One arrived with four of his men including Brian who'd helped out when JJ threatened us last May. Brian had slimmed down some and looked serious, dressed in black and sporting a matte watch just like Dex's. I was glad Dex hadn't fired the guy. Last May, I'd tricked him into letting me take a horse out to do some reconnaissance. He'd ridden Honey. We'd been shot at.

Can you say *Deja-vu all over again*? Although the idea of a silent knife scared me more than gunfire.

After consulting with Malcolm, Dex told his men where to patrol. I snapped a lead line on Noire to keep her from following them. She doesn't like being leashed, and keeping her by my side while also holding Willy was awkward at best. I tried shutting her in the tack room, but all the excitement and comings and goings had her agitated, and she barked nonstop until I let her out.

The preparations kept everyone busy and distracted. I called to check on Mrs. Erdman—she was fine—and to tell Zoe to stay away for now.

"Can you come pick me up for work in the morning?" she asked before I could explain.

"Erm...no. We have a situation here. No rides for a couple of days. Everyone gets vacation." I hoped our *situation* would be resolved within a day, that Dex would find Benito, that life would get back to normal.

When had I become such an optimist?

I heard a door close and assumed Zoe had gone into a different room for privacy. "I don't want a vacation. I don't have a car. I'll go crazy if I have to spend another day playing cards with Mrs. Erdman."

Sounded like she was already on the edge. I felt sorry for the kid but couldn't risk bringing her into our crazy world.

"No," I said. "Malcolm's orders." Not exactly true, but I knew if he knew I was talking to her, that's what he'd say.

I pictured Zoe's face, the frustration in her eyes as she tried to think of something to convince me.

"Don't you have any friends you can call?" I asked. "Go swimming or something?"

"I'm not from around here."

That wasn't really a huge revelation. I'd suspected she had secrets. "Look, Zoe, whatever *your* situation is, I can't deal with it at the same time I'm dealing with *our* situation. Okay?"

"No. What is your situation?"

"I'm not at liberty to say."

A long huffy breath came down the line.

"If I bring you my truck," I offered, "will you stay away until I say it's safe to come back?"

She hesitated, but said, "Yeah. Okay. I guess."

"Swear."

"I swear to stay away."

I promised to be there in a little while, hoping to convince Malcolm to let someone follow me over. I saw him conferring with Dex and decided it made more sense to not bother him with this little matter while they were in the middle of planning our siege defense. Instead, I snagged Brian from where he sat in the barn.

He held up a hand to ward me off before I could say anything. "Don't talk to me, Miss Parker. I'm working."

Well. Dex must have given him a *very* stern lecture after our last encounter.

"You look great," I said. "Been working out?"

He smiled. "Yes. And no."

"No?"

"Whatever you're going to ask, the answer is no."

"Not very neighborly today, are we?"

"C'mon. You know the deal. If I mess up again, Dex will can me."

"I just need you to follow me to a friend's house. It's five minutes away. Dex already okayed it."

He eyed me with distrust, as well he should.

"We'll be together," I added. "You'll be doing your job by keeping an eye on me. Nothing's going to happen here in broad daylight."

He snorted at that. We both knew it was a crock.

He stood. "I'll double check with Dex."

I leaned backwards out of the barn door to see if Dex was still talking to Malcolm. They were walking around the side of the house. "You sure you should interrupt him right now? He's talking to Malcolm."

Brian frowned and put his hands on his hips. Or as close as one of those bandolier thingies strung with weapons, tools, and communications devices would allow. I couldn't tell whether it was helping to hold his pants up or contributing to their gravity induced slide toward the ground. He tugged on his waistband.

"Okay. Let's make it quick."

Oh, how I love the smell of victory. Even small ones. I ran for my keys and we were off.

My truck complained the whole way, but at least it started, and if it kept Zoe out of our hair until this was over, it was worth it.

Ten minutes later, we pulled into Mrs. Erdman's long drive. Brian stopped near the road. Zoe came outside when I pulled up to the house.

"That was quick."

"And we're in a hurry." I threw the keys at her. She grabbed them out of the air.

"Who's that?" she asked with a tilt of her head toward the black SUV by the road.

"A friend. Sorry about this, but we have to go."

"I wish you'd tell me what's going on. I really could help."

"No can do." I slammed the truck door and a piece of rust popped off the wheel well. "Take good care of it."

"I seriously doubt I could do any more damage to it than you already have."

Smart ass.

"Just don't loan it to Mrs. Erdman, okay?"

"Ha ha." She peeked into the front seat. "Is this a manual?"

I stopped and turned. "Please tell me you know how to drive a stick."

She shook her head. "I'm sure I can figure it out."

"Oh, hell no. I can't afford a new transmission." I waved to Brian. "Slight delay. Need to give a quick lesson here." To Zoe, I said. "Get in the driver's seat." A glance over my shoulder showed me the door to the SUV opening. I shoved Zoe. "Hurry up."

"All right, all right," she grumbled as she climbed in.

I pointed at the floor. "See that pedal on the left? That's the clutch. You have to use that to shift gears. Got it?"

"I guess." She jammed the keys in the ignition.

"Press the clutch to the floor and keep it there before you start the engine."

She did as told.

"You're going to have to make a tight three-way turn to get out."

She looked keen, eager. "Okay."

"Look at the shifter. The knob shows you the gears. See? First, second, third, fourth, reverse, and neutral. You want reverse, so push it to the side and down."

She fiddled with the thing. Out of the corner of my eye, I saw Brian with one hand to the side of his head, talking into what I assumed was a spy-like ear thing. I put my hand over Zoe's and shoved the truck into reverse.

"Feel it?"

She nodded, put both hands on the wheel.

Keeping my eyes on Brian, I said, "Crank the steering wheel all the way left, give it a little gas and slowly ease out the clutch. Slowly. Then, push the clutch in again."

"Where do you think you're going?" Brian yelled.

By some miracle, we didn't stall as the truck swung around into the bushes along Mrs. Erdman's drive. Zoe let out a surprised little squeak. She looked from me to Brian and back.

I jammed it into first. "Turn the wheels right, give it gas, and let out the clutch again. You press the clutch when I tell you, and I'll shift. Got it?"

"Got it."

"Try not to hit that man."

She giggled, having entirely too much fun. "I'll try."

We jumped forward, jolted up on the front lawn around Brian, then bounced back to the driveway.

"Clutch!"

We rounded the SUV in second and screeched onto the pavement in third.

"Nice work," I said.

"Told you I could figure it out."

"You are smarter than the average bear."

"Huh?"

"Never mind. You should probably put a little gas in the tank."

"I can do that. Thanks, Vi. I appreciate this. Sure I can't come see the horses?"

"Nope." I pointed ahead. "When you get up there where the road straightens, shift it into fourth."

She did. The truck jerked us against the seat belts, then smoothed out. We drove a little farther and found a place to turn around just as Brian caught up and pulled behind us. I couldn't see his face through the tinted windows, and really, I didn't have to. But I waved.

It's the friendly thing to do.

Brian and I returned to Winterlight. The clouds passed over without dropping any rain on us, leaving the air sultry and still and hotter than ever. Late in the afternoon, when the sun turned the horse's shadows into elongated dinosaurs drifting around the pasture, my parents retired to the kitchen to start dinner. Malcolm and Dex took the front porch. Yes, I'd gotten a thorough dressing down from both of them. But all's well that ends well, right? Okay, it wasn't over yet. I'd displayed the appropriate remorse, and we'd let it go.

Giacomo and I sat by his garden. We seemed alone, but I knew one of Dex's men was in the garage, another in the old barn. Close, unobtrusive, deadly.

Willy leaned against the house, and the scattergun rested across Giacomo's lap.

"So, these are heirloom tomatoes?"

"Heirloom, *Sí*." He pointed at two plants on one end of the row that had longish fruits. "These are San Marzano. Good for canning. But this one," he indicated the one that needed my bra to hold it up. "Italian. Like me. Good for salad or sauce." He scooped one hand under the red cup of my bra, weighed it. "They will get bigger. A pound or more. " He put two fingers and his thumb to his lips, kissed them. "*Delizioso*."

I pointed at the spandex support. "That's one of only two non-sports bras I own, and it's my favorite."

He shrugged and leaned forward. "I no find the pantyhose. You leave it in apartment. I think you no need." He added a suggestive ogle of my chest.

My grandfather's a dirty old man. Great. I shot him a look to match his turn of thoughts.

He chuckled. "I find something else."

"Yes, you will."

We sat in silence for a while.

I love long summer evenings. Even though it was August, and the days were shorter than they'd been in late June, the light turned everything that warm red-gold color, and the air softened.

When I'd first arrived from the East coast, I'd never thought to get used to the open and sparsely populated countryside. I'd come to like the way the quiet isolation cocooned us. Obviously, given my sudden aversion to the traffic and pace back on the Island, I'd adapted.

Tonight, though, the coming dark hummed with menace, and despite the comparative safety of where I now lived versus where I used to live, I could wish for a little less sparseness, a little more population. There were miles of uninhabited woods out there where a cunning killer could hide. How long had Benito been spying on us? Despite the heat, I shivered.

Malcolm had called Clara and Hank and informed them of the heightened terror alert. We were all to join them for dinner tomorrow night.

That was, of course, assuming there were no attacks tomorrow.

Dex had brought night-vision goggles and planned to *go hunting* after dark. I didn't like the sound of that, but he promised to take his second in command. Malcolm, I could tell, itched to go with them, but he would stay, he said, guard his home, his family.

My family.

Still raw from losing Ed Todd, the thought of losing anyone else ate at me, stirring that greasy stew that curdled in my gut. I kept thinking of Giacomo's story about my grandmother, Josephine, about how much time and energy I'd wasted being angry at my parents. I would get to know them. Let them know me.

The mud room screen door squeaked open, and my father stuck his head out. "Time to eat."

We went in. Malcolm had taped up the window I'd broken. Someone had swept up the glass. That seemed so long ago, when I'd punched out the pane in my panic to get to him, but it was only the other night. My knuckles hurt and still wore bandaids. My toes were a little sore from when Smitty had stomped on them. My mother had a bruise on her forehead where Malcolm had grazed her with the butt of the shotgun. We were wounded, but determined.

Dinner was a roast and potatoes and broccoli and salad and good. The situation hadn't dulled anyone's appetite. And there was wine. Lots of wine, especially for Giacomo. He was glassy-eyed before the peach cobbler Clara made for us came to the table. Maybe we'd sleep.

Maybe not.

My father told a couple of stories about him and mom at dance competitions. Early on, in the states. Later, all over Europe and other parts of the world. They always won, he said.

"For a long time, that's how it was," my mother added. "We *were* the competition."

They were both extra quiet after that. We all were. We could keep thoughts of the bogeyman at bay for only so long, after all. But I knew, *knew* their quietude meant something. It was a clue to why they'd quit Europe and come back to the states when Giacomo contacted them. Had they stopped winning?

That mystery would have to wait.

We went to bed. Giacomo said he would help keep watch. But he slept. I know because he snored with the ferocity of a drunk elephant.

Malcolm wrapped himself around me, his front to my back. Needless to say, we didn't sleep naked like usual. Just the same, his erection—his *spear*—pressed against me, demanding attention. If the last couple of days didn't call for some good hard sex, I didn't know what did. And what the heck was it about being surrounded by people, by the possibility of discovery, that made me want him even more?

Carefully, I slid out of the bed, pulling him behind me. We padded down the hallway to the bathroom, turned on the shower and got in. It was an old house, and the walls weren't exactly well insulated, but there was a room between us and my parents. Hot water, slippery soap, a hotter man powerful enough to support me with one arm and still touch me the way I liked. Not that I needed that extra stimulation. I sank my teeth into the meat of his shoulder to keep from screaming my hallelujahs out loud.

Afterwards, back in bed, he held me until he thought I'd

slipped into dream time, then quietly went into the hall to relieve Brian, who tiptoed downstairs to nap on the couch.

Some time after midnight, the weather broke. Rain and wind scourged the house, thunder rattled the windows, lightning lit the walls. Usually, I enjoy lying in bed listening to a good storm, but that night each thunder thump made my whole body jerk.

Eventually, I slept.

We start the course with a large circle, Wastrel feeling a little unbalanced. It's that same jump course again, but I'm determined to ride it out, to see where Wastrel is taking me. Two strides from the first jump, he rotates hard to the right and we leave the ring. We're cantering through a marsh, yet the footing is good, not boggy at all. More like a shallow creek with a sandy bottom. With each stride, water splashes up to cool us. We jump into a large box floating above the water, halt. While standing there, Wastrel bobs his head and paws the hard floor. I know I'm supposed to pay attention, that there is meaning in his actions, but as usual, I don't get it.

He swishes his tail. I smell smoke and think of Ed Todd, imagine I can feel the heat of the fire and hear the screaming and kicking of the horses even though there is nothing inside the box with us. I force myself to sit and listen, to feel. I remember what Ed said about my gift, about his fire not being an accident.

We jump down, back to the marsh or river. It is dark, but the moon is out, glowing pale crystalline blue like a faceted gem and casting a long reflection on the water's surface. Wastrel stops and paws again causing the moon's light to scatter away from his hooves like mice leaving a flooded nest. We canter along the reflection, following it all the way to the moon, which we jump. As we come down on the other side, Wastrel kicks out, sending the orb bouncing along the water like a skipped rock to shatter into a thousand new moons to light our way.

Dawn brought fog, and we all groggily bounced off each other in the kitchen fixing our coffees. Giacomo took his black, complaining it was too weak. He usually drank espresso, he said, but I seriously doubted they served that at the nursing home. My mother added a pinch of artificial sweetener—which I didn't even know we had—no milk, and took hers at the kitchen table. My father, a tablespoon of real sugar, extra milk. He'd prefer one of those syrupy creamers, he said, then mumbled the old adage about beggars not being choosers as he took his cup down the hall to the living room.

Dex came in looking bedraggled and defeated. He'd seen several deer, every raccoon, possum, skunk, fox, coyote, bobcat, and owl in the county as well as a muskrat, but no Benito. Nor had he found any sign or tracks, but they could have been washed away by the rain. I handed him our largest mug fixed the way he liked with a little milk, no sugar.

Into the second largest mug we had, I added a generous serving of whipped cream to my coffee and did the same for Malcolm when he extended his cup. He gave me a lusty wink by way of thanks. I hid my smile behind my cup, but I think my mother picked up on the vibe.

"Sleep well, Vi?"

I sat at the table with her. "I did. How about you? Did the storm wake you?"

"A storm woke me, yes." *She* winked at me.

My face heated. I'll be damned. I'd have to remember there were no secrets in this house.

I'd just begun to relax when a scream rent the air.

"Shit!" Dex yelled and took off through the mud room.

"Who's missing?" Malcolm asked as he went after him.

Cups were set down too hard and coffee splashed over the table and counter when we all followed.

"Giacomo," I said. "Where's Giacomo?"

"*Merde*," I heard the old man shout from outside. "In the garden."

Dex skidded to a halt by the row of tomato plants. One-by-one we all ran into each other trying to pull up. The rain had made the grass slick and the ground soft.

Giacomo knelt in the mud peering into a hole.

The tomato plant with my bra entwined in its branches had been dug up and removed. Shoved where its roots had been, one of the plastic pots the plants had arrived in.

In the bottom of that sat another black marble.

CHAPTER TWENTY-EIGHT

D ex got on his two-way, ordered his men in, and stormed up the driveway, his jaw so tight I feared he might crack a molar. That left the rest of us standing around a wet hole staring at a marble. My mother and I were both barefoot. Her toes were perfectly manicured with light pink polish. Mine, not so much. When was the last time I'd pampered myself? No idea. Maybe never. My feet were usually in boots.

My father picked the plastic pot out of the hole. "How do you think he did this without waking anyone?"

Giacomo's skin looked like bleached parchment. "'E's a ghost."

"The real question," Malcolm said, "is how he got past Dex's men."

I glanced to the team assembled in front of the barn. "By the body language and raised voices, I'd say that's exactly what Dex is wondering."

Dex jabbed his finger in one direction, then another, then a third. Three men took off. Dex came toward us. Malcolm went to intercept him. They consulted, then Dex took off after the others. Poor guy hadn't had a chance to change into dry clothes or drink his coffee.

Malcolm came back, but his gaze followed Dex. "Brian hasn't checked in."

"Enough," Giacomo muttered. "I go." He dumped out the dregs of his coffee, tipped the shot gun over his shoulder, and started walking along the dirt road that led past the soy beans to the woods.

"Whoa, whoa." I chased after him, sticking to the grassy verge. But I wanted to go, too. To get on a horse and gallop out. I knew that wasn't going to happen.

"Hang on there, old man," Dad said.

"Oh, for pity's sake," Mom said.

Malcolm jogged by me, snatched the long gun off Giacomo's shoulder, and got in front of him, halting him in his tracks. The old man was tall, and I suspected in better shape than he let on, but Malcolm had six inches of height on him, not to mention being around forty years younger and in prime physical condition.

Still, Giacomo tried to duck around. "He wants me. Nobody else gets hurt."

Malcolm took Giacomo's arm. "Not how we do things here."

I caught up to them. "Maybe he's right. Maybe we should go."

Malcolm gave me that look, the one that said he did occasionally wonder why he kept me around but this wasn't open to discussion.

"Not to the woods," I explained, thinking he might have misunderstood my intent. "But away from here. To a hotel or something."

Dad came up. He wore flip-flops, and while his feet weren't as pretty as Mom's, they were well cared for. I guess ballroom dancers had to take good care of their tootsies.

"Agreed," he said. "Coming here wasn't a good idea. We're sorry for all the trouble."

Malcolm glared at us. "You'd be sitting ducks at a hotel. Benito found Giacomo after fifty years of being on the run." He looked at each of us in turn, waiting, no doubt, for someone to argue. No one did. "No," he said. "You stay."

My mother still stood by the tomatoes. "That's settled. I'll make breakfast." She went inside.

I watched her, wondering at how she'd changed in a couple of days. When they arrived, she'd been quiet and withdrawn, but this crisis had sparked a response in her. If I hadn't just experienced my personal revelation about how quickly someone could change, I wouldn't believe it.

I started for the barn. "I'm going to do the morning chores."

"No, you aren't," Malcolm said. "Not alone."

"I'll go with her," my father offered.

"Stop being so bossy," I said to Malcolm.

"I *am* the boss. And until Dex or one of his men is here, we stay together. We have only an inkling of what this guy is capable of or if he's working alone. In the house, now."

Adrian and Giacomo didn't disagree and headed for the side door.

I put my hands on my hips and glowered at him.

"Don't fight me on this, Vi. And don't try to sneak around me, either."

He knows me too well.

"Giacomo assumes he's Benito's only target," he continued, "but we don't know that for sure." He came over and pried one hand away from my body, pulled it to his lips and kissed my palm, smiling the whole time.

I fought every inch of the way. I'm strong but there's no denying he's way stronger. He almost never played the boss card, rarely lorded his superior strength over me, and only occasionally laughed at me. There was no way to win against that triple threat.

We both knew he was right. I wouldn't concede the point aloud, but I did let him take me inside.

Mom had made a rasher of bacon and fluffy veggie omelet for each of us. The eggs were courtesy of Clara and Hank's hens, the bacon from one of their hogs, the veggies from their garden. The omelets were very good, seasoned with dill. We refilled or reheated our discarded coffees, pulled in extra chairs, got cozy around the small kitchen table, and dug in.

I liked it. We didn't talk about dancing or horses or the eye thief or the fact that Brian was missing. We rubbed elbows and passed the salt, stole bacon from each other's plates, and laughed.

Halfway through, I realized Noire wasn't patrolling for dropped pieces of food. Out of habit, I'd let her out when I first got up and hadn't seen her since. I went to the side door and called. She didn't come. Prickly cold crept up my scalp.

"Giacomo, do we need to worry about any Godfather type action with regard to the animals?" I'd started thinking about Gemma and Adrian as Mom and Dad but still hadn't reconciled to referring to him as *Grandpa*.

He paused his chewing, leaned back from the table. "What you mean?"

"I mean, you know, the horse." I drew my fingers across my throat. "In the bed?"

He blinked at me a few times, then waved his knife. "Eh, no. Benny loves the animals. When we were kids, he had a dog he adored. Followed us everywhere. He fed the strays, too."

Forks and coffee cups froze in place. Every head swiveled to him.

"You grew up together?" my father asked.

"*Sí.* We are *cugini*—cousins through our mothers."

My dad looked at me, his eyes wide. I connected the dots.

"That means he's our cousin, too." I sat down again, feeling weak in the knees.

Giacomo had already shoved another bite of omelet into his mouth. "Of course," he said around it. "We have a big family."

Slowly, everyone resumed eating, needing to digest this news along with the food. I'm sure I wasn't the only one wondering why this hadn't been mentioned before. Maybe forty some years at sea scrambles a man's brain as surely as the eggs on our plates.

Before conversation could resume, I heard Noire barking out near the barn. Relieved, I went to the front door to call her inside. Another taxi rolled up the drive, this one a white minivan instead of a yellow car.

The chances of one public transportation vehicle coming to Winterlight were slim to none. The odds of a second one coming so soon after were zero. Yet, there it was. It couldn't be good.

When I didn't return to the kitchen right away, Malcolm joined me on the front porch.

"What now?" he asked.

"My thought exactly."

The taxi stopped outside the gate, the back window opened, and a young man with shoulder-length blonde hair stuck his head out. The top and sides were pulled up into a man bun. In heavily accented English, he asked, "Is this the ranch of Miss Viola Parker?"

He had bright blue eyes, high cheekbones, a straight nose, and full mouth. He reminded me of Harry. In other words, he was impossibly good looking.

I felt Malcolm tense beside me. He crossed his arms over his chest. "Who are you?"

"Oh, so sorry. I am Mr. Milanko Stanislaw."

The screen door squeaked behind us.

"Miko?" my mother said. "What—"

"Ah, my belle Gemma Maria. Thanks to the gods I found you."

"You know this guy?" I asked.

Miko hopped out and slung a backpack over his shoulder. He handed a wad of bills to the driver.

"Hang on," Malcolm said. "What do you think you're doing here?"

The screen door skreaked again.

"What the hell?" my father asked. "What is he doing here?"

Oh boy.

"Don't make a scene," my mother hissed.

"Don't make a scene?" My father's look was incredulous. "He's the one who made a scene. *You* made a scene with him."

"It wasn't like that. If you would just let me explain."

Malcolm and I took a step back.

"Don't bother," Dad said. "Get in the taxi and go with him if that's what you want." He stomped back into the house, slamming the inside door. The screen jumped off its top hinge again. I caught the edge and set the corner on the porch floor.

A bright pink spot bloomed on each of my mother's cheeks. Her eyes glittered.

"Miko," she wailed. "Why are you here? How did you find us? I told you to stay away."

The taxi began to back up.

"I cannot, my belle, my love. I miss you so much, I cry to sleep every night. My heart is paining and my eyes are too tired. I must find you. We must be together or I will be dead."

"Stick around," I muttered. "You can join the club."

Malcolm gave me a sharp *shut up* look.

"This cannot be, Miko. *We* cannot be. You shouldn't have come, and you can't stay here. Viola, stop that taxi and make sure he gets in it."

She went back inside, slamming the door again. The bottom hinge popped off the screen. Malcolm caught it before it landed on us and leaned it against the wall. "Not sure the old house can handle this much drama."

I stared at the space where my mother had been, then looked at Malcolm, then at Miko's sad face, then down the driveway. The taxi disappeared over the hill. I wasn't about to run it down.

Noire pranced onto the porch. The fog had lifted but the sky was still heavily overcast, and it started to drizzle, then quickly turned serious. Miko's backpack slipped to the ground as the downpour flattened his pretty hair. He looked at the door his love had gone through, and I believed his heart was paining him. My heart pained watching him.

"Jesus Christ," Malcolm said. He gestured to Miko. "There's some breakfast left. Get in out of the rain."

Miko smiled, grabbed his backpack, and came up the steps. Noire sniffed him, wagging her tail the whole time, so whatever had happened between him and my parents, he wasn't a bad guy. A tad misguided if he'd followed them here from Europe. The lovesick puppy couldn't be more than twenty years old.

He reached for the doorknob. Malcolm stopped him. At this point, I think Malcolm's patience must have been worn paper thin. Mine was long gone.

"Hang on," he said. "Before you go in, explain why you're here and what you intend to do?"

"What you mean?" Miko's face was all innocence. "I come for my woman, Gemma Maria."

CHAPTER TWENTY-NINE

Malcolm ran his hands through his hair. It was shorter than Miko's, darker—more golden—but wavy and plenty long enough to get my fingers into. When he was tired or frustrated or angry, he often scraped his hands over his scalp. Maybe it helped him think. More likely it kept him from punching someone.

"I don't think the lady is interested," he said to Miko. "And I don't want you bothering her or upsetting her and her *husband*."

His emphasis on the last word left no doubt as to whether Miko had a place in the family. Miko's hand dropped away from the door knob.

"I will convince her. We belong together."

At that moment, Dex came around the corner with his men. They supported Brian between them. He had one arm around Dex's shoulders and the other covered his face. There was blood —on his arm, on his shirt. He hopped on one leg, the other hung limp and dragged a trail through the wet ground behind him, and there was more blood on his pants.

"Sit. There." Malcolm pointed Miko to one of the chairs on the porch. "Don't move."

Heedless of the downpour, we ran out to meet Dex while one

of his men brought around an SUV. They got Brian into it. He grunted and groaned and hissed as they slid him across the back seat.

It was a good sign that he was walking, or hopping, but the blood...that cold sweat that had started when I realized Noire was missing flared again. "Shouldn't we call an ambulance?" I asked.

Dex shook his head. "This is faster." He slapped the roof and the car took off. "He's going to be all right."

I couldn't tell whether he believed that, said it to reassure himself, or us.

Malcolm squeezed Dex's shoulder. "What happened?"

Dex pressed his thumb and forefinger to his eyes for a moment, breathed deeply. "Benito got the jump on him after the storm started. He sliced his hamstring, tied him to a tree, gagged him. Cut an X across his left eye socket." He crossed his index fingers over his eye. "Didn't take the eye, though."

Without realizing , I stepped back, my hand to my throat. "Oh my God."

Malcolm put his free arm around me, pulled me against his side.

"But then, he put a tourniquet on his leg," Dex went on. "I think he wanted him to live. At least, long enough to tell us what happened."

"Did he say something?" Malcolm asked. "Benito?"

"Yes. He said, 'I will not take your eye. You tell him. Tell Giacomo. I will take his, and everything he cares about. An eye for an eye.'" Dex stamped his foot. "Shit. I'm getting too old for this."

I was too old for this. Or too young. Not sure. Either way, I needed to go to the house and make more coffee before I said or did something I shouldn't. Unfamiliar feelings battered me. Impotent rage because of what Benito did to Brian. Confusion about my parents and Giacomo and their place in my life, mine in theirs. Grief over Ed Todd kept sneaking up and wrapping cold hands around my throat. Fear, too, was like an icy finger tracing my spine. Helplessness. A desire to run so strong my feet itched.

I wanted to punch something, needed to go riding. A drink or two or six would help. Curling up into a ball held appeal. What had I been thinking taking my truck to Zoe? If I could get away for a while, I could track down a nice, dark bar, maybe with a mechanical bull. That way, I could drink, ride, and probably find someone to punch all in one spot. I could pass out in a corner and be at peace, if only for a while. No one would know where I was.

I sighed. It wouldn't last. Dex would find me. He was spooky that way.

Alternately, I could take a horse into the woods, find Benito and take him out. Even if he was my cousin once or twice removed. He had no right to terrorize us like this, to hurt people who were in no way involved with his vendetta. To hurt any of us. I stoked the flames of my anger to keep the welter of other emotions in the dark.

Raised voices came from inside, rising over the drumming of the rain like a Greek chorus run amok. Miko no longer sat on the porch where we'd left him. Few people dared disobey Malcolm when he used *that tone*. That Miko had ignored the Laird's directive spoke of either his determination or youthful stupidity. I stood there with my hand hovering over the doorknob, uncertain I wanted to step into whatever pile of steaming excrement had materialized now. As if we weren't already knee deep. Noire sat beside me wagging her tail, spinning water in an arc across the porch floor. She loved having so many new people around. For her it meant more treats and attention.

A smacking sound came from inside followed by a grunt and a screech. Had someone just been punched? The door opened, sucking me toward it. My mother reached out, grabbed my wrist, and yanked me in.

My father and Miko grappled with each other in the living room. They were well matched in height and build but it was obvious neither of them knew how to fight. Noire ran in and started barking, circling them. Whether she wanted in on the action or was trying to break it up is hard to say.

I covered my mouth and pretended the crazed yelp of laughter that wanted to escape was a cough. Miko hooked one foot behind my father's legs, they toppled to the couch, then the floor. I watched in horrified fascination as a lamp whirled off a side table and crashed against the wall.

My mother pinched my upper arm. "Do something!"

"What do you want me to do?" I yelled at her. The whole place had gone insane.

"Stop them."

I took a deep, calming breath, put Brian and Benito out of my mind. "Sometimes it's good to let men work things out like this." I pointed at them. "It appeals to their baser instincts."

What psychology Cliffs Notes had I been reading?

Miko and Adrian rolled to the other side of the room, knocking into another table. I grabbed the lamp on that one before it could meet the floor and set it up on the mantle. Noire bounced over them and barked some more. The men were yelling insults at each other in another language. French, I think.

"Don't we have enough to worry about?" my mother asked.

Although I'm pretty sure my dad wanted to kill Miko, and Miko was only trying to defend himself, I didn't think they were really going to hurt each other. I raised my voice to be heard over the din. "Dad's been very tense with all this stuff with Giacomo. Maybe it's good to let them burn off some energy."

"Are you serious?" She kicked Miko in the ass. "Stop it this instant."

They both ignored her, rolled back to the other side of the room, pushing the couch against the wall. Dad had Miko's bun now, and he jerked it hard. I think Miko was trying to bite him. Apparently dancers fight like adolescent girls. I'd concluded Miko was also a dancer, something in the way he held himself, his gait, but had yet to confirm that. My mother's eyes blazed at me.

"Okay, okay." I went to the kitchen, filled a pitcher with water, came back, and dumped it on them. They fell apart like coupling cats, sputtering and howling. Noire commenced to licking their faces. So helpful, my dog.

My father seized the moment to slap Miko on the ear. Geez. Boys. He got up, touching his lip, which was bleeding, and shot daggers at my mother, who didn't move toward either of them. Miko stayed on the floor, staring at my father like he hadn't expected the older man to put up such a fight. He touched his eyebrow, red with rug burn and beginning to swell.

"Who started it?" I asked.

"He did!" they both said.

Sorting this out would be like getting the truth out of a couple of toddler girls caught squabbling over Barbies. In other words, a waste of time.

My father would expect me to side with him. I wasn't the one to arbitrate this. But something had to be done, and Miko needed to leave. Whether that would be alone or with my mother in tow remained to be seen.

I turned to her. "Can you go get Malcolm and Dex and ask them to come in here?" I walked her toward the front door but didn't want to leave the boys unsupervised for long. "And then maybe you should go upstairs for a while, okay?"

"I'd like that."

"I'll come up in a bit. You want an iced tea or something?"

"What I want is a stiff drink."

"That makes two of us but maybe iced tea for now?" We hardly needed to add alcohol to the mix.

She lifted her slender arm and pushed a few stray hairs off her forehead. "Some cool water will do. But I can get it."

I patted her shoulder. "Okay. Good."

A few minutes later, I had Dad on the couch with a bag of

frozen corn on his lip, and Miko in a chair across the room with our only ice pack on his brow. Each of them looked anywhere but at the other. The similarity to the lull between rounds of a boxing match should have made me smile, but I wasn't exactly in a jokey mood, even if their spat was comic relief from the truly serious business of Benito and Giacomo.

And Brian. Jesus. I wanted to ask Dex how badly he was hurt but was afraid. I didn't think he'd be as sanguine as Malcolm about my responsibility for this mess.

The phone rang as my mother returned, Malcolm and Dex following. I answered with "Hold on a minute," as Mom got herself a glass of water and went upstairs. I covered the receiver and quickly explained to the men what they would find in the living room.

Dex grunted, Malcolm rolled his eyes, and they went down the hall. I returned to the call.

"Hello?"

"Miss Parker, how good it is to hear your voice. How is my Little Miss Bong?"

"Humphrey J. Dexter the Third," I said, forcing cheeriness into my tone. "It's good to hear your voice, too."

Dex Two didn't like the name Humphrey, which is why he went by Dex. But since we also had Dexter Hamill, retired mounted cop and sometime PI, we kept them sorted by referring to them as Dex One and Dex Two. When together, they always argued about who was really number one. The gray mare known as Little Miss Bong belonged to Dex Two. Which reminded me that I needed to get out to the barn and feed the horses and cats.

"Bongo is fat and sassy," I said, filling a glass of water for myself. "How are you?"

"Very well, thank you. And you?"

Dex Two is kind of old school in the manners department, which I find refreshing.

"I'm well," I lied, hoping he didn't want to come riding. There was no need to bring anyone else into our situation. At the same time, the interruption was welcome, gave me a few minutes to catch my breath. Not to mention an excuse to not be in the living room.

"I'm calling to let you know you should be receiving in the mail today your formal invitation to my annual Labor Day get together."

"Oh, right." I flipped the calendar from August to September. We had the event written in on the Saturday evening of the holiday weekend. Dex Two's *get together* was a formal affair for three hundred downtown. I still needed a dress.

"You haven't forgotten, have you? I'm looking forward to seeing you there. Both of you."

"No, of course not. Only..."

"Never say something has come up to prevent your attendance?"

"No," I squeaked, and took a drink to clear my throat. "No, of course not. We'll be there."

"Is everything all right, Miss Parker?"

"Yes." The low murmur of male voices hummed down the hallway from the living room but I couldn't make out what they were saying. "It's just that my parents have come to visit. And my grandfather."

"Wonderful. Give me their full names. I will have Daphne issue invitations."

Daphne was Dex Two's secretary. He's an attorney with a swanky office in a high-rise in the city. More to the point, he's Malcolm's attorney.

"Pardon me a moment, Miss Parker." I heard papers shuffling. Dex Two is a meticulous notetaker. "Do I remember correctly that you and your parents were...estranged?"

"You remember correctly. Their visit wasn't planned—"

Giacomo came into the kitchen scratching his head. "*Idiota,*" he said with a sharp hand gesture.

Who was the idiot? Adrian, Miko, himself?

"Miss Parker?" Dex Two prompted.

"I'm here. Their visit wasn't planned, but it's going surprisingly well. I'm not sure how long they're staying, but I'm certain they'd be delighted to attend your get together."

"You remember it's formal?"

"That won't be a problem."

Most of their luggage was empty, but surely they still had a couple of dressy outfits? Giacomo, on the other hand, we'd have to take shopping. I doubted he'd had much use for a tux on the cargo ships or at the nursing home. All depending on whether he was alive in another week, of course. Focusing on what we'd be doing when we got on the other side of this situation helped it feel temporary, surmountable.

The volume of the voices in the next room elevated. "I don't mean to be rude, Dex, but I need to go."

"Of course, Miss Parker. I know how busy you are. Always a pleasure. I'm not sure I'll be able to fit in a ride between now and the party—so many last-minute details, you know—but I will call if so."

More like he'd have Daphne call, but whatever.

"Sounds good. Thanks."

We hung up. I let out a long breath, hoping none of us would be needing Dex Two's services in the near future, and returned to the living room with Dex One's refilled coffee mug.

Dex had his back to the room and stared out one of the long windows. Malcolm stood like an angry referee, legs apart and arms across his chest. Dad and Miko had lapsed into French again.

I touched Dex's arm. He flinched. He's not easy to sneak up on, so I knew he was deep in thought. Certainly, he wasn't paying attention to the drama behind him.

"Have you heard anything?"

He rolled his shoulders. "They got him to the hospital. He's in the emergency room. That's all I know right now."

I handed him his mug. He took it with a grateful tip of his head and went back to staring out the window. He smelled of sweat and wet dirt. The knees of his khaki pants were dark with mud and had bits of soggy leaves stuck to them. Dried blood smeared his arms.

"I'm sorr—"

"Don't say it, Vi. This isn't your fault. I should have fired him after his last ill-advised encounter with you, but *this* isn't your fault." He jabbed his chin toward the out of doors.

Okay then. I shut my mouth, tired of trying to take the blame.

"Enough," Malcolm said to the other two. "I can't keep up. English or not at all."

Malcolm spoke both French and Spanish, but it's hard to stay fluent if you don't have others to use it with. I might have to finish my college degree if there was any chance of us staying together. Although when I'd started thinking there might be a future for us—hoping?—I don't know.

Giacomo wandered in, a tumbler of red wine in his hand, his fingertips stained brown. He'd been digging in the garden, probably removing any trace of Benito's visit. He leaned one shoulder against the doorway, his eyes twinkling with amusement. I wasn't the only one getting a kick out of this distraction from our other situation.

"It comes down to this," Dad said. "She tangoed with him." He nearly flung the bag of corn at Miko. "This whelp."

He returned the frozen vegetables to his lip and used his other hand to make a sharp dismissive motion that I'm pretty sure meant something crude in Italian. I glanced at Giacomo whose shaggy eyebrows had shot up.

Shaking his head, my father next spoke as if to himself. "After all we've been through together." He turned his head to the stairs, and yelled, "You tangoed with another man."

CHAPTER THIRTY

Evidently, tangoing with another man is tantamount to cheating. At least as far as my father was concerned. Had they done more than tango? We needed my mother's version of the tale. Though, I'm a big believer that there are three sides to every story. Hers, his, and the side you never hear.

But first, I really needed to get the horses taken care of.

"Come with me to the barn?" I asked Dex.

"Gladly."

"I'm going to take care of the horses," I said to Malcolm. "Dex is coming with me."

"Good. I'll keep on eye on these two." He swung his gaze around to Giacomo. "Three."

"Take this sorry excuse for a dancer with you," my father said. "Get him out of my sight."

"That's a good idea," Malcolm said. "Miko, go with Vi and Dex. Do as they say."

Miko rose and pulled himself tall without even a glance toward my father. He shook his hair out of his face. "I would be pleasured to go with you, daughter of my love."

Oh, brother.

"Just don't get in our way."

Dex took hold of Miko's arm. "Stick close to me, whelp."

Outside the barn, I opened a gate to let ten of the horses into stalls. Each of them knew where to go. Dex shut stall doors as the horses went in. The other five I fed outside. Everyone got an amount of grain according to their size, weight, and work level.

We were closed on Mondays, didn't have any rides. That was a blessing, but I figured we'd cancel Tuesday's as well. It was income we needed, but it couldn't be helped.

Or maybe we'd find Benito today.

Or he'd find us.

Either way, this situation would be resolved. The one with my parents I was less confident could be cleared up quickly.

"What can we do to help?" Dex asked.

"Throw three bales down from the loft, if you don't mind."

Cali finished eating, so I brought her out and put her on cross ties, got a hoof pick and brushes. It felt good to work, to focus on what I could do without thinking but always put my all into, the activity I loved more than anything.

By the time I had the mud cleaned out of Cali's feet, Dex and Miko were coming back down from the loft, and three bales sat in the middle of the aisle. I took the box knife we kept handy for this purpose and cut the twine holding the bales together.

"See how it comes off in sections?" I pointed this out for Miko's benefit, not Dex's.

He nodded. "I come from farm. I know hay."

"Great. Each horse gets two of these sections. Put some in each stall and six piles out in the field." I always put one extra because they often chased each from pile to pile like a horsey game of musical chairs.

Technically, two flakes of hay per horse wasn't accurate. If I were doing it myself, I would be more precise, adding a little or removing some according to the horse's size, but for today's purposes, nothing would be hurt by keeping it simple.

"Except Mikey," I said. "Pony in stall seven. He gets one."

Like most ponies, Mikey was an air fern constantly under explosion watch.

Dex and I watched Miko heft several flakes of hay and distribute them according to my orders. He looked like he'd done it before.

"Could be handy to have around," Dex said.

"I don't think it will be good for his health to hang around for too long."

Dex gave me a wry smile, got his gelding, Ciqala, put him on a second set of cross ties and started brushing him. I brought out Honey, known for falling asleep when being groomed, and clipped her to the third set of cross ties, figuring I'd see just how much Miko really knew.

When he'd finished putting hay out in the field, I handed him a set of tools.

"Did the farm you come from have horses?"

He nodded. "Yes. You know the Ukrainian Riding Horse?"

"No," I said. "I haven't heard of them. Is it a warmblood breed?"

"Yes, yes. From Hanoverian and Thoroughbred stock."

"That's a good cross. So, you have experience with them?"

"My uncle raised them. Before I become dancer, I want to be jumper rider. Like you, Viola Parker."

Small world. "Fantastic." I put my hand on Honey's neck. "This mare is an American quarter horse." She wasn't registered, but she had the right conformation. "They are also considered warmbloods because many of the breed's foundation sires were Thoroughbreds."

He stroked her back. "She is very beautiful. Like Russian doll."

"Clean her up and don't forget to pick out her feet."

Starting behind her ears, he flipped her mane to the opposite side of her neck and started brushing her with long, powerful strokes.

Honey's eyes rolled back in her head.

I fed the cats and went back to grooming Cali.

The rain had taken the edge off the scorching air, but it was humid. Before long, we were dripping, yet one by one, we put each horse on the cross ties and got them thoroughly groomed, something that didn't usually happen on a daily basis. Even Mikey, who Miko volunteered to take because he reminded him of his childhood, got polished up and his long mane and tail detangled. With the dust removed from his coat, his black patches shone, and his white parts gleamed.

I didn't want to like Miko but couldn't help it. Despite his fixation on my mother, he was good people. He had a gentle hand with the horses, worked tirelessly, and Noire approved of him, too. Considering the guy had probably been traveling for the past twenty-four hours, hadn't had breakfast, received a cool reception, been in a fight, and grilled by Malcolm, he was cheerful and uncomplaining.

It didn't hurt that he was easy on the eyes—a young, unsnarky, unsullied by drugs and alcohol version of Harry.

I was finishing up Fergus, Malcolm's old thoroughbred, when I heard Clara's Gator coming up the road.

I walked out to meet her. "Hey, Clara, you know we're on lockdown here."

"I know it. That's why I figured you could use some pie."

"I can always use some pie."

"Is that Dexter Hamill I see in there?"

Clara had once told me *that man can park his boots under my bed anytime.*

Dex came out and gave Clara a hug.

"How're you keeping, woman? You look younger every time I see you."

Seventy-some years old and she blushed.

"Fair to middlin, Dex. Yourself?"

"Truth be told, I've been better. But you shouldn't be out hot rodding on this thing alone."

"Now, Dexter Hamill, I appreciate your concern for these bones, but it's just a hop, skip and a jump from our place to here. Ain't nobody's gonna bother old Clara."

"I wouldn't be too sure about that. You stay alert, now, you hear?"

"I hear."

"I don't suppose you have any fresh-baked pie on you?"

Clara smiled coyly and pointed to a foil wrapped bundle on the passenger seat.

"I tried a new recipe—August pie. Because it's August. It's got peaches and raspberries in it."

The corners of Dex's coffee-colored eyes crinkled, and I was glad to see him smile.

"Sounds delicious," he said, injecting his tone with a sexy drawl.

Clara leaned around us to peer into the barn. "Got someone new working? Where's Zoe?"

"Erm...well, Zoe's off until we get our situation situated," I said.

Miko joined us. "I put Mikey to the field?"

"Yes," I answered. To Clara, I said, "This is Miko. He's..." How the hell did I explain this?

He wiped his hand on his jeans and stuck it out. "A friend of Miss Viola Parker's parents come to visit from Ukraine," he said. "Very cheerful to meet you I am."

"Oh." Clara fluttered her eyelashes. "The feeling's mutual, young man. Do you like pie?"

Miko's stomach rumbled by way of answer. "Yes, yes. Very much."

If he also liked whipped cream, that would seal the deal. I was keeping him.

"Well, it will be at the house when y'all are ready," Clara said.

"I need to get back to the garden. Them tomatoes won't can themselves."

She motored off. We went back to work. A few minutes later, I heard her go by again.

We filled the water trough, picked up poop, put the last of the horses out, swept the aisle, and hung up the tools. I glanced at the clock in the tack room. Only ten a.m. It promised to be a long day. But pie would help. We went to the house.

There, my father and Malcolm sat in the living room, reading the paper. It was a week old, and I know Malcolm they'd both already read it. Giacomo snored in the recliner. My mother, apparently, was still upstairs. Leaving Dex and Miko in the kitchen, I went up, hoping there would still be August pie left when I returned.

She was not in their bedroom.

She was not in our bedroom.

Or the bathroom or the storeroom.

I went downstairs, double-checked the living room and sitting room and even the office before returning to Malcolm.

"Where's my mother?"

He glanced up, brows scrunched. "Still upstairs."

"No. She isn't."

My father sat forward. "What do you mean she isn't? She hasn't come down."

"I checked every room. She isn't up there."

"The attic?" Malcolm suggested.

I hadn't thought of that. All three of us trooped to the second floor, then up the narrow and steep stair that led to a sauna-like cobwebby space filled with boxes.

Unless she'd floated, thereby leaving no marks on the dusty floor, then folded herself inside one of the larger packing boxes, she wasn't there, either.

The phone rang.

We hurried back down, but Dex answered it before we got there.

"Oh, hey Hank," he said as we reached the kitchen. "Nope. Clara left about twenty minutes ago." He shared an alarmed look with Malcolm. "Yes, I'm sure. We were in the barn and heard the Gator go by."

Hank's panicked voice boomed from the other end of the line. "Well, she ain't here neither."

"We're on it." He hung up and was already to the front door when he yelled, "Clara didn't make it back to the house."

"Wait," I shouted. "My mother's missing, too."

CHAPTER THIRTY-ONE

We bolted out of the house and ran down the driveway. After that, it was a hard right past the barn onto the gravel road that led to Hank and Clara's, a little less than a mile away. Malcolm, the ex-pentathlon guy, outstripped us. Dex was a close second, even with a prosthetic leg, but Adrian, in loafers, swore as he fell behind Miko who sprinted by in his running shoes. I ran as hard as I could, but it's not my thing, unless a horse is doing it beneath me.

As I went by the barn, I cut into the storage shed along the side. There, I hopped on the ATV and fired it up. I roared up behind my dad, skidded to a stop, and motioned him behind me.

He threw his leg over the seat.

"Hang on!" I yelled.

He grabbed my hips, and I gunned it. The road curved away from Winterlight and down into a densely forested ravine. It followed a creek for an eighth of a mile before ascending to level ground again where open fields spread to either side. Beyond that, it finally ended at Hank and Clara's. We caught up with the other three at the bottom of the hill. They bent over something on the road.

"Shit," I said.

"What? What is it?" my dad yelled, his voice strangled with fear. Either that or he'd swallowed a bug. "I can't see." His heart pounded my back.

I try not to panic until there's something to panic about. But Jesus God. My mother. Clara. I could barely breathe, didn't answer because I didn't know what was what.

I killed the engine and we joined them. Clara rolled on the ground, eyes wild, struggling against Dex and clearly screaming, "Get off me, get off me," even though she was gagged.

Malcolm always carried a multi-tool on his belt. He used it to cut the zip ties holding Clara's hands. She came up swinging.

"Clara!" Dex took her by the shoulders and shook her. "It's me, Dex. Calm down."

She blinked, took a breath, stilled, then went limp just as Hank came up the road from the opposite direction on their ATV. Dex and Malcolm eased Clara to a sitting position and untied the black bandana used to gag her.

"Oh my God," she wheezed, one hand covering her heart. "Oh my God."

Hank shuffle-ran to kneel at her side and touched her cheek. "Clara, it's me, Hank, your husband. Are you all right? Do you know me?"

She looked at him like he was a giant flopping fish that'd materialized out of thin air. "Of course I know you, you old fool. I got tied up, not bonked on the head."

Malcolm and Dex both let out a breath.

Dex crouched beside her, his good leg folded beneath him, the other straight out to the side. "Was Gemma with you?"

"'Course she was. She wanted to help with the tomatoes."

"What happened to the Gator?" I asked.

Clara looked around and then at each of our faces. "I don't know. It all happened so fast. He took Gemma..." She put her face in her hands. "Oh, no. It's all my fault."

"No," Hank soothed. "No it ain't."

"But she said you knew." She sent a pleading look at Dex. "Said you said it was okay for her to come with me back to our house." Her gaze landed on Adrian. "I'm so sorry." She started to cry.

Miko said, "I cannot understand what is happened. Where is my Gemma? Does she go to tango with another man?"

Too late, I saw a white-hot rage boil over in my father. He swung around and punched Miko in the jaw. Miko spun and face planted in the dirt. He flipped himself over only to find my father straddling him, flexing his fingers like he'd take any excuse to hit the boy again.

Malcolm and Dex grabbed Dad's arms, pulled him back.

"Let's be clear on what happened before anyone throws any more punches or accusations," Malcolm said. "Clara, the man who did this, did he say his name? Can you describe him?"

Clara put her hand over her heart. She still hadn't caught her breath. "He stopped us with a gun and made us get out and lie on the ground. Tied us up and gagged us. I mean, I guess he gagged Gemma. I couldn't really see."

"There, there, now," Hank said. "You couldn't have done nothin.'" He put his arm around her. "Can't you see she can hardly breathe? Give her a minute."

Frustrated with how long this was taking, I said, "I'm sorry, but I don't think we have a minute."

"You saw him, right?" Malcolm prompted gently. "Before he tied you up?"

She put one hand on Hank's shoulder to keep him calm. "Yeah. I seen him. Ugly old thing. One side of his face was scarred up bad." She touched her fingertips to her eyebrow as if to make sure it was still the same as it had been that morning. "He put that gun barrel right against my neck. Cold as death." She shivered.

"Did he say where he was taking her?" my father asked.

Clara shook her head. "He just said, 'You tell Giacomo I take everything he loves. He must come alone.'"

"Come where?" I asked.

"He didn't say. He just shoved me with that gun." She rubbed her neck. "I'll never forget how that felt." She got to her feet. "He was wearing a black eye patch. Does that help?"

I hadn't doubted it was Benito, but that confirmed it.

"Thanks, Clara, very helpful," Dex said. "If you remember anything else, let me know right away, okay?"

"There is one other thing," she said, brushing her hands together.

We all looked at her, hoping for the one piece of information that would lead us to my mother.

"He took my Gator."

CHAPTER THIRTY-TWO

Miko sprang to his feet. "This is bad. Who is this man who took her? Why he take her?" He'd been cradling his jaw, but he put his hands to either side of his head and turned in a circle. "Gemma," he yelled. Then louder, "Gemma!"

"I doubt she'd hear you," Clara said, "even if they was in range. That Gator's so loud it drowns out the cicadas."

Miko's arms dropped to his sides. My father shook out his hand. I imagined his knuckles stung. I flexed my fingers, still sore from punching in a window. The glass probably had more give than Miko's face.

"My father's cousin, Benito, is out for revenge over a long-ago killing," my father explained to Miko. "It's a long story."

Dex kicked at the underbrush along the edge of the shoulder. Shortly past Winterlight, the county maintenance ended and it became a private road. That meant it was more dirt than gravel. And that meant tracks would be a lot easier to see.

"Clara, that Gator has eight-inch heavy-duty field tires on it, right?

"I don't know." Clara looked at Hank.

"Yep. Just put new ones on." He went over to Dex and Malcolm. "Six of 'em set me back five hundred dollars."

They all studied the road surface. I held my breath.

"He didn't turn around," Malcolm said.

Adrian and Miko joined the party, so I figured I would as well.

"He went this way." Dex pointed toward Hank and Clara's place.

"He couldn't have gone far," my father said, "or he would have ended up there, right?"

Hank rubbed his chin. "I would have seen the Gator on my way here."

Malcolm's eyes narrowed. "There's a path off this road that runs along the creek and eventually hooks up with our trails." He traced a line in the air that must have followed the path through the woods. "It's rough in spots. We almost never use it, but the Gator could make it part of the way. After that, they'd have to be on foot."

I was already headed to the ATV. "I know the trail you mean. A horse could make it." We didn't have a moment to lose.

"Don't go off half cocked, Miss Parker," Dex yelled.

"She's right," Malcolm said. He followed me.

"Take our ATV," Hank said. "Clara, you can walk from here, right?"

Clara lifted her chin. "Of course."

"Benito probably has a car parked somewhere," my father said.

Malcolm jogged ahead of me and got the ATV started. "Hank, are you sure you two are all right?"

Hank nodded.

"Get that bastard," Clara said.

"Vi and Miko with me. Dex, bring Adrian."

We sped back to Winterlight.

At the barn, I took charge, grabbing tack for each horse and giving it to who needed it. I took Miko's arm as I handed him

Miss Bong's bridle. She was great for bulldozing through the woods, and I knew Dex Two would want us to use her.

"You really can ride, right? Not just ring stuff, but real riding?"

He grinned and pulled himself taller. "Yes, Viola Parker. I am like American cowboy."

Not really an answer. "We'll leave you if you can't keep up." I gave him a spare helmet.

He took the bridle and helmet from me. "I have boots in backpack. I can get?"

"Hurry up."

He sprinted out of the barn. Dex always wore boots, as did I, and Malcolm had a spare pair in the tack room. Each of us took our own horse. My father watched us, looking helpless. I realized we'd left Giacomo alone in the house. What a bunch of freaking *idiotas*.

"Dad, can you go check on Giacomo, make sure he hasn't gotten himself into trouble or wandered off?"

Malcolm came up. "Adrian, we need you at the house to man the phone. You good with that?"

Adrian nodded to both of us and turned to go to the house.

Noire stood on her toes and pirouetted around me, excited we were all going riding.

"You're the good girl," I said to her. "But you can't come with us today. Dad?" He stopped and looked at me. "Can you take Noire with you?" I attached a lead line to her collar to make it easier.

He took the leash, then jerked me against his chest. "Be careful and bring her back."

I blinked and nodded.

Dex had gone to his truck and returned carrying a duffle bag. He stopped my father on his way out and gave him a walkie-talkie, then brought one to each of us. He was limping more than usual, which meant the fake leg was bothering him. The run probably hadn't helped. I frowned at him, and he gave me a look, so I let it go and clipped the radio onto the back of my waistband. He'd communicated our plans with his second who'd been out patrolling. Unfortunately, not in the area where Benito had been. The guy was slippery.

"Miss Parker," Dex said. "You and Miko follow the trail they took. Let me know when you find the Gator."

I knew what Dex was thinking. This put me and Miko the farthest behind Benito. He and Malcolm would take point and hopefully catch up with them, rescue Gemma, and take down Benito without our involvement.

I guess I didn't answer fast enough, because he added, "This is important, Vi."

He almost never used my first name. "I got it. What do we do after that?"

"Keep going. We'll come around from the other direction."

Miko returned wearing a pair of highly polished oxblood paddock boots. "We close Benito in vise," he said.

Dex nodded to him. "Any chance you know how to handle a weapon?"

Miko shook his head. "I throw knife okay."

"Works for me," Dex said. He handed Miko a walkie-talkie, showed him how to use it, then produced a sheathed knife and gave that to him.

Dex looked at me. I lifted my hands. "I'll hold the horses."

"You'll also hold this." He crouched, strapped a small handgun to my ankle, and pulled my pants leg over it. "In case I lose mine."

"Right. In case you lose yours."

He cracked a half smile. "It's the same one you had last time. You remember how to use it?"

"I remember it has no nail." I said this on purpose to annoy him.

"No hammer," he said with a shake of his head.

Our radios sputtered and Dad's voice came through.

"Um, ten-four? The package is secure."

Oh brother. Someone had been watching too much television.

We mounted up. Malcolm brought Gaston alongside Cali, put his hand on my arm. "You have your phone, too?"

I patted myself down. "Nope. Don't know where it is."

"And if you did, it probably has no battery power."

"Too right."

"When this is over—"

"Are you going to spank me?"

He gave me a look. Neither of us were into that, but I liked to tease him.

"You're getting a new phone, and you're going to keep track of it."

I saluted. He dragged me close enough to kiss. With our helmets on, we had to tilt our heads to reach. Warmth washed through me at how he'd taken on my parents and this whole thing with Giacomo and Benito without a second thought. If he had second thoughts, he kept them to himself. I still couldn't believe he hadn't kicked us all out. With a final encouraging squeeze to my arm, he turned Gaston to catch up with Dex and Ciqala. I watched until they trotted past the house and disappeared around the bend.

I double checked Cali's girth and noticed Miko doing the same. So far, so good. I squeezed her straight into a solid working trot. Miko came alongside, moderating Miss Bong's huge stride to match Cali's. He posted in rhythm with me. His heels were down, his hands close together, but not too close, and he kept a light contact with Bongo's mouth. Good. She didn't need or like heavy hands.

Cali protested my inattention with a toss of her head. She sensed our edginess, curled her neck and champed the bit in anticipation of speed. I relaxed my fingers a hair. Miss Bong, older and half draft, would stay steady. She was very close in type to the horses Miko was used to riding. I nodded at him. He gave me a grim smile in return.

We stayed on the grassy shoulder until the gravel ran out and the footing became more forgiving, then picked up canter. At the top of the hill, I slowed to trot again for the descent, watching Miko out of the corner of my eye the whole way. He was fine.

We picked up canter at the bottom, found the trail, trotted the turn into the woods, then went back to canter. Soon, the path narrowed, so Miko pulled behind, and I gave Cali her head.

We galloped. Under normal circumstances, I love to ride after it rains and would give myself over to the sensory pleasure of my horse's stride, the sound of her hoofbeats thudding the ground, the scent of the forest. Today, I concentrated on the trees, the footing, the turns, and what lay ahead.

During one straight stretch, I spared a glance behind me. Both Miko and Miss Bong had clods of dirt on their faces and chest kicked up by Cali's hooves. Miko gave me a jaunty wave. I'm not sure he truly understood the seriousness of the situation. Maybe that was just as well.

The Gator tracks were easy to see in the low, muddy spots. Any grass and brush obscuring the ground had been squashed flat by the heavy vehicle. Clearly, Benito wasn't worried about being followed.

Maybe he wanted to be followed? If so, it changed nothing.

I slowed a little. Something on the ground at the side caught my eye.

"Hold up," I said so my sudden stop wouldn't cause a collision. I pulled Cali down to walk, circled back, and hopped to the ground.

"What is?"

"Hang on."

The horses snorted and shook themselves out, rattling the saddle flaps and stirrup leathers.

I leaned down. There, in a clump of tall yellow flowers, a cigarette, unsmoked. I plucked it out.

Miko dismounted, took it from me, and turned it between his

fingers, pointing at the brand name printed on the side. "This belong to Gemma. She tries to quit but still smoke on the bad day."

"The bad day?"

He shrugged. What were the bad days like, I wondered? It didn't matter right now. We already knew they came this way. Now we knew my mother was all right at least at this point.

We kept going.

Not much farther along we came upon the empty Gator parked where a large tree had fallen, blocking the path.

We stood there for a few minutes, listening, but the woods were quiet except for bird song. We dismounted again and walked around the vehicle. I radioed Dex and Malcolm our location. They were twenty minutes from the expected rendezvous point. Dex said to wait for further instructions.

I was examining the passenger side for any trace or clue when I heard Miko gasp. I looked over to him. He pointed at a red handprint on the driver's seat.

Blood.

CHAPTER THIRTY-THREE

All color seeped out of Miko's face like it'd been siphoned off by a hose. His eyelids fluttered.

"Oh, crap. Don't faint, don't—"

His fingers opened on Miss Bong's reins. He began to crumple to one side. With my reins looped around my shoulder, I hopped across the seat and shoved my hands into his armpits as he slid to the ground. But Cali didn't like being on one side of the Gator and me on the other. She shifted into reverse, taking me with her. I lost my grip on Miko as she wrenched me back. I let go of him to keep hold of Cali. Miss Bong wandered off in search of grass to nibble, her reins dragging on the ground. I wasn't confident she would stick around when she realized no one was paying attention, and I didn't need two horses to chase.

"Shit, shit, shit."

I scrambled off my side of the Gator and dragged Cali over to Miss Bong. The big mare let me catch her, thank goodness. I hate tying horses by the reins, but there was no choice. I found a sturdy tree and attached them to it as best I good, then went to Miko.

He lay on his side next to the Gator, out, and still very pale. I rolled him to his back, tapped his cheek. He felt cold.

"C'mon, Miko. Wake up." I unsnapped his helmet and slid it off, doing the same with mine.

The Gator had cup holders and one held a grubby half bottle of water. I opened it and splashed a little over his face.

Nothing.

I wriggled my arm under his shoulders, lifted him, and dribbled water into his mouth. Most of it ran over his chin.

No response.

Had he fainted because of the blood, or the thought it might be Gemma's—which I refused to consider—or simply because he was exhausted and hadn't eaten? We should have left him at the house, made him eat and rest. So stupid.

I reached for the walkie-talkie, but it wasn't attached to my waistband. Thinking I must have dropped it when Cali yanked me through the Gator, I climbed over the seats and looked, but it wasn't there. On the other side, I got on all fours and searched the ground.

A shadow fell across me at the same time something cold touched the back of my neck. For a moment, I thought the horses had gotten loose and Cali was nibbling on me.

But then my brain caught up and registered that sensation, one I'd felt before.

A gun barrel.

"Don't move and don't make a sound."

The voice was low and very close to my ear. It wasn't familiar, but I knew who it was. I'd like to say I whirled around and disarmed him, shot him in the knee and saved the day, but I'd stopped breathing when the cold metal touched my skin, and I could only do exactly what he said.

"Lie flat and put your hands behind you."

He pressed his foot to the small of my back to underscore his order. I dropped to my belly and crossed my wrists. The zip ties were tight and cut into my skin. I gritted my teeth as he tugged me to my knees, forced my mouth open, and tied a bandana around my face as a gag.

I still hadn't seen him. Didn't want to.

The whole time, I imagined Miko waking up and conking my assailant on the head.

He didn't.

Jabbing the pistol's muzzle between my shoulder blades, Benito shoved me forward, off the trail, and into the woods.

CHAPTER THIRTY-FOUR

Benito frogmarched me away from the trail at a steep angle and down into a ravine. We were quickly well out of sight of everyone and everything. Thick underbrush snagged at my jeans, and branches scraped my face. I turned my head into them, hoping some of my hair would get caught and leave a clue as to what direction we'd gone. I also scuffed the ground hard when I could.

Which reminded me I still had Dex's gun strapped to my ankle. I couldn't reach it and would probably shoot myself in the foot before I'd make good use of it.

Ed Todd hadn't liked guns, either. I don't know why I thought of him at that moment. But he hadn't been far from my thoughts since the call from Harry. Ed, though, he'd fought in Viet Nam, so he knew how to use all kinds of weapons and had been a good shot. He'd admitted it was a handy skill to have.

He often said it was better to have and not need than to need and not have.

If I got out of this alive, I'd let Malcolm and Dex teach me to shoot. I'd overcome my fear and revulsion of guns, get good at using them, and hope I never needed one again.

Ever.

Because once I did know how to use one, then I wouldn't need it, right? That's how it works.

Now, I tried to remember everything Dex had showed me last May. We'd practiced a stance and how to hold the weapon with two hands. To keep my finger off the trigger until I was ready to fire. Not to point it at anything I didn't intend to kill.

I'd wait. Maybe a chance would come when I could reach it and use it. I'd catch Benito off guard. As if. I had a bad feeling that Benito, like Dex, would be almost impossible to sneak up on.

Within a couple of minutes, we reached my mother. Profound relief dropped me to my knees in front of her where she sat tied to a tree. Like me, she wore a gag and her hands were zip tied behind her. The guy had come prepared. But then, he'd had about fifty years to plan.

I looked her over quick and didn't see any obvious injury. Nothing to account for the bloody handprint on the driver's seat. With my eyes, I tried to ask if she was all right. She nodded to confirm.

Benito had a bandana tied around his bicep. Blood had seeped through it. More ran down his arm. The print on the seat had been his. Had my mother done that to him? God, I hoped so. Or maybe it was Clara. She almost always had a knife on her. You never knew when you might have to slice up a pie. Or a murderer.

Benito untied Mom from the tree and lifted her to her feet. For a moment, he was distracted. I could have run. He probably wouldn't have shot me for fear of the sound drawing others to us.

More likely I'd trip and knock myself out.

Finally, I got a look at him. He was shorter than both of us and nearly as slim. Surely we could take him? We were at a disadvantage with our hands bound, but maybe. I forced myself to be hopeful.

Malcolm and Dex would find us.

Benito would make a mistake.

Mom and I would sit on him until help arrived.

He wore a patch over his left eye, just as Clara had said. His forehead, cheek, and temple were scarred and lumpy, his nose one sided, his cheek caved in. Even his hairline was uneven. Apparently, plastic surgery hadn't been an option. Giacomo had never said what kind of gun they'd had that terrible morning. I'd assumed a pistol but wondered now if it'd been a shotgun.

My thoughts swung to Josephine dying at the hands of the man who supposedly loved her while delivering new life.

Adrian. My father.

I shook it off, needed to stay focused, but then my thoughts swung to Clara and what he'd done to her. Then to Miko, lying alone and unconscious in an unfamiliar forest. The horses might or might not still be there when he awoke. If he awoke.

Benito didn't speak. He ran a narrow blue nylon rope through my arms and my mother's so we were connected to each other, pointed in the direction he wanted us to go, and drove us from behind.

My mother's pretty pleated white skirt had a scalloped edge at the hem. It was torn and dirty. Her bare arms and legs were scratched and bleeding, but it all looked superficial. The yellow espadrilles she wore weren't practical for traipsing through the woods, but they were better than sandals. They were soaked and dirty, though, so she'd been through the creek. Her small cross-body purse still hung at her hip. That must have been where the cigarette had come from. Much good it would do us.

I tried to talk around the bandana. It was stiff with newness, so at least I knew it was clean, but it didn't exactly taste good.

"Where are you taking us?" That's what I heard in my head, but to anyone listening, I'm sure it was unintelligible.

Apparently no one was listening, because I got no answer. My mother slid me a look with a slight shake of her head. She must have already tried talking to him. Benito was a cool customer. My guess was he was going to use us as bait to lure Giacomo to whatever he had planned for him.

Taking his eye, for starters.

Would he take ours?

Sweat broke out on my forehead and stung my eyes, making me keenly aware that I had two. Benito had only one. He wanted everyone to be like him. Half blind and disfigured.

None of this was insight. It was all supposition, all to keep myself from thinking about what might happen. I tried to pay attention to our direction but was lost once we were off the path. It was around midday, so the angle of the sun was no help.

I lost track of time, too. Neither my mother nor I wore a watch, and we couldn't have seen it if we were. But I'd guess we walked for at least an hour. We stopped once and crouched while Benito listened, but it wasn't anyone coming to save us, and we moved on.

My mother began to trip every few steps, and I did what I could to keep her from falling. I was hot and thirsty and beginning to feel light-headed. Where was a can of whipped cream when you needed it?

Eventually, we stepped out onto a trail I knew. It was far to the east end of the property and ended at Helen's house.

Helen was Malcolm's mother. He had his own weird and convoluted family history, and hadn't known until recently who his biological mother was. When Helen revealed the truth, he'd gifted her a few acres of land, and she'd installed a pre-manufactured home. We visited with her weekly. They'd become friends.

What did it mean that we were headed in that direction now? Perhaps that once we reached her house, we'd be at a paved road. Where Benito probably had a car, just as my father had said.

Once we were off the land, we'd be much harder to find. There had to be a way to keep that from happening or at least delay it.

We reached Helen's house, walked across the yard, and entered the back door. Benito wasn't worried about us seeing where we were, and there was no one nearby to see that there was a strange man going in and out of Helen's house.

Was she even still alive?

Bile rose in my throat. I stumbled over the threshold and fell on the hard floor of the kitchen, pulling my mother down beside me.

All looked in order.

Benito hauled us to our feet, dragged us into the living room and sat us on the couch. If he'd hurt Helen...

Where was she? If she'd been going out of town, she'd have told us. Her tabby cat, Sylvester, jumped up on the couch, purring.

Benito patted the cat's head, and the cat let him. I was seriously confused, even though Giacomo had said Benito liked animals.

Banging came from down the hall. Muffled cries. It could be Helen. Did he have her gagged and tied in the bathroom?

Benito disappeared around the corner and came back with her, trussed up just like us. He slit her zip ties with a wicked looking curved blade that had a very pointy tip. He removed her bandana as well.

"You bastard," she spat. "I've been in that room for days. I'm starving and I need clean underwear." She rubbed her wrists.

"Get them drinks." He waved his gun at her.

What the hell was going on?

He removed our bandanas.

"What the hell is going on?" I said. "Helen, are you all right?"

Helen scurried to the kitchen. Her ankles were hobbled so she could take only small steps, but she returned with a glass of water for each of us. "I'm all right. What the hell is going on?"

The question of the day.

She put a glass to my lips. I shook my head. "My mother, first."

Mom drank, then I did. "Has he told you anything?" I asked.

Helen shook her head.

"Why are you doing what he wants?" my mother asked her.

"He said he'd kill Robert if I didn't."

Sharp pain shot through my chest. Robert is Malcolm's first name. Her son. I've always used his last name, because most people do. When he asked me to call him by his first name, I tried. For about a day. It felt too intimate. Since he's still my boss, I needed the appearance of keeping my distance, even if it's only pretend.

I blew out a noisy breath. "Helen, this is my mother, Gemma." They nodded to each other. "And that's Benito, the eye thief."

Benito smiled with only one side of his mouth. "Benito Antonio Colombo," he said with a tip of his chin.

"Benito and my grandfather, Giacomo—"

"Wait," Helen said, "I thought you and your parents..."

"We were. They came to visit. It's a long story. What matters now is Benito and Giacomo were in love with the same woman, Josephine."

"Ah, Josephine," Benito said in much the same tone Giacomo had. She must have been quite a woman. "I have never loved another."

"Right," I said with a sarcastic frown at him. "But she loved and married Giacomo. And this dick, here, he killed her."

Benito sprung to his feet. "No!" He pointed both the gun and the knife at me. "It was Edwardo, the stupid *coglione*," he hissed. "He missed Giacomo and hit my Josephine."

"She wasn't your Josephine." The words crossed my lips that fast. I really needed to fix the broken connection between my brain and mouth.

One swift stride and he had the knife pressed to my left cheek.

"You're just like her. Beautiful and bold. If not for that, I would take your eye right now." He tucked the pistol under his arm, dug in his pocket, brought out a black marble, and held it in front of my face. "You want one of your own?" He pushed it closer. "Do you?"

Afraid to move, breathe, or blink, I whispered, "No."

He pocketed the marble and removed the knife. "Good. Then shut it."

I nodded, let out my breath. My mother exhaled, too.

Before he could make it back to the loveseat, I quietly said, "Still, she died because of you."

He whirled on me. "Because of Eduardo! And I shot him. My own brother. I killed him because he killed her."

Geez. Meanwhile, Giacomo had spent the rest of his life feeling guilty about the little brother.

"But Giacomo," he continued, "he did this." He tapped his eye patch. "He took Josephine from me, and he took my eye. Now, he will pay in kind."

I didn't like the sound of that, but I didn't like any of this.

After a few moments, my mother asked, "Now what?"

Benito sat on the love seat. He rested the pistol on one thigh and the long, curved knife on the other. "Contrary to what my cousin might have told you, I am not a barbarian." The good side of his face smiled. The bad side, the left, seemed frozen. "Now," he continued, "we take refreshment before moving on to the next leg of my journey." He paused to press his fist to his mouth. "The final stop. The end."

CHAPTER THIRTY-FIVE

Obedient as a pet dog, Helen made peanut butter and jelly sandwiches and fed them to us. If I were her, I'd do the same, especially if someone I loved was threatened. There was nothing about Benito that suggested he wouldn't follow up on his threat. Benito, thankfully, fed himself, his chewing awkward and messy. When we finished, he untied one of us at a time, and we got a potty break. I tried to find something in there to hit him over the head with, but the room had been stripped bare as a truck-stop toilet.

He zip tied Helen's hands again, gagged her and secured her in the bathroom. Our bandanas were stuffed in our mouths and tightened. He took us out the front, and shoved us through the back door of a windowless cargo van, slamming and locking it behind us. The van was old and rusty and had a business's name painted on the outside—nothing I could make sense of—nothing that connected it with the images in my dreams. Inside, it was dark and smelled of dirt, but once my eyes adjusted, a quick glance told me a sturdy plywood wall separated the front seats and the rear. The ceiling and sides were unfinished.

And there by the door, lying on its side, Giacomo's tomato

plant, one bra strap still tangled in its branches. It looked like the rest of my bra had been shut in the door. The plant needed more dirt and a good watering. Next to it, a plastic sandwich bag of black marbles. I shuddered.

Benito didn't get in the van right away. Was he going back to the house?

My mother mumbled something.

"Shhh," I forced through the bandana.

The front door of the house opened and a moment later, a *pop pop* came from inside.

A wail escaped me. "Nooo."

My mother's face scrunched into a question.

"I think he just killed Helen," I cried. "Oh my God, no."

Mom got the gist of what I said, and her eyes squeezed shut. A tear slipped out, then another. My cheeks were wet as well.

Benito really was a *bastardo* no matter his civilized pretense.

The driver's door of the van opened and the vehicle dipped as Benito got in. Bad shocks. A moment later, we were moving. We took a left out of the driveway. That direction led to the highway.

Shoving my desperation and horror aside, I communicated to my mother to lie down on her side with her back to me. I did the same so that my fingers were level with the back of her head. After nearly fifteen minutes of frustrated picking and accidental hair pulling, I got the knot in her bandana loosened enough for her to spit it out. She moved her jaw around to stretch it, then undid my bandana, getting it done more quickly then I had hers, probably because she had longer fingernails.

We were on the highway now, traveling fast. It was hot, but there was a vent in the partition, so a little cooler air leaked in.

It also meant Benito might be able to hear us, even over the sound of the engine, the air-conditioning fan on high, the radio blasting oldies, and the rusty vehicle's squeaks and rattles. There was no need for him to know we'd freed our voices.

Mom started to say something, but I shushed her and

motioned her to my side of the van so we could sit next to each other.

She leaned close and asked, "What's going to happen?"

Who could guess what was in the mind of someone like Benito? Keeping my voice low, I said, "I think he wants to lure Giacomo somewhere so he can kill him. Where and when, no idea."

He'd probably kill us, too, maybe as a way to torture Giacomo, but I saw no reason to say that out loud. Instead, I wriggled around to check every crevice and opening, looking for a way to cut through our restraints. To the side of the sliding door, there were a series of openings with a rough inside edge. Getting my wrists in there to saw through the plastic ties would be awkward, but I had to try.

I tilted my head to motion Mom close again, and whispered, "Are you all right? Did he hurt you?"

She shook her head. "I'm glad he didn't tie my ankles." She crossed them and stared at her feet.

She was probably imagining she'd dance again. With Miko? With Dad? Did it matter? I doubted Benito's future vision for us included gliding across the ballroom floor. Looking at my mother's feet, I couldn't help but picture Helen's bound ankles. Oh God, poor Helen.

"I'm sorry I ran away," my mother muttered. "I had to get out of the house. Adrian and Miko..." She frowned and shook her head again, sighed.

Too well, I knew that urge to run, to escape conflict, especially if I'd caused it. The muscles in my arms already hurt, so I stopped sawing for a minute.

"I have a gun," I whispered.

"You...what? Why haven't you used it?"

I gave her a look. "It's strapped to my ankle, so I can't reach it. Plus, I don't like guns, plus I'm not sure how to use it."

"Why do you have it if you don't like it?"

"Dex made me take it when we went looking for you."

Leaning on the hump made by the wheel well, she tilted her head back and looked at the ceiling, clearly feeling badly about her ill-conceived escape.

"How did you get out of the house?"

"Climbed out the window onto the back porch roof. Used that big bush next to it to get down."

More resourceful than I would have given her credit for.

"Is Clara all right?" she asked.

"She is. Miko I'm not so sure about."

"What do you mean?" Her voice rose. "Did Adrian—"

"Shhh. Not Dad. Miko and I were riding—"

"You went riding?"

"Not like that. Geez. Give me a minute to explain."

She pursed her lips but stayed quiet while I explained how we found Clara, then went out searching, leaving Dad and Giacomo at the house. When I told her Miko had passed out, she frowned.

"I keep telling him he has to eat. He's worried about gaining weight. It's ridiculous."

I started back to cut through the ties. "Mom, what, exactly, is your relationship with Miko? And why is Dad so upset?"

"*He's* upset?" She started getting loud again, I widened my eyes and she sputtered, "What about me? If it weren't for him—"

"Start at the beginning."

The van leaned hard as if careening around a curve, maybe getting off at an exit. The bag of marbles shifted and several rolled out, pinging around the interior and dropping into whatever pocket they came to like pin balls. We braced ourselves until the van leveled, following the course of the marbles with morbid fascination. Benito must have gone from one highway to another. I wasn't familiar enough with the road system to guess where we were or might be headed.

"Earlier," I said, trying again to cut the zip ties, "you told Dad not to eat whipped cream because it would make him fat. Don't you think you're sending mixed messages?"

"Miko is still growing. He doesn't have to worry about gaining weight. Your father is nearly fifty and starting to go soft around the middle."

"Oh my God, are you serious?" Now my volume rose. I took a breath to calm myself before continuing on a hush. "The man is lean as a sapling."

Mom rolled her eyes. "I see him naked."

"Too much information."

She also inhaled deeply through her nose, let it out slowly. I could tell not having her hands free was driving her crazy. She needed to clasp them, or drum her fingers. Maybe even chew her nails.

"Miko was your father's idea."

"What's that supposed to mean?"

"He hurt himself, your father. It's been several months ago now. He twisted his knee and tore his ACL. He had to rest and do physical therapy. But I needed to keep practicing."

I knew a thing or two about the stress of competition—how it wore on you both mentally and physically. "So, you've been competing all these years?"

"Yes, but not as much as in the past. We decided to open a studio in Paris and teach."

I rested my arms, couldn't tell if I was making progress other than chafing my wrists raw. "Sounds very romantic," I said, fighting my sarcastic tone, but losing. "I suppose your studio was upstairs from a bakery and had high ceilings and tall windows that opened onto charming Juliet balconies." Bitterness leaked out, even at a whisper, but I couldn't seem to stop myself. "And you ate fresh baguettes for breakfast topped with artisan cheese, and drank *chocolat*." I spat out the last with as close to a French accent as I could muster.

Her neck lengthened and her eyes narrowed slightly. There

was the haughty woman I knew. But I can't say I was proud of my childish display or my winning ability to bring out her worst.

"There *was* a bakery on the corner. That's not uncommon in Paris. We were struggling, but getting more clients all the time. Investors helped us get started. After all, we'd made quite a name for ourselves over the years."

Did any of this really matter given our situation? It did. I needed to know, even if learning the details hurt. "*So* happy for you." I renewed my sawing with extra energy. Sweat soaked my T-shirt and stung my eyes.

"Why are you so angry?" she hissed.

My arms stilled. My whole body went stiff, and the hurt child inside me roared awake. "Oh, I don't know, Mom, maybe it has to do with the way you left me to be raised by someone else and never—" My voice cracked. I cleared my throat. "You never made any effort to see me or know me." I despised how shaky I sounded.

Her breathing accelerated. I could practically hear her heart pounding inside her chest. "I tried. I wanted to. But Trudy..."

"Now you're going to blame it on Aunt Trudy? Like she didn't have enough to deal with caring for your infant when she was already pregnant with Penny and then having her own baby so it was like raising twins?"

"Is that what she told you?"

The radio up front suddenly cut out. I froze and bit down on what I'd been about to say while my mother and I held our breath. A tense minute later, the radio volume went back up, but not as loud as it had been before.

Keeping my voice down, I said, "Aunt Trudy didn't have to tell me. That's the way it was."

My mother shook her head slowly. She chewed her lip. She was always so tightly restrained. What I'd said rattled her. Her mind was racing. I saw it in her eyes.

Haltingly, she said, "That's not actually the way it was."

I let out a frustrated breath. "Okay. Tell me how it really was." I couldn't wait to hear her side of it.

Her mouth close to my ear, as if we were teenagers sharing a secret, she said, "Trudy is eight years older than me. She and Vic were about to celebrate their fifth anniversary, childless *again*. They wanted babies so badly. Then I got pregnant. Your father and I barely passed each other in the hallway—"

I pulled away from her. "You had to do a little more than that to get pregnant, Mom, come on."

"Of course we did. But I mean I got pregnant the first time. Trudy was so angry. Not just because I hadn't finished high school, but because she wanted to have a baby and couldn't, and I—"

"Didn't want a baby but got pregnant without trying. I get it."

"No."

Too loud, too loud.

Benito banged on the partition and yelled, "You'd better not be talking back there!"

He seemed to listen for a few minutes, but then forget about us as soon as Frank Sinatra's "New York, New York" came on, and he launched into a spirited singalong.

My mother and I relaxed a hair.

"No," she repeated. "You *don't* get it. It's not that I didn't want to have children, Vi, I did. But not that young."

"Fair enough. I can understand that. But if Aunt Trudy was already pregnant with Penny, what was the big deal?"

"That's just it. She wasn't."

"But..." Now I was the one baffled. "Our birthdays. Penny and I are only six months apart."

My mother gave a small shake of her head almost like she was trying to loosen something stuck in her ear, then put her lips near mine again. "She wasn't pregnant, or if she was, it was very early, and she didn't know yet. She insisted I give you to her to raise. Ordered it."

Aunt Trudy was very...*demanding* about what she wanted, so this didn't surprise me.

Mom continued. "Her pregnancy wasn't easy—whereas mine was—and she had Penny prematurely. That's why your birthdays are only six months apart."

Penny had been premature? How could I not know that? We both fell silent. The van had made another turn and began to slow. It stopped, then started again, stopped, started, bouncing every time Benito jammed the brakes. He honked his horn and cursed. We were stuck in traffic. Did that mean we were in the city?

"And then," my mother went on quickly, "Trudy said it would be best if I didn't contact you. It was too upsetting and confusing. You have to understand. I looked up to her. She's my big sister. And she was so happy to have children."

"And you were so young," I murmured, as much to myself as to her.

Adrift in a swirl of thoughts and feelings, I wondered why I couldn't have heard this story when I had Malcolm to hold on to.

Geez. Malcolm. Where was he? They'd surely found the Gator, horses, and Miko by now. Had they been able to follow us? Found Helen? What would Malcolm do when he found his mother dead? My throat got tight, and the pain in my chest made it hard to breathe. I pushed those thoughts away again, tried to concentrate on keeping our day from ending the same way.

Mom nodded. "It seemed to make sense at the time. Your father and I were free to pursue our dream. But..." She rose to her knees, sat on one hip, leaned.

The van jerked to the left as if Benito had abruptly changed lanes. She fell against me. I couldn't catch her, had made no progress freeing myself. All I could do was stick my shoulder out to keep her from falling flat.

She looked at me. In the dim interior of the van, her eyes were wide, glittering, her brow pinched.

My eyes, *my* brows.

She leaned her forehead against mine. "Vi, my sweet girl, my entire body ached for you, to hold you, to smell you, to feel your soft skin against mine. Your father, he didn't say much, but he was so sad." She wiped her face on my shoulder. "We were a sorry pair."

My heart constricted so hard I thought it would stop. My mother had missed me? "I...um..." Coherent thought fled. "It's going to take me a while to process this, Mom. It's so different from what I've thought my whole life."

"Trudy told me she had told you the truth."

It was my turn to look away, to turn from the pain within what she said. "No, she never told me."

My aunt, who had raised me and who I'd looked to as my mother for so long, had lied to me. For what? To punish her little sister? She'd kept that anger close, nurtured it, just as I had mine. Aunt Trudy had never exactly disparaged my parents, not in so many words, but she'd made it clear they didn't want me. That she had. That she was my true mother.

Was it possible the one person I'd thought responsible for my sanity was actually the one responsible for my insanity?

My hatred of my parents had made me who I was. Strong but resentful with a defensive attitude that kept people at more than arm's length. Unfailingly committed to my horses but trusting of critters more than people. So fearful of abandonment that I desert others before they can reject me, just as I'd been cast aside as a baby.

Or thought I'd been.

We hurtled toward God only knows what Benito had planned for us, I had yet to learn where Miko fit in, I'd probably never see Malcolm again—the one person I'd allowed inside my thick walls —and none of it really mattered because my entire freaking life was a lie.

CHAPTER THIRTY-SIX

A short time later, we must have gotten off the highway because we made turns and frequent stops, as though we were in an urban area. At one point, we stopped and someone else got in. Benito had an accomplice, someone who hadn't been at the farm. They talked but I couldn't make out what they were saying. My mother and I helped each other get the bandanas back in our mouths, even if they were hanging loose in the back.

Finally, we parked and the engine was turned off. Benito and his passenger got out but no one came to get us.

I tried to calm my heart, to keep my composure for my mother's sake, whose rapid blinking and fidgety legs made me think she was about to fly to pieces. My mind considered and rejected ideas for getting away. I might be able to get to my gun at some point, but he had one, too, not to mention that blade that could scoop out an eye with a flick of the wrist. The man was a cold-hearted killer and wouldn't hesitate to use either weapon. Or both.

If there was any chance of escape, it had to include getting my mother to safety as well, and that might prove challenging. She was in good shape from dancing, and properly motivated, but could I depend on her to keep it together?

The back door opened and Benito stuck the gun in before showing his face. Smart man. Stupid me. I should have been ready. I could have kicked him. But how far would we get with our hands tied? I had no idea where we were, if we could get help, or if we'd end up in worse trouble.

Benito motioned to us with the pistol.

Okay, maybe not worse trouble.

We slid out and landed in the weedy backyard of an abandoned brick two story with equally run-down buildings to either side, all flat-roofed and overgrown with vegetation. A short chain-link fence separated the parking area from the yard.

The wooden back porch sagged to one side. There were two doors, one with a boarded-up window to its left. The other was open, and I could see a stairway inside leading up.

The posts of the porch had once supported a second-level deck, but the left half of it had fallen down, kind of like Benito's face. Two upstairs windows, one with a few pieces of wood nailed over it, the other half glass, half open. A torn curtain fluttered over the sill.

Nothing about the place was familiar. I couldn't see to the front where there had to be a street. We could be anywhere. There was a certain similarity to Malcolm's father's old house in Soulard, but St. Louis was full of street upon street of two-story brick homes.

Benito herded us through a squeaky gate toward the open door. My mother whimpered as she stumbled forward. Her wrists were bleeding. Mine probably were as bad or worse, but they'd gone numb about a half hour before.

Even though it was hot, for a few moments, the temperature outside the van was a relief compared to the stuffy interior, and a light breeze sent a chill through me as we crossed the yard. Then, we were inside the narrow stairwell, where no air moved.

Shreds of oriental carpeting remained at the edges of the

stairs. Every step groaned and threatened to crack beneath our feet, and I was reminded of the one at home that creaked.

Home. Winterlight. I would kill to see it again.

I didn't like killing, hated to see anything suffer, but if it came to it, I would.

That realization made me surprisingly light and focused. I kept observing details, for all the good it would do. The interior walls of the stairwell were brick. There were no lights. The place reeked of decay and dust, mildew and rotten garbage.

Straight ahead at the top of the stairs, a hall continued into a dark unknown. To the right, a doorway opened onto what used to be a kitchen. A few scraps of gold-flecked linoleum stuck to the floor. The non-boarded window with the curtain let in light and provided a good view of the alley. Two wooden chairs sat in the middle of the room, back to back.

Benito tied us to these. Before he sat me down, I caught the tail end of a pickup rumbling down the alley, then the window was out of my line of sight.

Our captor dragged another chair over to face me, just out of my reach. Not that any of my limbs were free, but this man was careful. Calculating. As Giacomo had said, cunning.

He took out a flip phone, jerked the bandana out of my mouth.

"What is the number of the house where Giacomo is?"

I lifted my chin and stared at him, had no intention of making this easy. "It's in the book. Look it up."

"Stubborn, I see. Like your grandmother, God rest her soul." He brought out the curved knife. "That is not a problem."

"Is that how you were going to convince her to marry you? At knife-point?"

With the swiftness of a striking snake, his hand flicked forward, ice slid across my shoulder, and blood soaked into the sleeve of my white T-shirt.

My body jerked, and I hissed, "Shit."

"For God's sake, Vi," my mother cried around her bandana, "give him what he wants."

I gave him the number. Benito pushed keys and put the phone on speaker. "If Giacomo doesn't answer, say you need to speak to him. Nothing more, understand?"

I nodded. A thin dribble of blood reached my elbow.

It rang only once before my father picked up. "Gemma?"

Benito chuckled darkly, motioned at me with the knife.

"I need to speak to Giacomo."

"Vi? Thank Christ. Are you all right? Is Gemma with you?"

"Yes, Dad, and she's fine. Put Giacomo on now."

I wanted to ask if Malcolm was there, but if he had been, he'd have answered. Were they still out looking for us?

"Where are you?" he asked.

"In an abandoned house—"

Again, the cut was instant and precise. Blood trickled down both my arms.

"Adrian, get Giacomo now," my mother said with a hint of her normal commanding self.

He must have understood her because a moment later, "*Ciao*," came through the airwaves.

"*Ciao, cugino*. I have your lovely granddaughter with me. And her mother. Viola, she is like Josephine, no?"

A stream of angry Italian words spewed from the phone.

"Yes, yes, yes, always the same from you, cousin. Now, if you want to see them again alive, you must come. Alone. We will finally finish this. *Da uomo a uomo, Sì*? Man to man."

CHAPTER THIRTY-SEVEN

"I no have the driving license," Giacomo said.

"That has never stopped you before," Benito replied, serene, *civilized*.

Giacomo muttered in Italian. "I no have the car, Benito. How'm I supposed to get there?"

"Oh, cousin, you disappoint me. You used to be so ingenious. If you like, I can send you an eye. Will that help you find a way? Should it be your daughter-in-law's or your granddaughter's?" He took an exaggeratedly patient breath as if this conversation was too tiresome and pedestrian. "You choose."

My mother moaned.

Something like a growl came through the phone. "Address."

Benito told Giacomo where we were. "No police, Giacomo. Only you. Understand?"

"*Sí.*"

"It will take you almost two hours to get here. I will be waiting for you. It will be a reunion." He tapped his temple with his fore-finger as if something had just occurred to him. "On second thought, bring Josephine's son. The whole family should be together one last time." He touched a button on the phone's face to disconnect and tucked it into his breast pocket.

I stared at him, afraid to take my eyes away. He stared back. "So much like her," he said.

The blood on my arms had already dried. The cuts were remarkably shallow considering the blade. The man probably considered himself an artist with that knife. I wondered if he disinfected it after taking an eye. The thought made me gag.

Benito rose and moved the chair to the window, checked his watch, then walked past us and down the stairs. A few minutes later, he returned with the tomato plant, bag of marbles, and an old suitcase. He put the drooping plant and the remaining marbles on the kitchen counter. My bra finally came loose and dropped to the floor.

"Why did you take the tomato plant?" I asked him.

He let his head fall to one side as he considered the Big Italian plant. "Only to torment my cousin. I know how important they are to him. Something of Josephine's. Like that blue marble you found." He looked at me without smiling. "You are clever, like him. Maybe too much so."

Maybe. "You should give it some water."

Without taking his eyes from me, he put it in the sink and opened the tap. Nothing came out. He put his hands up in a mocking helpless gesture.

"Okay," I said. "Then why don't you do something useful with that knife and let me loose so I can strangle you?"

"Oh, Vi," my mother grumbled, making it obvious her bandana was loose. "Can't you just be quiet?"

Benito leaned against the counter, took out the knife and turned it as if considering it for the first time. He lifted it to his face and held it beneath his good eye. "Do not tempt me to use it on you."

I curled my lip at him. He chuckled.

"I could learn to like you, Viola *York*."

If he meant to rattle me by using my parents' name, it wouldn't work. I'd deliberately taken my uncle's last name of Parker when given the choice.

"You know where that name comes from?"

"Shakespeare," I said.

"Not Viola, but York?"

"No idea, but I have a feeling you're going to tell me."

"Nowhere," he said with a dark laugh. "Giacomo made it up to throw me off the trail. It worked, for a while. But it means nothing, has no...history."

He probably wanted me to ask him about his name's history, but I had no interest in that so decided to take my mother's advice and keep my mouth shut for a while.

Benito consulted his watch again and disappeared through a door into another room of the apartment, taking the suitcase with him. I let my head drop back until it rested on my mother's shoulder. She leaned her cheek against mine.

"Are we going to die today?" she asked with remarkable dignity.

"Will Dad contact Malcolm and Dex before coming here?"

"I think so."

"Then there's hope. Other than that, no idea."

"I'm sor—"

"Don't," I said, cutting her off like Dex had done with me earlier. "You can't be held responsible for the actions of one madman."

"Do you think he's crazy?"

"Don't you? Wouldn't you have a few screws loose if half your face had been blown away?"

She nodded. Between our backs, I brushed her hand with mine. She responded and we hooked our fingers together.

"Let's try to rest a little," I said, feeling drowsy.

"Okay," she said.

I let my eyes drift closed, wanting to escape this nightmare if only for a little while.

The only way I can describe what happened next is to say my entire body shifted left about an inch. Like when a big shudder goes through you, but somehow, my body paused mid-shud. The room brightened, and Wastrel stood before me, his breath warming my cheek. I darted my eyes hard to the side to see if my mother was aware that a horse now stood over us, but her eyes were closed, her breathing regular. At least one of us was getting a break.

I was not asleep, of that I'm sure. I lifted my head and put my nose to Wastrel's nostril, breathing with him. His whiskers tickled my lips.

The room transformed before me. Sunlight splashed against the shiny floor, filtered by new sheer curtains at the window. A woman stood at the sink, washing a head of iceberg lettuce. The tomato plant and marbles had been replaced by a green pepper, a cucumber, and a couple of carrots. She shook water off the lettuce, put it on a cutting board. Holding it with one hand, she used the other to open the lower cabinet to the left. There, on the inside wall was one of those magnetic bars that hold kitchen knives. She pulled a chef's knife off the strip and sliced the lettuce into neat ribbons.

Wastrel hadn't moved, but he made a whuffling noise as if to make sure I was paying attention. As in the dream—had that been just last night?—I smelled smoke.

The woman scraped the lettuce into a bowl, reminding me of my mother standing at the sink in the kitchen at Winterlight. Before slicing the other vegetables she had laid out, the woman reached for the stub of a cigarette hanging off the edge of the counter and took a long pull then blew smoke up toward the ceiling. As she flicked ash into the sink, she turned and blinked. Could she see Wastrel? She looked startled, then the room darkened, she faded, and so did Wastrel.

I didn't want him to go. "No—"

"Wha?" my mother murmured.

"Nothing," I said. "Rest."

My body shifted again, as if completing the earlier shudder. What the hell had just happened? It wasn't a dream. More like a vision. I stared at the lower cabinet to the left of the sink, wishing the door had fallen off like it had from a couple of the others. Was it possible? Had Wastrel just manifested in real time to tell me there was a knife in the cabinet? Or was it a symbol to do with Benito's blade? Either way, how was I supposed to get my hands on it?

And what about the smoke? I wished we were next to the cabinets just so I could bang my head against something.

I. Did. Not. Understand.

But if Wastrel was trying to communicate, surely there must be a way out of this situation. Surely, there was hope.

I thought through everything he'd showed me so far from the very first dream following Giacomo to the apartment he shared with Josephine, to the diving horse, to the toy stick horse, to riding over water and jumping the moon. And now this...vision of a knife and cigarette. What connected these ideas? What could be interpreted literally and what was a symbol?

I let my head fall back to my mother's shoulder, clenching my jaw to keep from groaning out loud in frustration.

Knowing Wastrel meant well, knowing there were important hints in his messages—hints that might save our lives—and deciphering the meaning of his visits were two very different things.

Focusing on my breathing, I tried to relax without falling asleep, to empty my mind and be in a meditative state of centered calm, the place I am in before entering the competition arena.

Soon enough, Benito returned. Perhaps he'd been meditating in the next room, preparing himself for what was to come next.

He'd changed into a black suit. The starched white shirt wasn't buttoned all the way up, exposing a vee of his chest and a milky oval stone hanging on a gold chain. He carried a bundle of cloth. This he shook out to reveal an old red shirtdress.

"You will put this on."

I narrowed my eyes. Was it a maternity dress? "No, I won't."

He carefully hung the dress over his arm, tipped my chair forward, jerked me up by the arms, and moved us in front of my mother. Her eyes were wide, blinking. She'd dozed off. She inhaled quickly through her nose, brought herself awake.

He lay the flat edge of the curved knife against her cheek. He didn't speak, didn't have to.

"Okay," I said. "But you'll have to untie me."

He backed us into the other room. I tried to give Mom a reassuring smile, but I'm pretty sure it was just an ugly grimace that had nothing encouraging in it.

Benito sliced the ties holding my hands and quickly stepped away from me. Grateful, I eased my arms to the front, my shoulders complaining the whole way, and rubbed my raw wrists.

He slid the knife into a leather sheath and took the pistol from his waistband.

I started to pull the dress over my head while assessing this new space. Two windows looked out on the next building's wall. Scarred wood floors, peeling wallpaper, a wire hanging from the middle of the ceiling. Two doors in the wall opposite the kitchen. A closet, maybe? And...

"No." He waggled the gun at me. "Take off your clothes. And your shoes and socks."

A chill went through me. What was this about, and what would he do to me when he saw Dex's gun? I couldn't risk it.

"Can I have some privacy?"

He kept the gun on me as he went to one of the doors on the other side of the room. "In here. Don't close the door all the way."

Perhaps there was something civilized left in him after all. I eased through the opening into what had been a small bathroom.

A few pieces of blue tile clung to the wall above what was left of the vanity. The sink was gone. The toilet as well. Only a hole in the floor to mark where it once had been. A tiny window above the tub let in enough light for me see my reflection in a cracked mirror—the kind you buy to put in your locker at school. It leaned on a piece of two-by-four cross bracing where a medicine cabinet had once been.

Despite my tan, I looked pale in the room's gray light, my eyes bloodshot. Most of my hair had escaped its tie, but not in any organized way. It clung to my damp cheeks and forehead.

Worried Benito would open the door at any moment, I first undid the gun and hid it behind the mirror. Somehow, I'd get my hands on it later. Then, I unlaced my boots and removed my socks. I stood on them, as if it mattered what the soles of my feet came in contact with at this point. With exaggerated care, I folded my jeans and T-shirt and stacked them on my boots in the corner.

Other than my arms, the rest of my body was even more pale than my face, not that I could see much of it in the tiny mirror. The fresh cuts on my shoulders gleamed like neon lights. I summoned enough spit to rub the dried blood off my arms.

I picked up the red dress and held it by the sleeves, looking at the back of it. It would be a tight fit.

I remembered the strip of fabric I'd found in the woods right before finding the blue marble. What had happened to it? I'd pocketed it and forgotten. Pulling one long sleeve straight, I examined it more closely. The dress was old, a pattern and style from the sixties. Hand made by the way the seams were finished. There, a recent tear in one elbow. I put it down and searched the pockets of my jeans. The last couple of days had gone by so fast, I hadn't had a chance to do laundry, had pulled on whatever pants were handy.

From my left back pocket, I pulled out the strip of fabric. It was a match. What the hell was Benito doing carrying around a dress everywhere he went? I picked it up again, held it at arm's length, turned it around.

The upper right front of the dress around the shoulder had a good-sized hole in it, surrounded by several smaller ones. I slipped my hand through the neck and stuck my fingers out the frayed openings, felt the stiffness of stained material.

Icy terror stole my breath, froze my bones, stopped my blood.

This was my grandmother's dress. The one she'd been wearing the day she died.

CHAPTER THIRTY-EIGHT

No, was my first thought.

I can't put this on, my second.

I forced air into my lungs, little sips, then a big gulp. My heart started beating again, wild, erratic. Blood rushed through my veins, warmed me, got my mind in gear.

What did this sick fuck have planned? Did he want to reenact that morning's events with me playing the part of Josephine?

"Come along, my sweet," Benito said.

His voice sounded different, cajoling, almost seductive, and that sent a new tendril of dread coiling through my gut.

I snatched the gun from where I'd hidden it and tried to strap it to my thigh. The holster was stretchy but too small.

"Hang on," I said. "I'm almost ready."

I pulled the gun. I could shoot him through the door. What caliber had Dex said this thing was? I turned it, trying to see some indication of its power, not that it would mean anything to me. I guess people who own guns know that kind of thing and don't need it stamped on the grip. With my luck, this was a pea-shooter and the bullet would barely dent the thick wood of the solid old door. Worse, it would ricochet and I'd shoot myself. Benito would get pissed and cut out my eye.

Or my mother's.

If I were alone, I'd chance it.

I put the weapon back behind the mirror, took a deep breath, and stepped out of the bathroom.

Benito looked me up and down, a strange smile curling the good side of his face. He canted his head, then circled his hand, indicating I should turn around. The thought of putting my back to him sent a shiver through my whole body, but I did as told.

Gently, he tugged out my hair tie and smoothed my hair down my back. I tried not to tremble at his touch on my scalp, forced myself to keep breathing, to stay still.

"Better," he said, taking my shoulders and turning me to face him once more.

I swallowed. He looked me over again, and his smile faded. He touched the hole above my right breast, put the backs of his fingers on my skin. His eye gleamed as he stared at the spot, but I'm not sure he was seeing it, or me, or this place.

"Don't touch me."

He didn't react.

"*Il mio cuore*, do you remember what you said when you gave me this?" He tapped the stone at his throat.

"No," I said, not willing to play into his fantasy.

"Ah," he sighed, then laughed softly. He chucked me under the chin. "Always the coy one."

I jerked away from him, but again, he didn't appear to notice. He took my hand and guided me to the kitchen. There, he dragged my chair over to his by the window. We sat side by side. His fingers were surprisingly soft.

My mother speared a question at me with her eyes. I flicked my free hand to let her know it was all right, to just be quiet for now.

Benito picked up where he'd left off. "We were in your father's garden, do you remember?"

I started to argue, realized a response wasn't really required.

"You said the rainbow moonstone would help to clear my mind and enable me to rest. You knew I had trouble sleeping. You liked to say that I kept forgetting who I really was on the inside. The moonstone, you said, would help me remember."

"And have you remembered?" I asked. "Who you are on the inside?"

"For a time, it did help, but I strayed, Josephine, after you went away. I took the moonstone off because it hurt too much to think of you. I almost never slept, and I forgot for a long time."

He flattened my hand on his thigh, stroked my fingers with his. It was all I could do not to jerk away. But it felt right to let him go on. Maybe I would learn something I could use against him. And it's not like I had a choice.

"Now, I know the moonstone connects us. What will bring us together again."

What the what?

Benito's phone chirped. He extracted it from the inside pocket of his jacket. I imagined he must be boiling inside his black suit. The polyester dress I wore was hot enough. I'd been keeping my eyes forward, searching the backyard and alley for any sign of help arriving, but it was quiet, not even a dumpster-diving stray dog. I took a quick sideways glance at Benito. His skin glistened with sweat, but he didn't seem to notice, or didn't care.

"Yes?" he said to his phone, his voice back to its normal clipped style. "Good." He listened for a moment. "No, no. All is prepared. Just do your part as we planned."

He rose.

"Was that your friend you picked up on the way here?" I asked.

Benito glanced around the room. "An associate," he said.

He yanked the tomato plant out of the pot, scooped my bra

off the floor, and took both out to the balcony. I was surprised the heavy fruit still clung to the stem. He used the bra to strap the plant to the railing so that it hung over the edge. That seemed exceptionally callous.

I took the moment to sidle over to the counter. Keeping my eyes on Benito and my hands behind me, I groped for the lower cabinet next to the sink and pulled on the knob. The door resisted, then made a loud pop as it came unstuck. Benito turned. He tilted his head to one side, a habit. Was he seeing me or Josephine at this point?

"Sit," he said.

I went back to the chair but got my mother's attention and tried to make her look in the cabinet. Was there a knife? I made a cutting motion with the edge of one hand against the other. She peered at me, concentrating hard, her elegant brows drawn tight. I pointed at the cabinet. She looked, looked back at me, shook her head.

Did she not understand? Couldn't see? Or was there no knife? What the hell, Wastrel? What was the point of that vision?

As Benito came back into the room, I realized I was free and could have shoved him off the balcony. What the hell, Vi?

But where was his associate and what was his part in this?

What did I have to lose? "So, where is this associate of yours?"

Benito dragged my mother's chair over to the counter so that she faced the door that led to the hallway. He removed his jacket and hung on the back of his chair. "In a strategic location," he said in answer to my question.

"I see. And what is his job?"

"Insurance."

Not helpful. "Why don't you let my mother go? You don't need her."

"Insurance."

Damn it. Had he thought of everything?

He adjusted the moonstone then stood next to my mother and pointed the gun at her head.

"Wait," I yelled, then realized something was off. Was he posing for some twisted selfie? I followed his line of vision to the top of the stairs. A full-length mirror had been placed there, angled in such a way that the reflection of my mother and Benito could probably be seen from down the stairs.

"Perfect," Benito said.

He went to the mirror and moved it into the kitchen, then came over to me and grabbed my hands. With the swiftness and precision of a cowboy roping a calf, he had my wrists zip tied together again. He led me to the top of the stairs. A little ways back in the dark hall, a rope hung from a rafter with a carabiner attached to the end. He snapped the carabiner to the zip ties, then yanked the other end of the rope to pull my hands over my head until I hung by them. He tied off the rope somewhere behind me.

"No," I said again, finally understanding his plan. Ignoring the pain in my wrists, I lifted myself by my hands and kicked at him. He wasn't very big, and I'm pretty strong. I tried to kick him down the stairs, but all he had to do was whip out that knife, nick my cheek, and I backed off. He pointed the gun at my mother for good measure.

She and I maintained eye contact while he gagged me once more, tied my ankles together, and caressed my hair one last time. If I could, I would have spit at him. He put the mirror in front of me, which left me helpless and in near total darkness.

Giacomo would spot his precious tomato plant hanging from the balcony. Enraged, he'd barrel up the stairs, notice Benito's reflection, and fire at him. Except he wouldn't hit Benito.

He'd hit the mirror and kill me.

CHAPTER THIRTY-NINE

I tried to swing my legs toward the mirror. But he'd attached them to something behind me to prevent that. He *had* thought of everything.

"It's almost time," Benito said.

I shouted every swear word I could through the bandana. Where was Giacomo? Where were Malcolm and Dex?

"You can be quiet," Benito said, using his bored voice, "or I can take your mother's eye. Your choice."

I shut it. There was a chance my mother would get out of this alive and intact. Me, not so much. That pissed me off. Everything I'd thought I'd known had turned out to be a lie. The truth was better, and the potential existed to build a new relationship with my parents. Like my dad had said, it was what it was, but it could be different. *We* could be different. Better. Combine that with Malcolm and the trust fund, and the future was worth looking forward to.

I wouldn't let Benito take it away.

But I couldn't think of way to stop this, either.

A few minutes later, I heard a car pull up out back. A door

opened and closed, then another. Hushed voices. My father and grandfather fighting about how to approach, probably Giacomo insisting Adrian stay back, and Adrian wanting to rush in and rescue Gemma.

Were they alone or were Dex and Malcolm nearby? I needed to scream. Didn't dare. Surely, they could hear my breathing. It echoed all around me off the old brick walls. Sweat stung my eyes. Blood thrummed my ears so hard it hurt.

I knew the moment Giacomo saw his tomato plant.

"I'm going to kill you, you son of a bitch," he yelled, all trace of accent and off-the-boat syntax gone.

"Why don't you come up and try," Benito said.

"Come down here and face me. *Da uomo a uomo*, like you said."

"Oh now, cousin. Don't be so hasty. You must come up the stairs, just like that day so long ago."

"Where are Vi and Gemma?"

"Come up and see old man."

Silence.

I jerked my legs. What the hell had he tied me to? I took a deep breath, tensed my whole body, jerked again. A crunching noise came from behind me. Had my legs moved closer to the mirror? Maybe. Had Benito heard the sound, too? Maybe not. The gate down below squeaked open and shut.

I had to kick that mirror down before Giacomo came in.

He mounted the porch steps. Again, I put everything into jerking whatever held me. Still not close enough.

The door at the bottom of the stairs slowly opened. From behind me came a scraping. I hadn't moved so what had caused it? I twisted, tried to fling myself around, thought I saw a shadow shift.

From down the stairs came the distinctive slide and click of a racking shotgun. I couldn't help it. I screamed.

My mother screamed.

The blast in the narrow brick stairwell was like having my eardrums pummeled with boxing gloves. A heavy thud banged me sideways against the wall, knocked the wind out of me. Glass shattered. Heat scorched my face. And just before everything went black, I heard Benito laughing.

CHAPTER FORTY

I came to, confused and in the middle of chaos. A heavy weight pinned me against the wall but I was no longer hanging from the ceiling. My hands were still tied, but I was sitting on the floor. Broken glass glittered everywhere. With my hearing muffled, I scanned the kitchen, but couldn't see my mother or Benito. I might have called out, but couldn't tell for sure, like in a bad dream. Distantly, it seemed, people were yelling and grunting. There might have been bodies getting punched or thrown, or both, in the next room.

Either I was in hell or still alive. The latter seemed unlikely, but as I was right where I last remembered being, it must be the case.

I tried to move. I'd thought the heavy object lying across me was a piece of the wall, but it was soft and warm. With my bound hands, I pushed against it. It rolled over.

I stared at the colorless face in shock.

"Zoe?" I shoved her shoulder.

Nothing.

"No, no, no. Zoe!"

What was she doing here? Her skin had flecks of blood on it

but I couldn't tell where it was coming from. I tried to shift, to get above her. Her chest felt hard. I shouted her name again and again.

Finally, she moaned.

"Zoe, Zoe, please be all right. What are you doing here? How did you get here? Are you hurt? Come on."

"Oh, shit," she slurred. "That hurt."

"Oh my God. What the hell are you doing here?"

I realized she must have been the heavy object that shoved me into the wall. I thought I'd been shot. But the shotgun had fired, the mirror had shattered...With my fingers, I picked at her shirt, encountering something heavy and stiff.

"Vest," she breathed.

"A bulletproof vest?"

She nodded, coughed, tried to sit up. I helped as best I could, hearing better, but very confused. I had to see where everyone else was, what was happening in the next room.

"I need a knife to get out of these." I held up my hands.

"No you don't."

"What?"

She slid the ties around until the connection was right between the tops of my wrists. "Just do this." Her breath came in short gasps, but she demonstrated putting her hands above her head then bringing her arms down sharply against her abdomen. "Hard as you can."

I scooted my butt around until I sat at the top of the stairs so my elbows wouldn't crash into the brick wall behind me and did what she'd shown. The zip ties snapped and I was free.

"Where were you a few hours ago?"

"Following you."

"You'll have to explain all this later. I need to get my feet free."

She pulled a multi-tool out of her pocket and sliced through the rope holding my feet. Which she could have done with the zip ties, too, danged show off.

"Who are you and what have you done with my Zoe?"

She fell back, holding her hands to her chest. "Later. I need to catch my breath."

"Are you sure you're all right? Let's get this thing off you and make sure." I unzipped the heavy vest—the kind cross-country riders wear—the sides came apart, and a large cast iron pan slipped out.

"What the—"

"Had to improvise." She felt around herself. "I'm okay. It worked like it was supposed to."

"*Supposed to?*" We'd be having a long talk. Later. I touched her face.

Zoe winced. "A few pellets must have hit me." She opened her eyes. "You too."

Or glass. I wasn't feeling any pain, though.

"Go," she said. "Make sure everyone else is okay."

I scrambled over her into the kitchen. It was empty. The shotgun lay on the floor.

In the next room, Benito lay across Giacomo's legs, half on his side, half on his back, wheezing as he tried to reach his nasty curved knife—a few inches from his fingertips. Blood glistened on his hands. His crisp white shirt was dotted with red. I couldn't see his pistol.

My mother stood over Benito, staring at him, her hands clutching her throat. Two eyes. No blood.

Giacomo sat against the wall, both hands covering his left eye, screaming and swearing. Lots of blood.

I sagged against the doorway, my legs buckling.

My mother saw me.

"Vi?" she sobbed. "I thought you were dead." She rushed over and put her arms around me.

I tried to hug her back but couldn't make my arms work. I began to think I'd been shot after all and just didn't realize. I felt so weak. "What happened? We need to call an ambulance." I squinted at my mother. Her features were fuzzy and dark spots floated in front of my eyes. "Do you have a phone?"

"Yes. Vi? Talk to me. Tell me what's wrong baby."

I took a deep breath. It didn't hurt. Maybe dying didn't hurt. "Giacomo...need to get help."

"Yes." She fumbled for her purse.

"Josephine?" Benito sounded feeble.

I breathed in again, certain I wasn't dying. On all fours, I crawled to him and Giacomo, flicking the knife away from Benito's fingers as I went.

With a watery hiss, he tried to collapse onto his back, but something prevented it. He gave up on reaching his curved blade and grasped the moonstone instead.

"Josephine, I'm coming."

Giacomo had gone quiet, his mouth drawn into a tight grimace, breathing heavy, right eye fixed on Benito. I forced myself up and to the bathroom, brought Giacomo my T-shirt. He pressed it against his eye socket. I couldn't tell whether he still had his eye or not. Either way, he had to get to an emergency room soon.

I leaned over to see why Benito couldn't lie flat. The handle and half the blade of a kitchen knife stuck out from his lower back. A growing pool of blood soaked into Giacomo's jeans and the scuffed wood floor. I looked at my mother. She held her cell phone but stared at us. The corners of her lips turned down. Had she done this to Benito? She stayed in the doorway, dipped her chin.

My mother had stabbed Benito in the back. The knife had been in the cabinet after all?

Benito reached a trembling hand toward my face. I slapped it away.

"Josephine isn't waiting for you," Giacomo gritted out. "The moonstone won't take you to her." He clenched his jaw, eased his legs from beneath Benito, and dragged himself closer. "I gave her that necklace." His thigh was also bleeding.

Benito blinked at Giacomo. He tried to speak, couldn't.

"Josephine said you needed it more than she did," Giacomo continued, his voice strained. "She asked to give it to you, and I let her." He sank to an awkward sitting position on the floor.

I got my socks and pressed them against the wound in Giacomo's leg.

"Josephine said you were *pazzo*," he said. "That we had to be careful. She was right. You *were* crazy. Crazy stupid. To come at me in my own home. You killed her. Took her from me. From all of us."

Benito's eye opened wide. He shook his head.

"He told me it was Eduardo," I said. "And he shot his brother because of it. You didn't kill Eduardo, he did."

"I loved her," Benito rasped. His grip on the moonstone loosened, his breathing grew faint.

Giacomo jerked the necklace off Benito's neck. "It doesn't matter who pulled the trigger. Your obsession killed her. You put my granddaughter in her dress and tried to make *me* kill *her*." His voice broke and his eye squeezed shut. "There is only one place for you." He pushed Benito down until the tip of the kitchen knife punctured the white shirt. "Go to hell."

Benito's eye closed forever

I stumbled back and away, retching.

Tires squealed outside, and in the distance, I heard sirens. My mother came out of the kitchen, took my arm, and got my butt into a chair next to Zoe. Some color had returned to the girl's cheeks. She really was okay. I hoped she hadn't looked into the next room.

"How are you so chill?" she asked in a feverish whisper.

I shook my head. "I'm not." My breath whistled in my tight throat.

Mom pushed my head down between my knees, and I slowly let air out. Then, inhaled, deeply, slowly.

"Benito?" a man yelled from the stairwell. "I've got him, Benito. What's next? You done up there?"

What the—?

Shit. The associate.

I lifted my head in time to see my father appear at the top of the stairs. Another man's arm wrapped around his neck. A gun pointed at his temple.

CHAPTER FORTY-ONE

"Adrian!" my mother shrieked.

"Nobody move or he gets it," the accomplice said, his voice high and nasal. "Where's Benito?"

I pointed toward the other room.

He cocked his head at my mother. "Get him."

I swallowed hard, tore my eyes from my father to my mother. "But—"

"Hurry up." He squeezed his arm tighter around Dad's neck for emphasis.

The guy was taller and broader than Dad, and even with his hair hanging in his face, I could see Dad's eyes bugging out of his head. His toes barely touched the floor.

The shotgun wasn't far from my feet, but I couldn't get to it and fire before Benito's accomplice pulled the trigger. Anyway, I'd kill my father at the same time.

"I..." my mother started. "He's..."

Sounding weak, Giacomo said, "Come and get him, Little Tony."

Little Tony? I wanted to return to Giacomo, feared he would bleed to death before help arrived.

Tony looked as baffled as I felt. "Giacomo?"

"Who else?" Giacomo answered.

"What'd you do to Benito?"

"Nothing he didn't deserve."

I hoped the sirens coming closer included an ambulance. And that we wouldn't need it for my father. Or me or my mother. Neither of us dared breathe.

"Why you still hanging around him after all these years?" Giacomo asked.

Little Tony relaxed a hair. Dad's feet touched down.

"Everything was a mess after you left, Giacomo. I didn't know what to do."

"If you have my son in a headlock, you need to let him go."

The gun barrel eased away from Dad's head. A smile creased Tony's face. He was younger than Benito and Giacomo. Another cousin? My lungs began to work again.

"Don't move!" Dex ordered from down below.

Tony jumped and released Dad. He fell hard onto his hands and knees.

"Don't shoot!" I yelled.

A gun went off.

Tony hit the floor screaming, "Jesus fucking Christ!" and grabbed his foot.

Dex came into view, arms out stiff, revolver pointed at Tony, then into the kitchen. He didn't give screaming Tony a second look as he kicked the accomplice's gun across the floor.

Dex's sweeping gaze took us in—me and Zoe on our rickety chairs. Mom and Dad standing next to each other after exchanging a brief hug—then he gave a curt nod and proceeded into the next room. I noticed Zoe's eyes following his every move like she was memorizing them.

Dex's second came up the stairs, stepped over Tony, and disappeared down the dark hall.

Dex crossed to the bathroom, kicked open the door, inspected that space, yelled, "Clear!"

His second echoed that from somewhere deeper in the building. I bolted into the next room, Dad right behind me. Giacomo lay flat and no longer held my T-shirt to his eye. What I could see of his skin had gone gray, like Ed Todd's. "No," I said.

Dex knelt beside me. With brisk, efficient movements, he took my bloody T-shirt, tore it apart and made a tourniquet for Giacomo's leg. He pressed another piece of it to the side of my grandfather's face and tied it around his head.

By the sound of pounding steps, Malcolm took the stairs two at a time. He must have hopped right over Tony.

Tony'd stopped screaming but still whimpered. "Hey, I'm bleeding here," he groused.

Malcolm came in, grabbed my arms, and pulled me against his chest where his heart beat madly. Mine hadn't exactly settled down, but it was good to know he was scared for me. For all of us. He didn't speak, but a great tremor went through him. He pressed my head against his shoulder and squeezed me like he'd never let go. I didn't want him to. Wasn't sure my legs could hold me any longer. He picked me up and carried me to the kitchen, set me on my feet but kept a protective arm around me. I turned my face into the safety of his chest.

Dex took Tony's arms and dragged him to one side. "Paramedics are coming up. Need to make room."

"Hey," Tony whined again. "I'm bleeding here."

"Shut up," Dex ordered. "You shot off your own toe. You'll live."

Dex assessed each of us until his eyes came to rest on Zoe. "What the hell are you doing here, young lady?"

I pulled my face away from Malcolm. "She saved my life."

Zoe blinked at Dex but held his gaze without flinching, unintimidated, and—smiling? I think the shotgun blast had addled her mind.

Dex's eyes snapped to me then back to Zoe. He was still hepped up on adrenaline, I could tell, needed to release it, to vent on someone. But it wasn't going to be Zoe. He turned to Tony.

"Who the hell are you?"

Miko had come in but stayed to one side, clearly unsure who he should be standing with at this point. Miko. He was okay! Dex and Malcolm must have found him. Didn't matter now. He had good color in his cheeks and looked fully recovered. Taking the seat I'd vacated, he introduced himself to Zoe. She offered a dazzling smile and they shook hands. I'd never seen her beam like that.

The paramedics came in. Dex led them to the next room. I kept hold of Malcolm's hand and followed them to Giacomo.

We crowded around him, ignoring the paramedics' efforts to shoo us away. They found a pulse, started oxygen, taped a bandage over his eye, put a collar around his neck, and were already relaying his condition over a radio as they lifted him onto a stretcher. They secured him and started moving out of the room. My father held his father's left hand. I held his right.

As we went through the kitchen, I leaned down and said, "You owe me a pot of sauce, old man. Don't forget."

I thought I felt him squeeze my fingers before they took him down the stairs.

CHAPTER FORTY-TWO

"All right," Dex said after the paramedics packed up and left. "This is a mess. Cops will be here any second. We need a simple, consistent story for what went down. I'll talk to them first, and hopefully, we can all go home before midnight."

In a calm voice, my mother asked, "Am I going to jail?"

"Why would you?" Dex asked.

She sniffed. "I stabbed Benito."

"Really?" Dex said. "It's harder to shove a knife into a person than most people realize." He stuck his bottom lip out and nodded. "Nicely done."

"She's stronger than she looks," I said.

"But—" my mother started.

"Was he attacking you?"

"No, he was attacking Giacomo, trying to cut out his eye." She reached for the back of a chair. Miko stood so she could sit. "And...and..." She swallowed, collecting herself. Her voice firmed with anger. "I thought he'd made Giacomo shoot my daughter."

I grabbed her hand and held it with both of mine. She'd kept it together and saved Giacomo. She hadn't flown to pieces. My grandmother survived a shooting long enough to deliver my father, and my mother, furious that I'd been shot, killed a man. The women in my family were kick ass powerful and resilient. I'd remember that the next time I thought of running away from my troubles.

"You're getting ahead of the story," Dex said, "but that's good to know. It's okay to use lethal force to defend an innocent party from lethal force. This falls within that description."

Everyone nodded in agreement. My mother took a big breath and let it out. Dad put his hand on her shoulder.

"Except—" I started, thinking about how Giacomo had forced Benito's body down onto that knife. The men in my family were tough, too.

Dex held up one finger to stop me. "Would it have changed the outcome?"

"Nope."

"Then I don't need to know. And neither do the police. Understand?"

I nodded.

I described what happened when we arrived at this abandoned house. My mother told us that after Giacomo fired, Benito met him at the top of the stairs, where Giacomo slammed the gun butt into Benito's face. He staggered into the other room, and they continued fighting. She was able to get hold of the knife in the cabinet, free herself, and stab Benito.

I whispered an apology to Wastrel for not believing him.

The police arrived, followed by a second set of paramedics. They started swabbing wounds. In addition to the neat slices Benito had given me, Zoe and I both had superficial cuts from the glass.

"I don't understand how we weren't shot," I said to Dex.

Hands on hips, he examined the hallway. "He aimed high," he said. "Shot through the rope holding you."

Zoe's improvised vest hadn't deflected the pellets, but a near perfect circular welt ringed her chest, ribs, and abdomen. Probably from the impact with me. The medic was stumped until Zoe produced Mrs. Erdman's iron skillet.

They got Tony's sneaker off and bandaged his foot. His right little toe was gone. My mother allowed them to disinfect the scratches on her legs and arms.

By silent agreement, we all declined a ride to the hospital.

I started explaining what had happened in the woods and at Helen's.

"Oh, God, Helen." I took Malcolm's hand. "I'm so sorry."

Malcolm and Dex exchanged a look. "Why?"

"You didn't find her?"

"What do you mean?" Malcolm asked. "What does my mother have to do with this?"

I sank to the floor. Just couldn't stand up anymore. My mother took over with how Benito had taken us through the woods. Malcolm crouched beside me, rubbed my back, and I broke the terrible news about Helen.

He stood and whipped out his cell phone, pressing the shortcut for her number. I heard her voicemail pick up. I left a curt message for her to call him immediately. Next, he called Hank, confirmed Clara was fine, then asked him to get to Helen's immediately, and call back as soon as he did. Third, he called the county sheriff and informed them there may have been foul play at Helen's address. He slid his phone into his pocket and stood by the window, staring at the wall of the house next door.

I put my head in my hands, and tried, unsuccessfully to keep the tears in. Now that the threat was gone, I felt shaky, exhausted, and like crying for days.

Tony corroborated everything we said about Benito and his intentions. For his part, he didn't seem to be guilty of anything much other than being stupid enough to follow Benito around, though I couldn't speak for what he might have done in years past. He *had* threatened my father. I had a feeling if Giacomo were here, he'd not want fingers pointed at Little Tony. Benito bore the guilt and responsibility for all this terror and mayhem.

I returned to the bathroom and pulled on my jeans. Dex had a spare polo shirt in his SUV, and I put that on, couldn't wait to get out of that dress. I needed to go outside. Even with broken windows, the tiny kitchen had grown stifling as the afternoon wore on and more people came in. I made for the stairs.

Malcolm's phone buzzed, and he answered before it was halfway through the first ring. He turned to me, eyes shining and face jubilant as he said, "Mom?"

I smiled my first real smile of the day and started down the stairs, then heard Malcolm say, "Sorry, sorry. I know. Okay. Just tell them it was a mistake."

Apparently, Helen wasn't too happy about having the sheriff at her door. That was a problem we could live with.

I sat on the bottom porch step, the only one I thought safe. The sun had moved around so that the back of the house was in shade. A light breeze ruffled the tall grass and weeds of the abandoned yard, taking with it the smells of decay, blood, and death.

Police cars jammed the alley, and two television news vans pulled in behind them. Oh, joy. Despite Dex's best efforts, we all had to answer questions, tell our part of the story. Yellow tape surrounded the house and yard. The coroner took Benito away.

Little Tony took the high road, candidly admitting his involvement in Benito's scheme for revenge. He said cooperating was best, sounding like he'd been in this predicament before. He shrugged and said maybe they'd cut him a deal. For sure he'd get a meal in an air-conditioned cell. He smiled cheerfully and waved at the reporters as the police cuffed him and put him in the back of a squad car. We promised to call Dex Two and do what we could for him. He said there was no rush.

After what seemed like hours, during which I went back inside to avoid having a reporter's microphone in my face, Dad asked if we could leave. He wanted to get to the hospital to check on Giacomo. We all did.

I wanted to know if we could take down the dehydrated tomato plant. I doubted my bra could be salvaged, but it was worth a try. And maybe Giacomo's prized plant could be revived with some tender loving care. Also doubtful.

Nope. Both were bagged as evidence along with Mrs. Erdman's frying pan. The black marbles were also tagged and taken. No one had tried to claim them. And Josephine's hand-made maternity dress. They took that, too.

It was near dark by the time Gemma, Adrian, and Dex got in Malcolm's truck. Dex's second—whose name I'd never gotten—drove Dex's SUV with Zoe and Miko. Malcolm took the wheel of my truck, pulling me across the torn bench seat to sit next to him. I had to straddle the shifter.

I didn't care.

We found the nearest Chinese buffet and stuffed ourselves before continuing to the hospital. On the way, I spotted an Italian restaurant. We pulled over, and I ran in and ordered an espresso to go.

The hospital was a gigantic complex on the edge of a park. Giacomo had already had surgery to clean up his socket. Although Benito hadn't managed to completely steal the eye, he'd damaged it beyond saving. In the future, my grandfather could opt for an ocular implant and a prosthetic eye, or he could wear an eye patch.

He'd been shot in the thigh, but it was only muscle damage, no tendons, ligaments, or bones were hit. He'd have a scar but full use of the leg. He must have been prepared to avoid the hamstring slice, but somehow, Benito had still gotten to his eye.

A doctor no older than me told us all this before we went into the room.

Giacomo was sedated and sleeping. Machines beeped, noting his pulse and respirations, and a bag dripped fluids and meds through a needle into his arm. We sat with him for a while, me and Dad on either side of the bed, while the others wandered in and out, went to the cafeteria to buy coffee, chatted. Malcolm spent most of the time on the phone with Dex Two.

Mom made herself scarce, whether out of deference to Dad or because they were still mad at each other, I didn't know. I was too tired to care at that point.

The television was on, sound off. I flipped through the stations. Something caught my eye, I went back.

And there it was. The tomato plant and my bra. Headlining the news.

I sighed. Then snorted. Then laughed. My father lifted his head. I pointed at the screen, and he smiled, chuckled. Life just didn't get any better than that.

Giacomo's color had improved, but sitting by him reminded me too much of the vigil I'd kept with Ed Todd. Except Giacomo was going to live. When my Dad's eyes started to droop, I decided we should go home and try to get some sleep. I left the espresso on Giacomo's over-bed table, and we left.

Zoe and Miko had opted to sit in the waiting room. They were talking animatedly and laughing when I picked them up for the ride home. The resilience of the young. I had only ten years on them but felt ancient. Miko hadn't tried to talk to Gemma. Perhaps he finally realized that ship had sailed. Or maybe a younger sloop had caught his attention.

If that were the case, I'd call him fickle and have to warn Zoe not to let her affections get involved too soon. As I watched them mooning at each other, I feared it might already be too late.

Meanwhile, Zoe had a lot of 'splainin' to do, and the long ride home was the perfect opportunity to quiz her. I made her ride with me and Malcolm. Miko waved and made a sad face when he got in the front seat with Dex's second—Trevor, I'd learned over sweet-and-sour chicken. Once we were on the highway, I feared

I'd be asleep against Malcolm's side before long, so I started quickly. "So, Zoe—"

"I know. But what was I supposed to do? First, you introduced me to Dex, then, after Mrs. Erdman burned down my car, I—"

"Wait. First of all, how did you find us? Did you say you were following us?"

"Right. You said I couldn't come to the farm, but I knew something was wrong, so I was driving around the area. I saw that van pull out from that house on the far side of Winterlight, and something didn't seem right."

Good instincts.

"What gave it away? Was my bra hanging out the side door?"

"That, and it was a pool service van. Same company my parents use. I know that house doesn't have a pool, and what would someone from that company be doing way out there, anyway? Plus, most of their workers are pool boys, if you know what mean."

I did. Benito didn't exactly fit the profile. I shook my head, marveling at how she'd put all that together. "Okay, so you followed us. Did you think to call the police or Malcolm?"

She hadn't hesitated to dial 911 when Giacomo fired the shotgun that first time.

"I didn't know you were in there. Don't have the house number on my phone. I tried the barn, but nobody answered."

At least she had a phone, one she probably kept charged.

"And what, exactly," Malcolm asked in his dad voice, "were you planning to do when you got to the house?"

"Did you have the vest and frying pan with you in my truck?" I asked.

"Yes, and I don't know. I saw the van parked behind the house, but I guess you guys were already inside, so I still wasn't sure it was you. That's why I went around the front and snuck in that way."

Malcolm took his arm from around my shoulders to run his

hand through his hair, then held it on the back of his neck. I could tell it was all he could do not to reach across me to smack the kid in the head.

"So," Malcolm said, his tone terse, "you snuck into what should be a condemned building, and then what?"

"Then I heard them talking, so I knew it was Vi and her mother."

"Do you have a weapon?" I asked.

She shook her head. Malcolm slid me a sideways look that said I shouldn't encourage her in whatever fantasy world she was living in.

"I got to the back of that hallway from the front apartment, and I saw what he had planned. At least, I was pretty sure what was going on. It all happened kind of fast after that."

No shit.

Malcolm grunted but somehow didn't comment.

"And what does Dex have to do with it?"

"You introduced me to him."

Why did I feel like she was blaming me for something? "I know, but—"

"Let me finish. I had a lot of time on my hands. Mrs. Erdman doesn't have cable, but she does have a good internet connection, so I started doing some research."

"Into bulletproof vests?"

"No. Well, yes. Did you know you can't just go to the store and buy them?"

I'd file that under information good to have and not need, like learning to use a gun. I waved my hand to get her to continue.

"Mostly, I researched what it takes to be a private investigator." She crossed her arms and nodded decisively. "Just like Dexter Hamill."

CHAPTER FORTY-THREE

If Zoe wanted to be a PI, that was fine. I was so drained, anything would have been fine. I suggested she discuss it with Dex. He would be straight about whether it was a good fit and what she could expect from that career.

All I wanted was a long, hot shower. As did everyone. We took turns taking short ones so we wouldn't run out of hot water.

I sent Miko to the apartment and told him to stay put until morning. Him on a one-way flight back to Paris was best for all concerned. My parents went to their room, but I heard their door open and close shortly after we were in bed, and someone went down the stairs.

We weren't sleeping, simply holding each other, grateful to be home and safe. Noire sighed at the foot of the bed.

After a minute, Malcolm said, "You should go see who that is and if he or she needs something."

A few days ago, I would have begged him to go with me. After what we'd just been through, everything else seemed easy.

My mother sat in the living room, in the dark. I switched on a lamp and joined her.

"How are you doing?"

One delicate shoulder lifted. She'd stabbed a man. A bad man, but still. Whatever she'd imagined when they left Paris, it wasn't that. In her lap, she gripped an object I couldn't see.

"I'm worried about you and Dad."

"That makes two of us."

"Want a drink? Water? Something stronger?"

She nodded. I poured her a short Scotch and set it in front of her, got myself a glass of water.

"He was really scared for you," I said after sitting across from her again.

"Yes. But he won't bend on this Miko thing."

"Did something happen between you?"

"Nothing but dancing."

"The tango."

"Not just the tango, the Argentine tango."

"Oh." I began to understand.

"Adrian thought he saw something."

"Apparently Miko thought so, too."

"It's impossible to dance without becoming close. I put my all into it as always. Miko misinterpreted that as something more than it was."

She sipped her drink, wrinkled her nose. "I'm not as young as I used to be. I enjoyed his attention. There's nothing wrong with that."

It wasn't news that she was vain. "Mom. The man followed you here from Paris."

"Youthful exuberance. Plus, his parents have money and indulge his every whim."

"He mentioned he wanted to be a jumper rider before he discovered dance."

"See? Your father just won't listen."

Dad found it best to not argue with her. She said he didn't listen. Pride and stubbornness went along with my family's strength.

I drank my water and went for a refill. Back in the living room, I asked, "Has Dad danced since he got hurt?"

"A few steps to demonstrate nuances to Miko."

"I think I know what part of the problem is."

"Do you? Please explain, because I've wracked my mind trying to figure out what to say."

"Dad was young like Miko when you two first met, right? Young and handsome and talented?"

A soft smile played at the corners of her mouth, almost painful in its private remembrance. The sparks must have really flown when they were first together. She didn't have to answer.

"You two were magical together, unstoppable."

"We were."

"Maybe he's feeling his age, too. He sees himself in Miko, but Dad was a poor kid from an orphanage sweeping up the dance studio at night. It's not much of a stretch to imagine him thinking Miko could steal you away."

She made a scoffing sound.

"Mom, no matter what you think, you're still gorgeous. Dad's never loved anyone but you. Have you ever worried about him straying?"

She picked up her drink, stared at it, put it down. In a small voice, she said, "No."

After a few silent minutes, I said, "I'm going to try to get some sleep."

We stood, she reached for me. We hugged, awkward, but getting more natural each time. She handed me a stuffed animal.

"What's this?" I could see it was a palm-sized teddy bear, but...

"One of our first big competitions was in Stuttgart. It's not far from Giengen where the Stief bears come from." She ran her fingertip over the bear's ear. "You were about two years old."

"I...you..." Tears clogged my throat. "But..."

"Trudy said not to send it. That you had plenty."

"Oh, Mom." I pulled her back into a hug. "I'm so sorry she did that to you."

"To us," she said. "She did it to us."

I guided us back to the couch. We sat and held each other.

"Could you talk to him?" she asked.

"To the bear? What's his name?"

She swatted my shoulder. "No. Your father."

I understood her fear, but thinking back to how Malcolm had encouraged me to talk to them, I said, "This is something you have to do yourself."

"But how?"

"Maybe you have to show him."

"I don't know what that means."

She'd never had to work for his affection. Maybe she had taken him for granted.

"I don't know, Mom, but I'm sure an opportunity will come."

I hoped an opportunity would come. Soon.

Another storm came through, leaving the morning air refreshing and cool. The horses snorted, flicked their tails, and shook rain out of their manes when we brought them in to have their breakfast. Noire ran down to the creek and came back sparkling with water droplets and carrying a giant stick. Miko threw it for her for as long as she wanted, which was a long time.

I hadn't slept much. I don't know if anyone did. But after I went back upstairs, Malcolm put his arms around me, I didn't dream, and that made it okay.

Clara cooked a huge breakfast of egg casseroles, sausage, and fresh-baked bread. Helen joined us, sharing the details of how Benito had ordered her to crouch in the tub, then shot two holes in her ceiling. It'd scared her nearly to death, she said, but he hadn't killed her. That shred of civilization in him had manifested at the right time.

And even though it appeared that one look at Zoe had gotten Miko over his moonstruck devotion to Mom, my parents were still stiff and standoffish with each other. I'm sure it hadn't helped that Mom slept on the couch. For all Dad knew, she'd rendezvoused with Miko.

We took our time with chores. No one had to be anywhere. We napped. Dad went for a walk after calling Giacomo. He told us not to drive all that way to visit. He was resting, too.

Malcolm disappeared into his office to work but surfaced every hour or so to check on each of us, trying to be unobtrusive, I'm sure, but I knew what he was up to.

Clara insisted on making supper as well. Dessert was a fresh August pie. I never had gotten a piece of the first one. I'd forgotten to bring whipped cream. It was delicious without any.

That night, I slept.

As soon as I had the work done on Wednesday, made lighter with Miko's help, me and my parents left to visit Giacomo. We would leave Dad at the hospital, then Mom and I were going dress shopping for Dex Two's gala.

Such a mother-daughter thing to do. When I was young, Aunt Trudy would drop me off at the mall by myself. This new experience had my stomach acting foolish, doing a girlish dance of excited anticipation. We would have lunch, too. Heck, maybe we'd get pedicures. I wouldn't mind having pretty feet for a change.

I also felt guilty. Sandy and Zoe were both attending the party, and we'd talked about going shopping. We would still need shoes. Maybe we could do that. Mom had plenty of them, she said.

As it turned out, Zoe didn't care. She and Miko were going riding, and she could wear one of her prom dresses. Sandy called to apologize because someone at work had lent her a dress. By the time we left, I felt better.

Malcolm gave us his SUV to drive, the one I'd flipped back in May avoiding a doe and fawn. The brake lines had been cut, too, but that's another story. The body shop had had it for weeks, and now it was all smooth and shiny. The brakes were fixed. The inside even smelled new.

We got on the road, my mother sitting up front with me, Dad in the back. I needed to get them talking and jumped to the topic that'd had me burning with curiosity since they'd arrived.

"So, guys, the empty suitcases? Don't you have mountains of clothes from years of competition?"

"Simple," Dad said. "We sold all of it to buy our tickets."

"It's true, Vi," Mom said. "We'd invested a lot getting the Paris studio set up."

"I thought you said you had backers."

"They backed out when your mother took up with Mr. Milanko Stanislaw."

My mother's lips tightened into a white line. My father's tone about frosted the windows.

"Why don't you use the trust fund?" The words came out without much forethought, as usual, but upon testing the idea, I didn't regret making the offer. If it would make things better, they could have it. It probably wasn't enough to make much of a difference to any of us.

"It's. Not. About. The. Money."

I fired up the defroster, thinking that maybe my mother was right, that I needed to talk to Dad. Underneath that glacial exterior, I guessed his heart was deeply wounded. And he was afraid.

"It's an irrevocable trust," my mother explained. Her long fingers pleated her black skirt. "We set it up a few years ago when we had quite a bit saved. We can't touch it. You're the sole beneficiary."

"Then I'll sign it over to you. Whatever."

What did she mean by *quite a bit*? At this point, knowing

they'd wanted me and had thought to create the trust was more than enough.

"The rules governing these things are strict. You can't get the money until you're thirty."

That was only nine months away. "But then I can do whatever I want with it, right?"

My mother stared out her window. "I suppose."

"It's for you, Vi," my father said from the back, his tone warmer. "For you to set yourself up. You're ready for that now."

"Originally, it was a revocable trust," Mom said.

"But then Victor..." Dad's voice trailed off.

Uncle Vic. He'd never approved of my obsession with horses. I could imagine what he'd told them. Probably the truth, but he had a way of spinning honesty that made it something else entirely. It explained the provisions of the trust.

"It's okay. At first, I *was* upset by the whole *keep a job for one year and earn a glowing letter of recommendation* thing. Not to mention the *amount undisclosed* part. It made me really mad. But coming to Winterlight has been good."

"Until we showed up," Dad said.

I tilted my head from side to side as if considering. "Even that."

Especially that. I'd shut out the events of Monday. I think everyone was avoiding thinking about Benito. We could make a therapist rich. We drove in silence for a time, me mulling all they'd said, them lost to their own thoughts.

We were in the city when my mother spoke again. "Last I inquired, the value was around one hundred thousand." She turned toward me and smiled. "American dollars. But I haven't checked the balance in months."

I stared at her. A car honked its horn. I jerked the wheel to bring us back into our lane.

I'd been operating under the safest assumption—the one that kept me from being disappointed—that the trust was crap.

A hundred thousand dollars is *not* crap.

I focused on breathing in and out before I blacked out. "That's...more than I expected."

More then I'd ever dared imagine. I couldn't wrap my mind around that many zeroes. Like the truth of my parents' feelings for me, it would take a while for this to sink in.

Dad squeezed my shoulder. "We never forgot about you, kid."

I patted his hand, grinned at him in the rear-view mirror. He winked.

"What's it like," I asked, "suddenly having a father after all this time? Giacomo's complicated."

He gave my shoulder a playful pat. "That he is. Life will never be dull with him around. But I bet you have an inkling of how I feel."

I did. "Speaking of," I said. "Who's paying his hospital bill?"

"He is," Mom said. "*He* won't be a burden."

The emphasis she put on the word *he* made me think she worried they would be. Or she would be. Their relationship had to be fixable. They'd always been so connected. Not that I'd spent much time around them, but there had been a few months during the summer I was thirteen that they'd been stateside. They'd rented a space, were giving lessons. I went every day after riding and worked hard to master several ballroom dances. *Master* is too strong a word, but I grew competent. Not that I have much use for the waltz.

I thought back to how against it Aunt Trudy had been. I'd thought she was trying to protect me. She'd been right because they'd returned to the international circuit and never looked back.

Or so I'd thought.

I'd thought so many wrong things. Been led to believe so many falsehoods. Now, I understood that Aunt Trudy was only protecting herself, or once again, punishing her little sister.

Before that, though, I'd believed they were home, that we'd finally live together as a family. It'd crushed me when they left. I'd screamed and cried and begged them to take me with them. Been physically ill and unable to eat or sleep.

How that must have infuriated Aunt Trudy. She'd never treated me the same after that.

But watching them, how they looked at each other, still so in love. *So* romantic. The dance moves were sensuous and seductive. They moved as one, like me and a horse, only better. Alone at night, I'd practiced the precise tilt of her head, the provocative swing of her hips, the sultry, smoldering look in her eyes when he spun and dipped her. I'd wanted to be her. Wanted someone to look at me the way Dad looked at her.

After they left, I'd wanted to be the exact opposite. *I'd* never looked back.

I shook myself. We were at the hospital.

Giacomo sat up in bed chatting with a nurse.

She laughed and patted his arm. "You old charmer. Well, you have visitors, and I should get back to work." She smiled at us, her eyes darting around as if she were embarrassed, and went out.

He opened his arms wide. "*La famiglia*. Come."

He hugged me and Dad. Mom kissed his cheek.

"Wow," I said. "You look great."

"A couple of good nights' sleep is all I needed, but they want to keep me *for observation*." He made an extravagant dismissive gesture with one hand.

"A friend is having a party this weekend," I told him. "You have to be well rested."

He narrowed his eye. "What kind of party?"

"A fancy one," Dad said. "I have a spare tux that will fit you perfectly."

"Will there be wine?"

"If I know Dex," I said, "only the best and plenty of it."

"*Bene*," Giacomo said. "The same man who was at the farm? I knew I liked him."

"A different Dex. I'll explain later. Have the police been here, yet?"

His face grew serious. "No. Why? Is there more trouble? Hey, what happened to our cousin Little Tony? I didn't get to see him."

"Tony confessed to being Benito's accomplice. I think he's being sent back to New York."

"Oh. That's too bad. He was a good kid."

Debatable, but whatever. "So, someone will probably be here to question you." I was surprised they hadn't come already. "Dex One said to remember that Gemma stabbed Benito."

"I know she did." He reached for her hand, raised it to his lips, kissed it. "You saved my life."

My father came by his suave charisma naturally. My mother paled a little, though, and I was sorry to remind her of what she'd done.

"Mom, they have a Starbuck's here. Could you get Giacomo an espresso?" I gave her my wallet. "On me."

"*Grazie.* The one you brought me Monday, it was cold by the time I found it."

"How did you know it was from me?"

He lifted his shoulders. "Who else?"

I took a fortifying breath. "Do you remember talking to Benito before he died?"

"The snake blamed Eduardo."

"Okay. Do you remember *how* Benito died?"

His eye lit with cold satisfaction. "*Sí.* I pushed him down on the knife. Sent him to hell."

I was so hoping he'd blacked out and forgotten.

"He was done for, anyway, wasn't he?" my father asked.

"Unfortunately, that's not the point," I explained. "Giacomo, could you leave out that detail when the police question you?"

"Why? It's the truth." He smiled and patted my arm. "Why don't you call me *nonno*?"

I closed the door. "Okay, *grandpa*. It seems you can use lethal force to defend an innocent party from lethal force." I tried to remember exactly how Dex had put it. "But once the bad guy's quietly bleeding out, if you strike at that point—"

There was a knock at the door, it opened, and two uniformed police officers came in. Crap.

"Don't worry," Giacomo said. "I love you."

Dad and I went out into the hallway. "What the hell was that about?" I asked.

"He's not the bumbling gardener character he portrayed. Trust him."

"Like you trust Mom?"

"I don't want to talk about that."

Exasperated with them, I said, "You're going to have to," my tone more caustic then intended.

I'm not sure what gave me the courage to speak to him sharply or why I thought I had the right to intervene, but now that I had them, I wanted to keep them. Together.

Mom came down the hallway with the espresso. I almost drank it myself. Tempting as that was, I entered the room and put it by Giacomo's bed.

"Dad will be outside if you need anything." I kissed his cheek, whispered, "*Nonno.*"

He winked at me.

We left Dad sitting in the hallway.

Mom and I hit the swankiest mall in town. I might not have had the trust fund yet, but I felt flush and could afford to splurge. Malcolm paid me a decent wage, and I'd spent very little of it since arriving at Winterlight.

After trying on almost everything in our size, we both ended up with jewel tones. Hers was a brilliant sapphire blue column, one shouldered, crepe, with a high slit to show off her amazing legs. Simple and elegant with a touch of crystal trim to give it a little glitz. For me, a dark emerald green with a square neckline, cutouts on the sides, and a chiffon skirt of tiny pleats. It would be easy to walk in, my main criteria. Plus, it would blend well with Malcolm's kilt, which I knew he'd be wearing Saturday night, the darling man.

We had lunch and didn't talk about anything in particular. I wanted to tell her about Wastrel's part in all this, but I'd exceeded my stress limit, at least for a few days. She had too, if her reaction in the hospital was any indication. Plus, I don't think I could handle one of her withering looks when I told her of my dreams and visions. We'd come a long way in a short amount of time, but that might be pushing our fragile rapport too far.

Purchases stashed in the back of the SUV, we returned to the hospital to collect Dad. There, we found Giacomo watching a soccer game on TV and Dad asleep in the chair by the bed. The events of the past few days were fast catching up with me as well, and I grabbed a coffee before we got back on the road to home.

Mom and Dad both slept, both snored. I listened to the radio, quietly humming along with a few songs so as not to wake them.

Near dark, when I pulled into Winterlight, my truck was parked in its usual spot, which meant Zoe was still here. Dex's truck sat next to the house. A strange car had pulled right up to the barn doorway—an expensive-looking sedan—and right behind it, a sheriff's SUV.

Assuming it had to do with Benito and maybe Helen, I got out but heard angry voices inside, men and women talking over each other.

An unfamiliar female shouted, "Calm down," over and over in a strident tone.

Above them, Zoe screamed, "No, I won't go back. You can't make me!"

CHAPTER FORTY-FOUR

Without waking my parents, I rushed toward our newest drama. Deputy Joe stood to one side of the barn aisle looking bemused. A woman had Zoe by the arm. A man had the woman by the arm. Miko stood beside Zoe, a look of fierce concentration on his face, trying, and failing, to keep up with the argument, whatever it was.

"What's going on?" I asked Joe.

"They saw her on the news and came to collect her."

"What? Who are they?"

"Her parents. She was supposed to be spending the summer with a friend in Chicago."

That explained why she was so skittish and hyper aware.

"And your job here?"

He shrugged. "Her parents want her to go with them, but I can't make her. She's eighteen."

What? "She told me she was sixteen."

"Lied about her name, too. It's Emily. Emily Frobisher."

The name she'd put on the job application was Zoe Frost. What the hell?

"Where's Malcolm?"

Joe shrugged again.

"Vi, tell them they can't take me."

I waded in with my hand out. "Hi there, I'm Vi Parker, manager of Winterlight. Zoe works for us." The mother had to unhand her daughter to shake with me. "Is there a problem?"

"Her name is Emily. Not Zoe," her mother said. "And she is supposed to start medical school tomorrow."

"I'm sorry, I didn't catch your names," I said, trying to diffuse some of the tension.

"Dr. Leon Frobisher." Emily's dad shook my hand. "This is my wife, Dr. Crystal Frobisher."

Oh brother, double MDs. This might be challenging. Good manners were a good start, though.

"Why don't we go inside where we can sit?" I showed them toward the tack room.

As I went by Miko, I told him to get Malcolm. He sprinted off.

Crystal wore capri length running pants with a silky blouse, looking like she'd run out of the house mid costume change. Leon wore stretchy khakis and a polo shirt with a country club logo above the breast pocket, looking like he'd just come off the golf course. They both viewed the tack room's questionable furniture with distaste, but sat. It almost made me laugh because they reminded me of my parents.

I looked at Zoe. *Emily.* "Medical school?"

"Pre-med. But I don't want to go to medical school. Never have." She sat in the lounger, arms crossed, a mutinous expression on her face. "It's what *they* want."

"You were accepted to Wash U, honey," her dad said. "That's not an easy school to get into."

"You only want me to go there because that's where you went. None of this has to do with me." Tears laced her voice.

Tears of frustration, I'd guess. They'd probably had this conversation several times before.

"Young lady, you are not going to waste your life playing with horses."

This from the mother.

"It was good enough when you could brag to your friends about my expensive horse and all the ribbons I brought home, all the shows my students went to."

Wait, she had her own horse? Students? Was anyone around me what they seemed? Sometimes, I longed for my old life where Ed Todd made crude jokes and Harry drank too much. I knew what to expect. Life was simpler.

"That's a hobby," her mother said, "not a way to make a living."

I felt one eyebrow creep up toward my hairline. Crystal breezed on, not realizing she'd insulted me. I doubted she would have cared if she did.

"You agreed to go to Wash U."

Miko came in with Malcolm and Dex, and I instantly relaxed.

"Everything all right here?" Malcolm asked. He and Dex took up positions on either side of Zoe...*Emily*. Miko stood behind her. If the Frobisher's thought they had the upper hand by bringing the sheriff, they appeared less sure now. Especially because Joe stayed outside. I smiled.

"Apparently, Doctor and Doctor Frobisher were surprised to see their daughter, Zoe—whose real name is Emily by the way—on the news because they thought she was spending the summer in Chicago."

On the news at the scene of a stabbing and shooting in an abandoned house in a crappy part of the city, to be precise. They must have been horrified. Shocked. I would have been. No wonder they'd rushed out without changing their clothes. The only surprise was they didn't have their lawyer in tow.

"They've come to take her home where she's supposed to be attending medical school at Wash U. Do I have that right?"

"Medical school," Dex said. "That's big stuff, Miss Emily."

"And you are?" Mr. Doctor Frobisher asked.

I watched Dex ooze into his southern gentleman persona as he stuck out his hand and drawled, "Dexter Hamill, Private Investigator. I'm considering taking Miss Emily as an apprentice. While she goes to school, of course."

I glanced at Emily. She looked as surprised as I did. But eager and excited, too.

"That's ridiculous," Mrs. Doctor Frobisher said.

Her father looked perplexed. Of the two, I sensed he was the softer one, possibly more open to other directions for his daughter.

"And dangerous," he said. "Is that what this is about?"

"The danger?" Emily asked. "No. It's interesting. And I'm good at it."

"How could you possibly know?" her mother asked.

"Excuse me," Malcolm said. "Let me introduce myself. I'm Robert Malcolm, and this is my estate."

Oh for pity's sake. He never referred to Winterlight as his *estate*. Between him and Dex, I'm not sure who was more crafty when it came to playing a part.

"I think we'd be more comfortable at the house." He opened the door to the tack room, leaving them little choice, good manners and all, but to go through it.

They trouped out. Malcolm and Dex followed, but Malcolm gave me a roll of the eyes over his shoulder before he did. Zoe— Emily—and I followed a little ways back, which gave me a chance to talk to her before we got to the house.

"Okay, pretty little liar, what's this all about?"

"I'm sorry I didn't tell you the truth. I just had to get away from them for a while to think."

"Let me make sure I understand. You have a horse. You've competed extensively, you give lessons, and take students to shows? What the hell, girl?"

"I needed to relax and figure out who I really am, not try to live up to anyone's expectations."

"Except your own."

"Except my own, right. At least someone understands me."

"Better than you know. On that, you didn't discuss this apprenticeship thing with Dex?"

"No. I told him what I'm interested in, and he gave me advice about what to study, but I was as shocked by that as you."

My mind whirred, happy to churn on something other than blades, blood, and tango.

"Just go with the flow in here, okay?" We mounted the porch steps. "This could turn out all right."

My parents were nowhere in sight. They hadn't been in the car, and they weren't downstairs. Maybe they were talking. I could hope.

Deputy Joe had also snuck away. Smart man.

Malcolm had the Frobishers all comfy in the living room with a glass of iced tea in front of each of them.

"I don't understand this apprenticeship," Crystal said.

"It's simple," Dex explained. "Miss Emily will work for me part time—in the office only—while she attends school for a criminal justice degree."

As far as I knew, Dex didn't have an office. I'm not sure what he was up to.

The Frobishers looked like they'd been hit with a bat, but otherwise, they were taking it well.

"You can move your horse here," I said. "If you want."

Zoe couldn't stop smiling. "I do. And I can still live with Mrs. Erdman. She needs me."

"We don't know any of you," Mr. Doctor Frobisher said.

"It doesn't matter," Mrs. Doctor Frobisher said. "This conversation is over. Emma, get your things. You're coming home right now."

Oh. Apparently she wasn't taking it as well as I thought.

"No, Mom. I already called them and dropped out. I don't want to go home, and you can't make me." She looked at Dex, adulation and gratitude shining in her eyes. "This is what I want. This is what I'm going to do."

All things considered, her voice was even, reasonable.

The doctors sat side by side on the couch. Mr. Doctor Frobisher's eyes rested on his daughter for a long time, then he looked at Dex, then Malcolm, then me. He put his hand on his wife's.

Miko must have stayed at the barn, realizing he didn't have a place in this convo, that his presence might only complicate things. Smart boy.

"I believe that Emily is fine here, dear," Mr. Doctor said. "She has been for months. These people obviously care about her. One more day won't make a difference. Why don't we get some dinner. We can talk more tomorrow."

Crystal pulled in her lips but surprised me by not arguing.

Mr. Doctor turned to Malcolm. "You can understand what a shock it was for us to see her on the news, I'm sure." He turned to me. "I understand she saved your life?"

"She did."

He looked at his daughter. "We're very proud of you, Emily. You gave us quite a scare. Please don't do that again." He rose and pulled Mrs. Doctor up with him. "Thank you for your hospitality, Mr. Malcolm. We can see ourselves out."

"Before you go," Dex said with a reassuring smile, "take my card. Feel free to do a background check on me."

Mr. Doctor took the card with a smile that said he'd get his attorney on that first thing.

Emily went after them. "Does this mean—?"

"We'll talk tomorrow," her father said firmly.

They left.

"I don't know whether that was acquiescence or a strategic retreat to regroup," Dex said. "He might be back with his lawyer."

"That's what I'm afraid of," I said with a yawn. I had sat in one of the side chairs and felt unable to get out of it.

Zoe—Emily, came back down the hall. "Thank you so much Mr. Hamill. You won't regret it." She picked up her purse. "I'm going home—to Mrs. Erdman's—see you tomorrow."

I forced myself up to walk her to my truck.

"I have a car, by the way," she said as we walked down the driveway. "It's in my name, so they can't take it away. I had to leave it home because I took the train to Chicago."

"Did you ever really go to Chicago? Wait, you mean another car besides the one that burned?"

"Yeah, that was my brother's old car."

"Listen, I'm exhausted but have one question. Would you consider giving lessons here?"

"Sure," she said.

At my truck, she gave me a quick hug.

"Thanks for everything, Vi. You're the best. Well, Dex is the best."

"He is. Have a good night."

I watched her drive away, then went out to the blacktop to see if anyone had picked up the mail. By the size of the stack, no one had been to the mailbox in a couple of days. I brought it to the house, passing Dex on his way out. He waved. I found Malcolm in his recliner, a Scotch at his elbow. I slid over the armrest onto his lap. He put his arms around me and picked through the mail.

"There's something for you."

I took it from him, peered at the return address. It was from Ed Todd's sister.

"It's probably a thankyou for being there when Ed...died." My heart still stuttered when I said the words. "She didn't have to do that."

I opened it. It was a letter. She did thank me. But that wasn't all. The words on the page blurred as my eyes filled with tears.

"Vi, what is it? What's wrong?"

I handed it to him. He read it, then looked at me, and what I saw in his eyes made my heart melt.

It was fear. After that came a flash of uncertainty and something else, something that made me want to run out once again. It looked a lot like selfish possessiveness. I suppose, under the circumstances, I could understand that.

Ed Todd had left his farm to me.

CHAPTER FORTY-FIVE

Saturday arrived and you'd think one of us was getting married with the amount of nervous energy and fluttering tummies we all shared. Me, Mom, Sandy, and Emily—I still had to mentally shift from Zoe to Emily each time I thought of her—went and got pedicures in the morning.

The previous two days had been busy. Emily and her parents had reached an agreement. She would work part time for Dex One and part time for us, and continue to live with Mrs. Erdman. She'd already started the fall semester at a college in Hannibal, taking classes toward a degree in criminal justice. She had her car, and her horse was due to arrive on Sunday. At the end of the first semester, they would reassess.

I'd be going back to the Island in the next week to sign papers to transfer ownership of Ed's farm into my name. I was still in shock about this turn of events and walked around in a denial daze, unsure what it meant for my future. Every time I thought about it, I saw that fear in Malcolm's eyes. Of course, I'd finish my year's contract at Winterlight. But I understood his fear. I'd felt something similar every time I'd thought he was going to fire me.

Miko would go to the Island with me. He would stay at Ed's

and keep an eye on things until I figured out what the next steps were. He had a six-month tourist visa, so we'd have to decide something before then. There had been discussion of his applying for a green card. Or possibly a student visa.

A shiny new smart phone arrived addressed to me. I'd assumed Malcolm ordered it, but he hadn't. It came from Harry with a note that he was tired of not being able to reach me. He hoped this new phone would inspire me to keep in closer touch. Or at least motivate me to keep it charged so it could receive a message. I wasn't entirely sure how I felt about this gift. I'd pay him back, but it made me uneasy.

I guess I did need a communication device. My old phone had disappeared, or I'd left it somewhere and forgotten, or dropped it. The last time I remembered having it was the week before at Penny's.

Speaking of, she'd had her baby! A girl. They'd named her Isabella. I received beautiful pictures and videos of Isabella on my new phone, and that made me feel better about the device.

I talked to my beloved sis-co, but didn't share everything that had happened. Anything that had happened. Not even how Aunt Trudy had lied to me. Especially that. I saw no reason to darken the joy of Penny's first days as a mother.

Brian had been released from the hospital. He got to keep his eye but would have a heck of scar to tell stories about. He'd have to do physical therapy after his leg healed.

Giacomo had also been released. He had a bandage over his eye socket and a rakish patch over that. It suited him.

Everyone couldn't fit in Malcolm's SUV for the drive to St. Louis, so we split up. Dex took one of his SUVs with Emily, Miko, Sandy, and Renee. I'd been so delighted to see her again, had missed her wisdom. We hugged and promised to catch up later. Malcolm's mother, Helen, had been invited to the gala, but she politely declined, saying fancy parties weren't her thing.

My parents and Giacomo—my *nonno*—rode with me and

Malcolm. Dad and his dad were resplendent in their tuxes. Dad's was basic black with satin lapels but Giacomo's was a deep damson plum color. The old guy wore it well, appeared comfortable in the snug formal attire, and it made me think there was even more to him than I suspected. He hadn't wanted to take the prescription pain killers they'd given him at the hospital, but we insisted—the eye socket obviously hurt—and he acquiesced. I had a feeling Dex Two's female guests would be swooning over him.

Malcolm wore his dress kilt and Prince Charlie jacket, matching waistcoat, tuxedo shirt, and black bow tie. Along with that, his dress sporran hung in front. My breath caught when he came down the stairs, casually shooting his French cuffs, and my tummy did several aroused backflips.

When he saw me, he froze, one foot on the last step, the other in midair. His right hand clutched the banister as if he needed support. My mother had tamed and pinned my hair into a one-sided chignon, and decorated it with a sparkly comb. I wore makeup. Not much, but I rarely wore any, so I knew I looked different. She'd lent me a diamond and emerald choker—a good fake, she'd clarified, a copy of one by Faberge—and matching dangly earrings. I felt like a princess.

He'd never seen me dressed up. Cleaned up, but not like this. His eyes flicked to my mother, who looked magnificent in her blue dress. She'd piled her hair high and wore dramatic makeup. Not as much as she would for competition, but more than me.

After clearing his throat, he said, "Gemma, you look stunning."

She thanked him with a regal nod, taking his compliment as her due. But she needed it, I could tell, because Dad hadn't said a thing.

Malcolm came down the last step nodding to Dad and Giacomo, and they acknowledged him—man speak for *don't we look swell?*—then reached for me.

"Come here, gorgeous."

"Okay, my scorching hot highlander. Since you put it that way." I grinned and put my hand in his.

Dex Two had valet parking so all we had to do when we arrived was alight and walk up the stone steps between a pair of chubby bears who guarded the entrance to the Peabody. The flat stone face of the building had a balcony carved into the second story with eight tall columns across the front.

Dex One drove in shortly after us. Miko helped both Emily and Sandy out. Sandy stared at the building and the people and the cars for a long time until Renee leaned close and whispered something in her ear. Sandy pulled up her jaw, lifted her skirt, and came up the stairs in a simple black dress with a low neckline and snug waist that showed off her curves.

Thanks to Harry's family, I'd attended events like this before. Though far from jaded, I wasn't agog either. I waved to them and waited while they caught up.

Emily's prom dress had a flowing purple skirt and intricately beaded high-necked top. Sleeveless. Renee glowed in a gray, strapless mermaid gown. Dex sported a silver bow tie to go with it.

Altogether, we looked like royalty. Not bad for a bunch of barn rats.

Malcolm pulled our invitations from his sporran to show the door man. We crossed the ticket area to a sweeping staircase that took us to the grand lobby, a two-story high art deco space with marble floor and gold accents. A balcony circled the entire second floor. Very elegant. Cocktail hour was in full swing.

Tables were set up on both levels. Bars were placed around the edges. At the opposite end, a live band played. Our table was on the first level near the dance floor. Each accommodated ten, so our group fit perfectly.

I watched my parents. Dad did all the right things. Escorted Mom, pulled out her chair, asked if she wanted something to drink, but I could tell by the pinched look around her eyes and the set of his jaw, things were tense. I suppose we could have requested to have Miko seated elsewhere, but that wasn't fair to Dex Two, or more likely, Daphne. It was enough that he'd accommodated all of us on such short notice.

Giacomo put himself at Sandy's disposal, getting both of them a glass of wine. Red for him, white for her. She blushed at his attention, and fluttered her eyelashes, although I think it was nerves rather than artifice. If he weren't my grandfather, I'd be half in love with him myself. I smiled my thanks. He shifted his eye to leer at Sandy's cleavage, then winked at me, the devil.

Dex Two swung by. I introduced him to my family, including Emily and Miko. He kissed the back of my mother's hand.

"I am so pleased to finally meet you," he said. "I do hope you will save a dance for me. A waltz perhaps? The band can play anything, anything at all."

"Of course," she said, though her eyes skated nervously to Adrian for a brief moment before she smiled at Dex Two.

Thankfully, he hadn't requested the tango.

He opened his arms to include the entire table. "Let me know if you need something. Most importantly, relax and enjoy the evening."

Dinner consisted of our choice of a filet mignon, salmon, or chicken piccata. Most of us had the salmon, Giacomo grumbling that he doubted the piccata would meet the standards of his palate. Malcolm went for the steak, then complained at the petite serving size. The high-ceilinged room rang with the clink of table, flat and glassware, the rise and fall of voices, and an undertone of soft jazz from the ensemble.

For dessert, four ice cream sundae bars were set up. My mother declined. Dad indulged in a bowl of strawberries buried in whipped cream, and I feared I'd created a monster. Mom wouldn't even look his way while he ate. Sandy and Zoe—dang it—*Emily Emily Emily* went full bore with three flavors of ice cream, fruit, nuts, whipped cream, chocolate sauce, walnuts, and M&Ms.

The concept was new to Miko. He kept it simple with vanilla

ice cream, a few crumpled Oreos, hot fudge, and sprinkles. Malcolm and I both skipped, but there were plates of cookies out, and I thought I might snag one of them later. Giacomo had plain chocolate ice cream. A simple choice for a not-so-simple man.

Dinner wound down, and the service staff cleared tables as the musicians launched into a big-band era swing piece that encouraged a lot of people to get up and dance. It had me tapping my feet.

"You will dance with me?" Miko asked Emily.

"Oh...I don't know how. Not like that." Her eyes flitted over the dance floor.

Miko looked over the twirling couples. "Look," he said, "No one can dance. I show you."

I could tell she wanted to. "Go on," I said. "How often do you get the chance to look gorgeous, attend a gala at a beautiful place, and have such a cute guy offer to teach you to dance? Go for it, girl."

She jumped up. "Okay. Let's do it."

Miko led them out. I could tell he'd prefer to have more room, but he began leading her through the steps, and she picked it up pretty quickly, giggling the whole time. They were cute.

Dex One and Renee danced slowly because of his leg. Sandy had gone to the lady's room, Giacomo to refill his coffee cup. The infectious beat drummed through my parents, I could tell, even though they tried to ignore it. I thought it must be like the sound of hoofbeats to me, a primordial force that makes the heart thump, blood course more quickly. It was impossible not to heed its call.

Leaning close to Malcolm so I could whisper in his ear, I asked, "Can you cha cha?"

"It's been a while, why? I'm rusty, but I can."

"Perfect." I hid my mouth behind my hand. "It's my parents' favorite," I said. "Can you do me a favor?"

He gave me a conspiratorial smile. "What do you have in mind?"

I explained. He nodded. "Don't go away. I'll be back in a few minutes. Be ready."

No wonder I loved him. Wait. Love?

Maybe.

The feeling rushing through my body, centering in my chest. Unfamiliar yet recognized. My feet itched some, but not to run.

I tried to keep track of his progress as he wended through the crowd, stopping to talk to people here and there, but he was on a mission and never stayed long. Eventually, I lost track of him.

A few minutes later, I saw him in close conversation with the band leader. The band leader nodded. Malcolm said something else. The other guy smiled and nodded again. As Malcolm made his way back to the table, the swing song ended. There was pause. Several couples left the floor. He stopped to talk to Miko, who took Emily's hand and led her...somewhere. Not to our table.

Then, the unmistakable opening rhythm of Santana's Oye Como Va started up, a classic slow cha cha song. Malcolm's eyes were already dancing as he shook out of his jacket and took my hand.

"How's your cha cha?" he asked.

A quick glance at my mother showed her drawn forward, as if the music had the power to bring her to her feet. It probably did.

"Rusty," I said. It was one of the dances I'd learned, but it'd been a long time.

He twirled me out to the floor just as the melody began.

My hips picked up the beat as he pulled me into hold, bringing his hips close to mine, closer than they should be in cha cha, but I wasn't complaining.

We started with some basic walk steps forward and backward. I fell into time with him. Side steps, rock steps, hip twists, chasse. Dang. I remembered, and I loved it. Why hadn't we done this before now?

"Very nice, Miss Parker," he said as we did some cross steps.

He held my gaze with his, very intense, not unlike the way my parents used to look at each other. My tummy did more gymnastics. If he kept it up, I'd lose the rhythm.

"Is there anything you can't do, Robert Malcolm?"

His kilt flipped around his thighs as he worked his hips. "Live without you," he said without smiling.

Shit. I blundered an underarm turn, brushing the top of my head on his arm, my heart pounding harder than the dance could account for, then tripped through the alemana. That's when I saw my mother's hand slap the tabletop. She shot to her feet, looked down at her husband, and began to back toward the dance floor, arms out, hands beckoning, keeping her eyes on him the whole time.

Had the opportunity come?

Unable to resist the call of the dance, my father rose. He took his wife's hand.

They walked out to the middle of the floor as if the music hadn't started yet, as if they were entering a competition.

Or a battle.

They faced each other, not touching. And then, by some unseen signal, they began dancing.

Which made what we were doing look like a freaking demolition derby.

They danced around each other, and side by side, then Dad spun Mom into hold and led her around the floor, legs flashing hips bumping. Back and forth, together, apart, they showed everyone how it's supposed to be done. Malcolm turned me into his chest and led me off the floor.

"You did it," he said. " You got them up on the dance floor," he said.

"Let's hope it works."

Giacomo came to my side, his coffee cup cradled in one hand. He lifted it toward the couple on the floor. "Well done."

"We're not finished yet," I said.

I watched and waited, breathless, as I think many were. The floor was clear now except for my parents, and they didn't seem to notice, or were simply used to it.

The final beats signaled the end of the song, and they finished with Mom in a lunge. They were magnificent. Everyone watching clapped and cheered. That didn't include every person in the place, but as those who were sitting farther back realized something was going on, they came closer. People upstairs lined the railing.

As my parents straightened out of their final position, a single violin began a haunting melody. Then, a concertina started. What contemporary band has a concertina? One that can play tango music, that's what. Dex Two hadn't been kidding when he said they could play anything.

Dismay briefly tightened the corners of my mother's mouth but she recovered quickly. She didn't glance at my father, just waited, waited for him to make the first move. He began to walk away. Where the hell was he going? My mother hung her head and walked in the opposite direction. What the...no!

The lights dimmed. When my father reached the far side of the dance floor, he turned to stare at my mother's back. She lifted her eyes, found mine. I smiled, hoping it was something like that secret smile she had shown me a few days before when talking about my father. I gave an encouraging nod. Returning her eyes to the floor, she pivoted on the ball of one foot, so graceful, kicking her dress behind her. Slowly, almost dragging her feet but in time with the music, she made her way back to center, where my father now stood.

She lifted her arms as if she might embrace him, but then put her back to him and gradually moved one leg out to the side, bending the other as she slid her body down his front, her face rapt. He gazed into the distance as if he didn't care, but as she rose and took one step forward, he grabbed her wrist, pulled her around and dipped her, all in perfectly controlled slow motion.

Sandy came up beside me. "What's going on?" she asked.

"Just watch," I said.

Dad viewed her exposed throat as if he wanted to bite her. The music swelled and sped up, he drew her into him, and they floated across the floor, chest to chest, legs flicking up and down, hers between his, his between hers.

That summer I was thirteen, I'd wanted to learn to tango. My mother said no. Adamantly. I was too young, she said, to understand the nuances of the dance.

Watching them now, I understood. They made walking look like seduction, the quick-quick, slow-slow steps building toward a climax, staring into each other's eyes as if they were the only two in the room, in the world. Then my mother would lower her gaze again, yielding to him, her hand around his neck as if he were her only hope of survival. His hand would be high on her back, possessive, then down at his side as if unsure he could contain her spirit. This was soul-searing intimacy laid bare for everyone to see.

It wasn't only her reluctance to teach me tango that I understood. Life and relationships were nuanced as well, too complicated for a child to comprehend. Yet, I'd been going through adulthood letting a child's anger and hurt guide me.

No more.

They had come home, come for me, not turned away when I lashed out. They'd gifted me with love and forgiveness. I could do the same for them.

Dex One and Renee came to stand on the other side of Malcolm. Renee reached behind the men and touched my arm.

"Hey, New York, now I know where your fire comes from." She watched my parents for a moment, turned back to me. "They're fantastic."

"Yeah," I said, "they kind of are."

My parents' lips came near to touching, then he twirled her away, and anguish filled her eyes. I could feel it. Everyone did. The entire place leaned toward them, pulled by their passion, as if they were the center, the sun, and all else revolved around them. Dad held her tight, her leg rode up to his hip, and he caressed her calf before she extended her foot out to the side and around, and then dropped into another lunge, bent backwards nearly double.

They came together, and it looked like they would finally kiss, but again she put her back to him, slid down his front, her hands stroking his thighs. His face showed a mix of agony and arousal.

"Jesus Christ," Sandy said in a hoarse whisper. "I think I just wet my panties."

"Don't be gross," I hissed. "You're watching a spiritual experience."

She snorted. "If you say so. But I know foreplay when I see it."

"Hey, these are my parents we're talking about."

"Whatever. They made you, didn't they?"

Indeed they had.

Mom collapsed into Dad's arms. He dragged her across the floor, her legs looking like she could no longer support herself. But it was all part of the dance, the give and take of life, the push of the past, the pull of the future. Malcolm's arm slid around my waist, his fingers warm on my hip.

"What do you think?" he asked. "Mission accomplished?"

They danced across the floor quickly again, spinning around each other, their legs kicking with nearly every step, the hem of Mom's dress snapping as Dad led them round and round. They rode the music like I ride a horse, one with it, as though it gave them life or sprung from them fully formed. Quick-quick, slow-slow. He lifted her onto his hip, she slid down, swiveled. The music built to a crescendo, and then it ended. They were in each other's arms, chest to chest, their lips so, so close.

The room was hushed, the anticipation palpable. The wait staff stilled, entranced. Not even the tinkle of crystal stemware broke the spell. My mouth had gone dry. I could smell Giacomo's coffee and the whiskey on Malcolm's breath.

My parents breathed hard. Dad closed his eyes and leaned his forehead into Mom's, whispered words only she could hear. She nodded as a sob convulsed her body. Her hands skimmed up the back of his head. She drew him to her. They kissed.

A thrill rushed through me to squeeze my heart with euphoria. The silence broke, the applause so wild it almost hurt.

The truth is, my parents are alive.

I used to pretend they were dead to make their absence in my life tolerable. But they are very much alive, present. Welcome.

Dabbing at sudden tears, I leaned close to Malcolm. In a choked whisper, I answered his question—and many others.

"Mission accomplished."

- THE END -

A vulture pecked at a lump of road kill a short distance ahead. Some might take finding a dead body in the morning as a bad sign. Not me. Not anymore. I've learned to look on the bright side, to be grateful.

A few minutes before, my ancient pickup began to chug, the temperature gauge screamed *overheating imminent* and the oil pressure flicked to zero.

Not exactly what I needed five days before a life-changing deadline.

I had guided the truck to the narrow slice of gravel between the crumbling edge of blacktop and grassy drainage ditch. That's when I spied the vulture.

Leaning on the steering wheel, I shifted my gaze to my dog, Noire, who sat on the seat beside me, her ears pricked to the winter wheat outside, her nose at the gap above the window.

"Stay," I said.

She snapped her big black head to me, brown eyes questioning.

"I'm sure there are rabbits and other critters out there, but I need you to stay."

She sighed and turned back to pondering the fields.

I rummaged around until I found a couple of used napkins, popped the hood, and got out. The liquid clinging to the dipstick resembled milky tea rather than black coffee. I'm no motor head, but even I could guess this did not bode well for my engine's state of health.

I shouldered my purse, strung a piece of baling twine through Noire's collar by way of a leash, and locked up the vehicle. With my dog at my heels, I started walking, knowing the bags of horse feed in the bed would be safe out here in God's country, also known as rural Missouri.

I could call my boss, Robert Malcolm. He'd come get me. But it was a soft spring morning, would be barely seventy degrees at midday. Birds sang to each other, and only a few cotton ball clouds hung in the sky.

Anyway, Malcolm was super stressed lately, working more than ever. Sometimes I thought he was hiding from me, from us, afraid of what would happen in less than a week.

To be fair, I hadn't given him any indication of what I planned to do when our one-year contract concluded.

That's because I wasn't sure, and I'd taken to falling asleep in the tack room or on the couch in his living room, rather than climbing into bed with him as I had for nearly a year.

Avoiding each other. He probably thought he was giving me space. I probably thought I needed space. He hadn't exactly begged me to stay.

I needed to decide. Should I stay with him at Winterlight, or return to my farm back on Long Island? Ed Todd's farm, that is. I'd never get used to thinking of it as mine, even though I'd fantasized for years about owning it.

He'd died the previous summer. A couple of weeks later, I'd gotten a shock when I found out he'd left the valuable piece of real estate to me. Unfortunately, he hadn't left any money to pay for upkeep or taxes, let alone feed the retired horses who lived there. Insurance covered some of the damage left by the fire, but I really didn't know what to do. No matter how many lists of the pros and cons of each option I made, I was no closer to knowing than I had been six months ago.

Except, except...I might want to stay in Missouri. Part of me thought I should want to return to my roots, but whenever I imagined going to the East coast, a squirmy sensation invaded the pit of my stomach. Sometimes it felt like excited anticipation, others, more like worried apprehension.

The vulture abandoned his breakfast at our approach. He sat on a fence post, patiently waiting for us to move along. Taking a deep breath and exhaling noisily, I tugged Noire away from the dead possum before she could roll in it, and steered us onto the road to get over a culvert.

A warning tingle zipped up my neck like the feeling right before a horse spooks. I heard it the same moment it was on us. A speeding car coming from behind, the engine roaring at the top of its gear.

Jerking Noire's rope, I hopped over the ditch, turned my ankle, and fell. My purse slingshotted over the wire fence into a cow pasture.

A sports car zoomed by, the whoosh of wind kicking up leaves and sucking the breath out of me.

I looked in time to see it was black, foreign, and had New York plates.

Get Wrong Lead today!

ABOUT THE AUTHOR

WWW.CANDACECARRABUS.COM

Long Island native Candace Carrabus spent her formative years in the saddle, just imagining. She still rides horses and writes stories —frequently simultaneously—and many of these stories are imbued with the magic and mystery horses have brought to her life. She shares a farm in the Midwest with her family, which includes several four-legged critters.

Sign up for her newsletter at candacecarrabus.com

facebook.com/AuthorCandaceCarrabus

twitter.com/CandaceCarrabus

instagram.com/candace_carrabus

ALSO BY CANDACE CARRABUS

FANTASY

Raver, The Horsecaller: Book One

The Roar of Smoke, A Book of the Meldborn

DREAM HORSE MYSTERIES

Cold Backed, A Dream Horse Mystery Prequel

On the Buckle, Dream Horse Mystery #1

Wrong Lead, Dream Horse Mystery #3

THE WITTING WOMAN NOVELLAS

The Man, The Dog, His Owner & Her Lover

The Good Horse, The Bad Man & The Ugly Woman